PENNIE PINCHING

Deborah Marcum

Printed in the United States of America

For my mom, the real Pennie.

For Ms. Judy and Karol, for inspiring real life characters.

CONTENTS

PENNIE PINCHING

MONDAY, JUNE 20

Every hair stood on end as Pennie felt the evil eyes watching her every move. The grisly smell of death surrounded her, filling her nostrils with the aroma of decay and putrefaction. The creaking of a floorboard under her feet momentarily quieted the buzzing of the flies in the tiny room. What if the noise startled the angry creatures? Was another attack imminent? While backing out of the room as quietly as possible, Pennie's heart almost exploded from terror when she bumped into the last person she expected to find.

"What the meth-lab is this, Pennie?!"

She finished pushing Chip outside and slammed the door to the small building.

"This is supposed to be the new office for the garden center, but it needs some work," Pennie explained.

Chip shook his head as he eyeballed the building. "It needs to be burned to the ground."

"What're you even doing here?"

"I brought my mom to get some new flowers for her hanging planters. I was just letting you know we're here, but you can get back to work now." Turning his back, he haughtily added, "Sorry for interrupting your very important job."

Pennie watched Chip's handsome backside as he walked across the property to the rows of flowers that extended past the Avocado Farms sign. She currently stood on the newly purchased tract of land that the owners hoped to use for a future Christmas tree farm, pumpkin patch, and hayrides. The little building came with the property, as well as a host of challenges.

When Adriana and Oscar Acevedo hired Pennie to manage the busy nursery and landscape center last month, she had no idea what her employment would entail.

Day one, during her attempt to clean up the small building, she disturbed a racoon's nest. Big mistake. Three stitches and one rabies vaccine later, she returned to work.

Day two, she met with the critter control people to remove the racoons and place poison around for the plethora of rats and mice.

Day three, Pennie tried to vacuum and shampoo the carpets only to have hundreds of vampiric fleas suck the blood from her ankles and lower legs.

Day four, she stayed outside to pressure wash the exterior of the little house only to be viciously stung by a wasp. Thankful it was only one wasp, she returned for day five.

So forth and so on. It had been four weeks, and the racoons were back. Carcasses of other unwelcome animals decomposed within the walls. Just now, Pennie managed to sneak in and out without angering the momma coon who watched intently from a hole in the ceiling, but the bug bomb to kill the newest infestation of fleas might agitate all the varmints as well as their lingering ghosts. She found herself in an endless cycle of trying to get this stupid building in order. Frustrated didn't even begin to describe her mood.

Joining her young coworker, Pennie entered the smaller shed currently housing the cashier station of the busy nursery. She perched on a stool, hoping the little fan would help her cool down despite the relentless sun breathing heavily on her. The town of Bartlett, a suburb directly outside of

Memphis, Tennessee, promised residents excessive heat and humidity every summer. At age twenty-eight, Pennie had never experienced a June that could be categorized as pleasant.

The sweltering temperatures made the flea bites on her ankles look worse than they were, and her face was flushed from the heat. Why did Chip have to see her this way? Not that he was interested in her romantically, but Pennie's imagination still held onto the idea that he could see her as more than a reluctant partner one of these days. As it were, her dirty t-shirt, shorts, messy bun, and lack of makeup wouldn't attract any man. The dirt under her nails might even scare away any potential suitors.

Oh well. When Pennie's husband died in a workplace accident over two years ago, she didn't think she'd ever be interested in love again. When she participated in a low-risk undercover assignment with Chip last year, the woman inside her woke up. That country-boy sexy voice, mesmerizing hazel eyes, and chiseled body… Even though he was a butthead most of the time, Chip worked his way into Pennie's fantasy. Distance would be better so Pennie could move on, but he undoubtedly enforced his squatter's rights to remain in her daydreams.

As she sat back with her eyes closed, allowing the breeze to cool off her sweaty neck, Chip addressed her from the window of the shed.

"Hey, don't forget to be on time tomorrow. We're leaving in two weeks, and we still have a few details to work out."

Pennie nodded as Chip left with his mom.

"Oooh, Pennie, where're you going with him? He's a stud," Lupe asked when they were left alone.

The nineteen-year-old was sweet, but she never impressed Pennie with her work ethic. Rather than entertain any gossip with the girl, she tried to get back into manager mode. "We're going on a cruise, but for now, you need to get back to watering the annuals. The petunias are drooping over there."

Getting back to her own work, Pennie's mind wandered… All the events of the past year floated through her subconscious while her hands filled a pot with garden soil and colorful flowers to create seasonal mixed arrangements. Chip's position with the Bartlett Police Department allowed him several opportunities to do some undercover work. They posed as a couple in love last August on a cruise ship to bust up a scheme to sell stolen art. In February, she joined him again to gather information to locate a missing girl on the Atlantic Coast.

Recently, Chip had been promoted to work with the investigative division of the Bartlett Police Department, where he could rekindle a relationship with her arch nemesis, Detective Pietra Russo. Working in such proximity to the Latina beauty, Chip would be eating out of her hand in no time. A couple of months ago, Pietra specifically told Pennie to stay away from Chip. Pietra had no qualms about fighting dirty to get what she wanted, and she showed her petty side more than once.

Rather than become a cut-throat competitor, Pennie bowed out. Would finding love ever require that much work? Would she ever have to compete for a man? Would a man just identify with her and fall in love without all the rivalry and struggles?

After watering the new flowerpot of mixed annuals, Pennie used the hose to rinse the soil off her hands. Using her thumb, she rubbed the bare ring finger of her left hand. No tan line or indentation indicated where she wore a wedding ring for five years.

Marrying her high school sweetheart at age twenty-one was a no brainer. Johnny always chose Pennie first. He never looked at another woman for Pennie to feel in competition with. He was a keeper, and she knew God blessed her with the ideal husband. His laid-back personality never conflicted with Pennie's aggressive temperament. They complemented each other perfectly.

Chip, on the other hand, argued with her. He called her out when she acted brashly. He rebuked her when he thought she was out of line. He tested her patience. The flip side of Chip though… He was protective, strong, and dedicated. Oh, but he confessed that he was relationship averse. Why was Pietra the only woman on the face of the earth to convince him that a relationship was worth a try? Pennie had no idea if they were actively dating again, but it was only a matter of time before Pietra got her perfectly manicured claws back into Chip.

A customer provided a welcome distraction from where her imagination was headed. Pennie checked out the lady who purchased flats upon flats of perennials. Just then, her boss and neighbor Adriana Acevedo walked up.

"Hola, Pennie! How's the building looking?"

"Adriana, I might set fire to it. If I get attacked by anything else, that building will be *en fuego*!" Pennie threw her hands in the air to show how big the potential fire would be.

"Oh no! What's going on now?"

"Momma coon is back, and the fleas are something fierce. It looks like I have boils on my legs, and if any frogs or locusts show up, I'll know for sure the Old Testament plagues are back."

Adrian softly laughed at Pennie's dramatics. "The water hasn't turned to blood, has it?"

"No, but my legs need to heal up before I go on my cruise. Are you sure you're good with me taking off for a few weeks? I don't feel like I've gotten much done here."

"No worries, *amiga*. I'm excited for you to visit my home country. Most of our springtime projects are finishing up so I can spend more time here. Go ahead and leave. I'll make sure Lupe stays busy."

As Pennie walked towards her truck, a Channel Four news van pulled into the parking lot. She enjoyed watching the "on your side" reporter Judy Thomas most evenings, and she lingered to see who might be in the van. Eventually, a camera man opened the rear doors to unload some equipment. Approaching the man, Pennie asked, "Are you here to cover a story of some sort?"

The man lifted his Channel Four ballcap enough to make eye contact before saying, "Yea, ma'am. Ms. Thomas will be here shortly."

His keen blue eyes and soft Cajun accent made Pennie smile. Without further acknowledging her, the man continued with his tasks. A moment later, an electric-blue Prius pulled into the adjacent space. For a sixty-year-old woman, Judy Thomas handled herself like a royal runway model. Erect posture, flattering dress suit, and four-inch pumps. Her dark auburn hair had a few silver streaks that added sophistication rather than age.

Pennie didn't realize she was staring until Judy's own onyx eyes pierced through her. "Can I help you?" Her polished dialect couldn't quite disguise the Southern drawl. The years had been kind to her. Smile lines and crow's feet were the only indicators of her age. Other than that, her high cheek bones, steeply arched brows, and bow-shaped lips made her a sophisticated beauty.

"Hi, Ms. Thomas," Pennie extended her left hand. "I enjoy your segments on the news. Are you covering a story here?"

After releasing her hand, the reporter responded, "Yes. In fact, I have it on good authority this property contains a historic burial ground. Do you know if the owners Adriana or Oscar Acevedo are here? I need to find out their intentions for the acreage they recently purchased."

Yikes! A cemetery! Pennie hadn't walked the entire property, but most of the twenty acres was overgrown. "Adriana is at the cashier station." She pointed across the field and ducked out before the reporter shared that horrific news with the feisty Dominican.

In her already-sweaty state, Pennie took her mutt Peach for a jog when she got home that afternoon. Putting thoughts of old burial grounds out of her mind, she allowed the pounding of her sneakers on the pavement to soothe her soul. Routine exercise kept her from becoming irritable, so she made it a point to run almost every day, as well as attend self-defense classes several times a week. Nothing like a few rounds of sparring to work the aggressive energy out of her system.

Finally, a refreshing shower and delivery pizza. Nothing was on television. The news story about the burial ground wasn't showing on Channel Four yet, so she flipped it to ESPN. Football and basketball seasons had come to an end. Baseball didn't hold her interest. Highlights of the weekend's golf tournament made her reminisce a little. After seeing her favorite golfer Kendall Lui win the tournament, she changed the station again.

National Lampoon's Vacation caught her attention. During the Griswold family road trip across the USA, they encountered one ill-fated event after another. Two weeks from now, Pennie would be on her own road trip with Chip. Oh yea, Pietra too. To make things complete, Pennie's exchange student would join them as well. They won't be on a quest to visit *Walley World*. They'd be taking a road trip and a cruise for another quest all together. The safety of a young lady depended on the success of their trip. Unlike the unfortunate *Aunt Edna* and her dog *Dinky*, Pennie hoped for everyone to return from this *vacation* safe and in one piece.

TUESDAY, JUNE 21

"Mom, come on. We're going to be late," Karolina insisted as Pennie ironed her strawberry-blond hair.

"Almost done," Pennie patiently replied, refusing to be hurried. Pennie instilled the need to be on time in her daughter, which was counterintuitive in the Brazilian culture, so she wasn't mad about the prodding. Karolina rolled her eyes from the vanity stool in the bathroom. Ignoring her daughter, she gave herself a final perusal in the mirror. To atone for her haggard appearance yesterday, Pennie paid special attention to her makeup. Her freckles were concealed, while her blue eyes were accented. The cute top emphasized her curves, while the wedge sandals added three inches to her five-foot-six height. Too bad she had to wear long pants to cover the inflamed insect bites on her ankles instead of wearing one of her stylish dresses.

Karolina, the typical Brazilian, wore shredded short shorts with a cropped t-shirt and slide sandals. The only thing American about her outfit was that the shirt featured a University of Memphis Tiger. This was a source of pride for Pennie since she was a Memphis alum herself. Giving one last glance in the mirror, Pennie conceded it was time to go. No matter how much time she spent preening, her looks would only ever be average. In the *looks* department, she could never compete with the exotic Latina beauty Pietra Russo anyway.

The short drive to the Bartlett Justice Center was spent with Karolina singing along with AmberLou tunes on the radio. The way Pennie was raised, the driver got to select the music, but here she was now, driving her own Ford truck, and unable to relinquish control from the stubborn twenty-year-old. How did Karolina manage to connect her own phone to Pennie's truck anyway? The caterwauling of the popular country star threatened to make her ears bleed. Fortunately, the drive only lasted long enough to hear two songs.

"Are you taking me to the AmberLou concert when she comes to Memphis in October?" Karolina asked as they walked through the parking lot.

"I bought eight tickets for my nieces, for you, and a few of your friends, but I don't plan on going." Pennie couldn't understand the overwhelming fame bestowed upon the mediocrely talented singer, and she certainly couldn't understand why her multi-talented daughter jumped on the bandwagon. AmberLou Sharp had an astounding fan base of *Sharpees* all over the nation.

The conversation ended as they entered the cavernous lobby of the Bartlett Justice Center. Detective Pietra Russo met them at the door and led them deep into the building where a conference room awaited their meeting. Pennie and Karolina sat at the large table where only one man and two other ladies found their own seats. Feeling slightly intimidated by the professionally dressed attendees, Pennie focused her attention on pulling a notebook from the satchel she carried, avoiding eye contact with anyone in the room. *Why didn't I choose a more professional outfit to wear today?*

From behind her, a rich baritone greeted her by name. "Pennie, it's good to see you again," Deputy Police Chief Tony Lawrence said. His voice echoed just a little in the sterile environment. Pennie jumped up to accept a hug from the chief who helped coordinate the other two undercover missions she participated in. His milk-chocolate skin looked as delicious as ever, and what was it about a man in uniform? Tony was in a serious relationship these days, so Pennie never fixated on him like she did on Chip.

Speaking of the devil, Chip entered the room. He took the chair next to Pietra, which was across from Pennie. *Dang it.* Squashing her jealousy, she kept her mouth shut while an older suited woman who reeked of authority stood to start the meeting.

"Thank you all for meeting us today. Since this is our first time gathering in person, I'll start by introducing myself. I'm Valentina Hernandez, and I work as an ambassador from the Dominican Republic. I've previously met Deputy Police Chief Tony Lawrence, Lieutenant Chip Jordan, and Detective Pietra Russo. I'm assuming you are Detective Russo's sister?" she asked of the lady who could easily pass for the sister of Detective Hotstuff.

"Yes, I'm Bianca Covey. My husband Archie is here with me."

Valentina turned her attention to Pennie, the palest face in the room. "You must be Penelope Nichols?"

"I go by Pennie." Now, not only was she underdressed, but her name wasn't as cool as the other ladies'.

"Noted. I go by Vale, so we can all be informal here. And this young lady must be Karolina?"

In that instant, Vale switched from perfect English to

perfect Portuguese. She carried on a brief conversation with Karolina, speaking too quickly for Pennie to follow along at all. After they finished the exchange, Vale addressed the group.

"I have to say this is very unorthodox. Given the sensitivity of the situation, I've elected to handle all communication personally. Our new Dominican president, Daniela Vasquez, considers it a blessing that someone would reach out to help in such a unique way. As a mother, I understand that the safety of our children is always the highest of priorities, and my goal is to help President Vasquez and her daughter Francelia as a friend and a mother. Now that I'm here, can someone please tell me exactly how this plan came about?"

Standing, and practically glowing in the spotlight, Pietra smiled as she individually made eye contact with everyone sitting around the table. The smile faltered a tad when she reached Pennie, but she recovered quickly. She shook her shiny umber-colored hair behind her shoulders before she addressed the group. Pennie wondered what it would be like to have an exotic appearance with olive skin tone and golden eyes.

"When I heard about the death threats against President Vasquez's daughter, I immediately felt compelled to help. My family spends a lot of time yachting between the Caribbean islands, and the Dominican people have always been gracious and welcoming. I asked my chief to talk to his cousin in the CIA to see if they were formulating a plan to help. As it turns out, if they were making any plans, they weren't sharing them with us.

"Of course, we understand if they wanted to do this without broadcasting her travel plans to keep her safe until the threat had been appropriately dealt with. That's why I wasn't surprised when they declined to share any information with us. Fast forward a month, while I visited my friend Penelope," an impish grin accompanied Pietra's use of Pennie's given name, "I noticed a picture of her Brazilian exchange student who resembled Francelia perfectly. That's when I looped in Chief Lawrence who contacted you, Vale. We decided to skip the CIA and the secretary of state altogether, and let you discuss the opportunity directly with President Vasquez. The plan was too good to pass up when we found out they had already booked a cruise that stops in the Dominican Republic next month."

Vale nodded. "President Vasquez gave me permission to pursue the possible extraction of her daughter at that time since no other satisfactory plan had been proposed. I used my own resources to verify the integrity of everyone involved here today, and I've included the cooperation of some higher ups in DC to ensure Francelia's safety once she arrives on US soil. Typically, the responsibility of protecting foreign visitors falls on the Bureau of Diplomatic Security, but we've had to be creative to bring this young lady to safety without any advertisement of her whereabouts. For this endeavor, I've reached out to Victoria Peele, the Under Secretary for Civilian Security, Democracy, and Human Rights. She's arranging a safehouse for Francelia."

Vale sat and exhaled before continuing, "For the safety of all involved, Ms. Peele and her staff do not know about any of your involvement or any details of our extraction plan. Vice versa, none of you will know anything about the safehouse or protective detail once Francelia arrives. We'll only give you the exact information you need to drop her off at the right location to go into protective custody. Please tell me Pennie, are you comfortable with allowing Karolina to participate in this mission?"

"The decision to help was ultimately up to Karolina. She turned twenty in February, and I was willing to support whatever she wanted to do as long her safety's never compromised."

Vale spoke again. “I believe we’ve worked out everything to keep Karolina safe and completely removed from any further involvement once her part of the extraction is complete.”

The details of the extraction were laid out in detail, ensuring every team member knew precisely what they had to do.

WEDNESDAY, JUNE 22

"Why are we making cookies for the police? They should be giving you treats," Karolina asked with a little giggle.

Pennie grinned as she stirred chocolate chips into the batter. "I'd say you're the undercover agent, not me." Karolina had no knowledge of Pennie's two other assignments, and now wasn't the time to tell her. She agreed to keep her prior involvement, as well as Chip's, secret so that Chip could be considered for future undercover operations. She had no idea she'd be selected to assist with this additional assignment, but she welcomed the excitement in her otherwise boring life.

"I want to document everything like it's a news story," Karolina said with a gleam in her eye. "I think I want to become an investigative journalist."

"I thought you wanted to do something like become a diplomat, like Vale Hernandez."

"Not really. I double majored in political science and multimedia journalism so I could create human interest pieces to publish on whatever platform suited the story. But now I realize that everyday people need an advocate. I want to be that advocate... to be the voice of the oppressed. As an investigative reporter, I'll have backing and resources to represent the citizens of Bartlett and Memphis. Or another city if I choose to relocate in the future."

"That's very noble, Karolina. I thought you were

bonding with Vale yesterday, making a path to becoming a diplomat."

"Could you understand our conversation?"

"No, I was impressed that she knew Portuguese at all, then she spoke so fast. I caught the word *Segura*, which I guess means safety. And the word *Deus* which means God."

"She wants us all to stay safe. She grew up in a travelling missionary family and learned several languages," Karolina said without elaborating about their conversation.

Refusing to pry into their private exchange, Pennie replied, "Well, we should have a few relaxing days on the cruise before the extraction takes place."

"What do we need to do before we leave?"

"Nothing, I guess. Pack. Next weekend, my nieces are coming over. I'm only taking off work because these bug bites need to heal."

"Come on, Mom. If you want to win back Chip, you might have to do some tanning or something more than letting bug bites heal."

Karolina assumed, just like everyone else, that Pennie had a brief romance with Chip. If only Karolina knew the truth of their fabricated relationship.

"I think our time has passed. Pietra has all his attention these days."

Karolina slowly shook her head, "We'll see what we can do about that."

SUNDAY, JULY 3

After church, Pennie's nieces went home with their parents, leaving her alone with Karolina. They ate a quick lunch and headed to the salon.

"This AmberLou style sure has been popular lately," Christy said as she took in the details of the picture Karolina provided. "It's a shame to color your virgin hair, but we can change it back if you get tired of the chunky golden streaks. I'll make sure the layers are good for growing out as well. You'll have to add some styling products when you curl your hair to get this exact look."

Pennie listened to her stylist talking to Karolina from the adjacent salon chair. Since Christy would take hours to get the Brazilian's hair cut and colored, she took an appointment with another stylist to get her medium-length hair trimmed and dyed a deeper shade of auburn. Despite being colored every few months, it always faded back to strawberry blonde so quickly.

They both got pedicures and manicures before leaving the salon. The next day would just be a cookout at her brother's house. Then they had to finish packing for the trip.

TUESDAY, JULY 5

"Does everyone have their passport?" Chip asked as he put the rental SUV into drive without waiting for any replies.

"I double-checked before we left the house. I have mine, and Karolina has hers along with her visa paperwork," Pennie answered from the backseat. Karolina had already inserted Airpods to drown out any conversations from the old folks.

"Did you pack the clothes you're gonna need?" Chip continued questioning, just like her dad used to do at the onset of any road trip.

Without thinking, Pennie answered with more attitude than she intended, "Yes, Daddy. I also dropped off Peach at the dogsitter, I brought plenty of snacks, and I peed before I left the house."

Pietra snarled a coral lip and turned in her seat to face Pennie. "Really? There's no reason to be crude. We have a fifteen-hour drive ahead of us."

She turned back around in the shotgun seat, adjusting the oversized sunglasses on her perfect nose. Who wears lipstick for a road trip? And the sun wasn't even up yet to need the glasses. Pennie stuck to her t-shirt, shorts, and a messy bun. Since their day was starting before the sun even rose, she hoped to catch a good nap before lunchtime.

"Pennie," Chip said her name and made eye contact through the rearview mirror. "Did you speak to the Acevedos about what we had planned?"

"Of course not. I asked them more about the Dominican Republic in general since they knew I was visiting there, but I'd never compromise what we're doing. Especially not with my daughter involved."

"Did they tell you anything we don't already know?" Pietra asked.

"I had to guide the conversation a little, saying how progressive the Dominicans have become to elect a female president, but they told me some of their personal experiences with the *machismo* culture that's still rampant throughout the country."

Pietra's eyebrows shot up above her glasses. "Like what?"

Still making eye contact through the rearview, Pennie elaborated, "You'd think there's just pockets of this super-masculine attitude, but it's prevalent in lots of Latin American countries. Pietra, what country is your family from? They might have their own personal stories."

Again, Pietra turned all the way around in her seat. She used her freshly manicured thumb and index finger to lift her glasses so she could make actual eye contact. "My family is from Italy."

What!? Pennie swallowed hard, feeling utterly embarrassed. For almost nine months now, she assumed Pietra was Latina of some sort. She made up nicknames for her based on this false heritage. Even Chip rolled his eyes before refocusing on the road. Faltering a little, she finally answered, "Oh, um, I didn't realize you were Italian. Most people wouldn't look at me and guess that my dad's side of the family is Native American. People only see the Irish genes I inherited from my mom."

Without responding, Pietra lowered her glasses and

turned back around.

"Anyway, Adriana told me about her great-aunt Juana who lived in another city in the Dominican Republic. The first time she met Juana, she was freaked out about her aunt's disfigured face. Adriana was only a teenager at the time, but she asked her mom about it later. Her mom explained that Juana married some misogynistic jerk, and after they had five kids together, he threw acid in her face and moved another woman into the house to act as his wife. Juana could never leave because she had no way to financially support her kids, so she was stuck with him, basically becoming a servant in the house."

"Her mother didn't help? Or anyone else in the family?" Pietra asked.

"No, the machismo culture is so deep rooted, this is almost normal. Her mom would always say something to the effect of 'you married him, so you're stuck with him.' In fact, acid attacks are common along with just blatantly murdering women. In a marriage or partnership, femicide happens all the time and is rarely investigated. I saw a recent statistic... one year, out of over ten thousand reported incidents of domestic violence, less than five hundred were prosecuted, and less than a hundred were convicted. Hundreds of children each year are orphaned just from femicide alone in the Dominican Republic."

From the seat beside her, Karolina decided to join in, *"Ese es el hombre ella escogió y tiene que quedarse con él."*

"What does that mean?" Pennie understood something about "he's the man," and it sounded like Spanish. Pennie couldn't always be sure what language that was since Karolina could fluently speak five.

Karolina smiled. "That's the saying in Spanish. *He's the man she chose so she must stay with him.* This is a problem in Brazil also. A few years ago, our president defended a professional soccer player who raped a woman, saying that all women want to spend time with him. Violence and oppression of women still happens there. Why do you think so many exchange students come from Brazil?"

Pietra seemed to soften with this information. She turned slightly to address Karolina. "Do you know anyone who's suffered like this?"

"We all know someone. My family is different, but we're from a small town. In middle school, I had a friend who watched her dad murder her mom."

"That's so sad. What happened to your friend?"

"Rebekah became a burden to her dad after he killed her mom. Rather than put her on the street, he contacted an agency to send her away as an exchange student. She was fifteen, and she lived with a family close to Nashville. I came here the next year when I turned sixteen. I kept hoping I could connect with Rebekah, but we lost touch. Can we stop to use the restroom soon? I need to refill my water bottle also."

Chip audibly exhaled from the front seat. They barely made it an hour into the trip before the first pee break was requested. They all grabbed a breakfast item from the gas station, including some dairy-free yogurt for Karolina, before heading further south.

Pennie slept through the next couple of hours of boring landscape that carried them from Tennessee through Mississippi into Alabama. They stopped at Taco Bell for a hearty lunch and the third pee break for Karolina. Even though her Brazilian daughter was lactose intolerant, gluten intolerant, and vegetarian by choice, Taco Bell was always a good option for her. They gladly made her a black bean and rice bowl to go with her vegan Crunchwrap.

After everyone made a mess with their fast-food lunches, Karolina started a new conversation with the front seat occupants. She was typically very quiet, so the amount of talking from the young Brazilian surprised Pennie.

"So, both of you are police officers, right?"

"Yes..." both officers answered hesitantly.

"I don't have to drive much since my apartment is next door to campus, but I have some questions about driving rules."

Pennie glanced at her backseat passenger. "Questions you couldn't ask me?"

"No offense, Mom. I wanted to ask the officers."

"What questions?" Pietra prodded, still harboring a little hesitation in her tone.

"Well, if the light is red, can I still make a right turn?"

"You can after you come to a complete stop and make sure the way is clear."

"Even if a police car is next to me?" Karolina asked to be sure.

"Yes," Pietra answered, not sure if she should laugh or be relieved with the silly question.

"What do I do when a police car is riding behind me while I'm driving down the street?"

"You just drive normal."

"Are you sure? I almost had a heart attack last week when I drove to Mom's house. A police car followed me, then changed lanes, then got back behind me. I didn't have any cash if he gave me a ticket. I didn't have my visa or passport with me. What if he pulled me over and sent me back to Brazil?"

Trying to suppress her laugh, Pennie interjected, "Holy moly, Karolina! You've been with me at least three times when I've gotten pulled over for speeding. Say you're sorry and show them your license. If you get a ticket, let me know, and I'll show you how to pay it later. You don't give cash to an officer."

"You have a clean record, Pennie. When've you gotten pulled over?" Chip asked.

"I get pulled over at least once every few months for speeding. I don't really like speed limits or stop signs either for that matter. But I always apologize and admit my guilt. I've never argued with an officer over why he stopped me. They choose to let me go with a warning every time."

"I don't know whether that makes you a good role model or a bad one for Karolina. You may want to get that lead foot under control before you have any kids of your own," Pietra commented before turning around to speak to Karolina directly. She obviously wanted a change in conversation. "This hotel we're staying in tonight is very nice. I plan to take a long bubble bath. I suggest you do the same so you can be relaxed for tomorrow."

"Bath. No," she answered with the shake of her head. "What if I drown?"

"Drown?" Pietra looked confused. "Can't you swim? How deep do you think the tub is?"

"I don't take baths. I listened to a podcast about accidents in tubs, and I don't want to become a statistic."

"Did you take baths in Brazil before you got here?" Pietra asked, entertaining a very similar conversation to one Pennie shared with Karolina when she first arrived in the States.

"Houses in Brazil don't usually have bathtubs. I'll stick to my showers."

With one unsure nod, Pietra turned her gaze towards the windshield without bothering to continue the dialogue.

After another pit stop in Valdosta, Georgia, the topic in the car turned back to the mission at hand.

Pennie opened with a question. "What do we know about the group that's specifically threatening Francelia? I found them on the internet, but it was only basic info."

"*Mata Cacatas*," Pietra sighed from the front seat. "That loosely translates to the *cockatoo killer*, but it refers to a species of wasp that's nicknamed the *tarantula killer*. This group's been extremely bold and violent towards the political parties in the Dominican lately. Most of the Caribbean and Hispanic countries have been making strides in representing women better. Similar to equal opportunity and affirmative action, some countries are requiring a minimum number of females to be elected or appointed in political positions. The Wasps, as we've been calling them, have been outspoken against this, promoting male dominance."

"So basically, their women belong in the kitchen, barefoot and pregnant," Pennie said with disgust.

"Yep. Across the board, the machismo culture has used murder, abuse, and rape to terrorize and control women. Any woman who tries to speak out would either disappear or turn up dead. Such as the wife of the Wasps' leader. Adolfo Cabral was never even charged when his wife was found stabbed to death in their home ten years ago. Since then, he's been on a rampage to restore the stronghold of machismo in his country. Even his little brother Julio is on the warpath with him."

Pennie had seen some recent stories featuring the Cabral brothers. Judging by their pictures, they could be Rico Suave kind of guys. Latino male models or something similar. But a pretty exterior can't make up for a hateful interior. "What kind of upbringing did they have to become terrorists like this?" she asked.

Chip joined in at this point, "I saw a statement from Cabral where he said his group isn't terrorists, murderers, kidnappers, or any of that. They're just fighting for social justice."

"That's what he says when he burns all the ballot boxes and forces the shutdown of a hospital for two days," Pietra spouted off. "They're terrorists who act like they're doing something for the greater good, but they're nothing but womanhaters, and they suck."

Pennie felt a little kinship towards Pietra at that moment. Regardless of the competitiveness or petty showings in their history, they were women fighting for other women today. They were on the same team as of six weeks ago. "How widespread is the group?"

"They seem to have small pockets throughout the country." Pietra appeared to have most of the answers. "Originally, they were a small offshoot of one of the violent gangs from Haiti, and we assume that's where they got a lot of their original members. As a nation, Haiti is still dealing with so much political unrest, they've had a string of assassinations along with the recent earthquake. The gangs wanted to see if they could take over the entire island by reaching into the Dominican Republic. In the rankings of corrupt countries, Haiti is at the top of the list where the Dominican is closer to the bottom. Amid all the corruption, the Dominican closed their border to Haiti."

"But right now, the Wasps are only a problem in the Dominican?" Pennie asked to be sure.

"Yes, but their violence has been escalating, especially with the death threats against Francelia. It's a bold move to threaten your president; it's a scum-of-the-earth move to threaten her daughter. The Wasps think that Vasquez will just step down as president, but she won't be safe even if she does that. Their violence knows no bounds."

Karolina, who had remained quiet for the past few minutes, asked her own question, "What happened to Vasquez's husband?"

"That's the question on everyone's mind." Pietra sighed. "He was abducted about a decade ago. Several gangs took responsibility for his abduction, and he received threats all the time. Carlos Vasquez received a lot of threats because he led his own political activist movement. Instead of promoting hate, he promoted equality for women. In his younger years, he considered himself a machismo kind of guy. Having a daughter changed things for him. His activism wasn't limited to creating awareness to gender bias, but he worked to create programs to educate females and teach them skills. He set up mentors for women. This went against the grain, even within his own family. His brothers and father practically disowned him, but Carlos didn't care."

Pennie could see where this was headed. "I'm guessing the police didn't care to investigate his abduction."

"The crime was swept under the rug. Machismo still had a stronghold on the rural police, and guys like Carlos Vasquez were considered a nuisance."

"Men are pigs," Karolina spouted off.

"Hey, hey, hey," Chip reacted quickly. "Not all men are pigs. As the lone male representative in this vehicle, let me assure you that I'm here to protect you and bring you home safe."

Karolina wasn't done. "That still sounds machismo

to me. Not that you're doing something wrong, but your assumption is that women can't take care of themselves."

Pennie decided to play peacemaker before her super-independent daughter picked a fight she couldn't win. "Okay, Karolina, we're going against the Wasps. We need all the muscle we can get. Chip's intentions are pure when he says he wants to protect us. In the machismo world, they use the guise of protection to control women. That's not what's going on here."

"I still don't like it. Chip thinks he has to drive because he's the man, and I bet he thinks he's in charge because he's the man," Karolina said quietly and turned her head to watch the scenery passing by.

"Chip, let's jump off the interstate up here and stretch our legs. I'm texting you an address to head to," Pennie suggested.

Once they were back on the road in Gainesville, Karolina appeared much happier eating her gluten-free, vegan brownie from the bakery just off the interstate. Pennie felt responsible for teaching her Brazilian daughter how to spout off and speak before thinking. She was trying to correct that behavior in herself, and she'd have to help Karolina learn to be more tactful as well. Anytime her typically quiet daughter got snappy, some source of sugar was the key to calming her down.

If Karolina ever chose to get serious with a guy, Pennie would have to share the secret of her sweet tooth. That would be the only way her relationship could last.

From the front seat, Pietra prattled on about growing up

in the Gainesville area. Her family hailed from all over Florida. Beaches, Gators, yachts…

Pennie couldn't spend much time on a beach without getting burned. Not just a little pink but crispy burnt.

She was a Memphis Tiger fan through and through, so she mentally booed the Gators in her head.

Yachts… now that was a different story. The couple of weeks she spent on a yacht with Chip back in February opened her eyes to a whole new way of life. It was only a short-term undercover assignment, but Pennie would always cherish the experience.

They drove in silence for a while. Everyone remained lost in thought as they entered the final five hours of the journey south. Reminiscing about their boating trip in February, Pennie considered how she could feasibly spend some retirement years with a man. It didn't necessarily have to be on a boat. A camper might be nice… Just a way to travel and focus on the experience rather than possessions. Accumulating memories instead of stuff.

She internally laughed at herself. Here she was trying to plan out retirement. She still needed to find a man to fall in love with, marry, birth out a few kids, raise a family… then retirement. That was thirty years away.

Karolina continued to listen to her AirPods, avoiding any conversation. Pennie wondered what music she chose for the drive and tapped her daughter on the arm. Using terrible sign language, Pennie asked what she was listening to. The Brazilian turned her phone to show a podcast instead of music.

After seeing the surprised look on Pennie's face, Karolina removed the earbuds and spoke in a serious tone, "This podcast is talking about the lack of integrity in nursing homes in the USA. Elderly people are malnourished, mental disorders are going undiagnosed, and they're dying of loneliness."

"Honey, why are you listening to that?" Pennie asked with genuine curiosity.

"When I have to choose your nursing home, I need to be informed."

Pietra and Chip both snickered from the front seat.

What a strange conversation. Pennie was just thinking of traveling during her retirement years, and Karolina was looking for an old folks' home to stick her in. "While I appreciate you becoming informed, you may be jumping the gun a little bit. You know I'm only eight years older than you are."

"Next month, you'll turn twenty-nine, making you nine years older. Anyway, when we get back home, can we join the ministry at church that visits nursing homes?"

"They just paint the ladies' nails at a local home, but we can do it. They only meet once a month."

"I want an inside look at a nursing home," Karolina said to Pennie before she addressed Chip. "Can we find a restroom please? I need more water, too."

"Is she really ready for this?" Chip asked as they stood outside the gas station. Pietra and Karolina were inside, relieving their full bladders and finding beverages to fill them back up.

"Her part of it is easy. Our role in this extraction is hands off, Chip. Karolina is stubborn. She sticks to her commitments, and she wants to make the world a better place."

"She isn't prone to freak out once we get there?"

"Nope. She's the definition of fearless," Pennie assured him.

"Fearless until a police car is driving behind her?" he implored with a light laugh and a sideways glance.

Rather than give into a light-hearted banter, Pennie sighed. "Given our conversation earlier, we know that Karolina saw a fair amount of machismo culture in Brazil. It's ingrained in her to think the police are influenced by corruption and gender bias. The first time I made her take cookies to the police station with me, she couldn't wrap her head around it. She thought I was bribing the police department for some kind of immunity from brutality."

"I guess we take things for granted here in the States even though male dominance is a real thing worldwide. In any case, please talk to Karolina tonight. Make sure she isn't getting cold feet."

Hitting the road for the last two hours of the trip, Pennie felt her stomach growling. She quickly clasped her hands over her belly, hoping no one could hear. Then her belly decided to perform its best rendition of the silverback gorilla's mating call.

Chip responded to her stomach's request for food. "Pennie, you could've gotten a snack at the gas station. We already lost an hour thanks to the time change, and another hour thanks to all the pit stops and the Mickey Mouse traffic near Orlando. I'm making it to the hotel before we eat dinner."

Darkness had already fallen along with Pennie's hopes for a good meal. She reached into her backpack for some snack crackers. It would be nine before they checked into the hotel. She handed one of her granola bars to Karolina. Packing snacks appropriate for her daughter's dietary limitations always seemed necessary.

Even though Pennie had done absolutely nothing physical that day, she felt exhausted. Checking her exercise app, she realized she had burned less than a thousand calories. After a good night's sleep, she could make up for it tomorrow.

The city lights, palm trees, and skyscrapers came into view as they approached Miami. Pennie knew when they arrived at the hotel, Chip would drop her off at the door with Karolina to check in first. He would check in with Pietra separately after they parked the vehicle. Their part of the mission wasn't quite undercover work at this point, but they didn't want to make it obvious they were a team for anyone who might be paying attention to such details.

They had no idea who would be in Miami a week from now to take Francelia to her safehouse. Ambassador Vale Hernandez stressed that she was the lone person who knew the identity of the team members from Bartlett that included Pennie and company. She also was the only person who knew the State Department was involved. Vale wanted everyone to stay removed from each other to protect Francelia once she arrived.

Pennie wondered if anyone involved in the US government would be prone to help the Wasps. She understood that secrecy was important, but most people in the United States wouldn't know Daniela Vasquez or her daughter if they met them today. Francelia could undoubtedly blend in under the radar if she chose to. Getting out of the country seemed to be the hardest thing to accomplish, and they were helping with that this week.

If any clandestine government operatives were hanging out in Miami a week in advance to give Francelia a ride to the safehouse, they wouldn't notice the Bartlett team hanging out together other than arriving in the same vehicle. When they got back to Miami in another week, the drop off would be a little trickier, but they'd be ready.

"I have a question," Pennie said, trying to make eye contact with either of the front seat occupants through the rearview mirror.

"What, Pennie?" Pietra sounded irritated that the silence was broken.

"If Vasquez and her daughter have been in lockdown for the past three months, not leaving the presidential palace in Santo Domingo, how is Francelia getting out of the house unnoticed?"

"That's not for us to know. The less people who know, the safer she'll be. It's less than a ninety-minute drive from Santo Domingo to La Romana. I anticipate that once she's out of the palace, it'll be a straight shot to the meeting point. They can only protect her by keeping the identity of everyone involved secret from each other. You don't need to be asking questions like that."

The last hour passed in silence. Pennie didn't like being chastised by Pietra. Chip did almost zero talking in the last seventeen hours. Karolina nodded off with her Memphis Tiger neck pillow for support.

The warm air of the Miami night greeted Pennie and Karolina as they stepped out of the vehicle. As expected, Chip didn't get out to help with their suitcases. They both grabbed their own bags and headed into the gorgeous boutique hotel.

After dropping off their bags. Karolina and Pennie managed to order a light dinner in the quaint little restaurant where they'd be eating breakfast ten hours from now.

"Are Chip and Pietra eating here?" Karolina asked as she sipped on her water.

"No, he texted a minute ago to say they were walking around to find something to eat."

"Are you jealous?"

Pennie grimaced at the question. "What? No. Seriously, why would you ask that?"

"I think you like the idea of a man protecting you. It's not what I'd ever want in a relationship. But if you want it, and Chip looks like he enjoys protecting people, why don't you fight for him?"

Pennie shook her head and focused out the windows overlooking the pool area. Under the darkness of night, the lights glowed, turning the area into something romantic. The idea of Chip and Pietra walking around the sensational streets of Miami together almost made Pennie lose her appetite. Pietra was better suited for him, and she was a cut-throat wench when it came to competing for a man.

Does Karolina have it right, though? Is it that simple? Do I want a strong man protecting me? Other men could be protective in a healthy way. Chip proved to be a butthead more than once. Other than a little begrudged respect, Chip never acted like he cared about Pennie as anything more than a partner on a mission. He was simply the one who spurred the notion that she should get back into the dating game. Evicting him from her daydreams proved harder than she anticipated.

"Answer me, Mom. Why don't you fight for him?"

She was spared answering for another minute while the food was served, and the waitress ensured everything looked good.

Pennie noticed a little cut-throat spirit in Karolina. The same spiritedness that her best friend Jenna possessed. A few months ago, Jenna started a committed relationship for the first time in her life. The bulldog attitude was now used to defend her relationship instead of being used to keep Cole in his place. Would Pietra's attitude eventually scare Chip off? Would it make him feel safe with Pietra? Pennie had no way of knowing.

Whatever he had going with Pietra would have to play out without Pennie fighting for him. She knew that for a fact.

"Mom, I can see your wheels turning. As soon as you swallow that bite of burger, I want an answer."

Purposely, Pennie slowed down chewing. The burger was delicious, so she needed to savor it anyway. After taking a sip of non-fresh-brewed sweet tea, she thought about what to say.

"Karolina... They like each other. I'm not going to ruin their chances at love because I can't seem to find someone else to date."

"That's not true. You tried to date that guy George, then that golfer Kendall. I don't think either of them was manly enough for you. Daddy Johnny was very protective of us, and you want that again. I'm not telling you to throw yourself at Chip. But you could style your hair and put on some lipstick. Maybe—"

Pennie cut her off, "I'll find love with someone else, Karolina. Now let's finish eating and get some rest."

Rest. What a joke. Midnight came and went. *Get some rest,* Pennie told her brain to no avail. Thoughts of Pietra and Chip walking hand-in-hand through the otherworldly downtown Miami... Thoughts of them laughing at an inside joke... Thoughts of them splitting a gelato... One bowl with two spoons... No visions of sugarplums tonight.

Even when Pennie's brain switched gears, nothing relaxing took over. Thoughts of Karolina replaced the prior thoughts. The mission. The death threats. She allowed her daughter to sign up for something potentially dangerous. Karolina resembled Francelia so closely, she wondered if her safety would be compromised by just stepping off the cruise ship at their stop in La Romana.

At some point, Pennie did fall asleep, only to succumb to crazy dreams. Chip kissing her on their last mission. It was all for show, but it still invaded her subconscious. The smell of his cologne. The huskiness of his voice. Then a more realistic version of her relationship took over the dream.

In this phase of the dream, Pennie watched Pietra and Chip through a restaurant window. The couple in love shared a sundae, while Pennie observed with a messy bun, shapeless jogging pants, and no makeup. Jenna helped her find new stylish clothes and showed her how to wear makeup. Why couldn't she follow instructions? From Chip's perspective, he must assume that Pennie didn't care. Using her reflection in the window, Pennie tried to fix her hair, but in typical nightmare fashion, she managed to pull a plug of hair from her scalp in time for Chip to look up and laugh at her. Pennie willed herself to wake up or dream about something else.

Then her dream took an evil tangent. The beaches of the Dominican Republic should've been peaceful, but terrorists dressed like ninjas stormed the resort. Chip whisked Pietra away to safety, leaving Karolina and Pennie to fend for themselves. One of the terrorists, dressed in black from head to toe, had the silhouette of a red wasp on his chest and a malicious gleam in his eye. He closed in on Karolina, reaching out to snatch her... Pennie couldn't breathe... she couldn't move...

WEDNESDAY, JULY 6

"Mom, wake up!"

"Oh, Karolina. I had the worst nightmare," Pennie said as she tried to shake off the terrors.

"I didn't sleep well either. Let's go to the gym before we eat."

Although she didn't give birth to Karolina, they shared quite a few traits. One of those traits was the need to work the aggressiveness out of their system through exercise. A trait they didn't share was their method of exercise. Pennie preferred running and self-defense classes, while Karolina was a true gym rat. Weights. Lifts. Presses. Other stuff that Pennie didn't know the name of. She observed her daughter doing reps from her viewpoint on the treadmill. She finished with some pushups and sit ups just to add a little resistance to the workout.

They both sipped on water at the end of the workout in time to see Pietra and Chip walk by, laughing about something. They walked on without noticing Pennie just inside the gym. Before Pennie's imagination could get bogged down, Karolina said, "Let's get ready for the day. I'll help with your makeup."

After room service delivered some morning sustenance, Karolina ate her vegan oats while scrutinizing Pennie's outfit. "You can't wear athletic shorts today. Put on one of those sundresses."

"We're fixing to shuttle to the port and go through check in. I'd rather be comfortable," Pennie argued.

"Put on the dress. Those sandals are fine. I know you can wear heels or wedges all day without a problem."

"Shouldn't we be focusing on your mission and not on my wardrobe?"

Karolina rolled her eyes. "No. I know exactly what to do. Let's look at your makeup options. I have more nail supplies than makeup, so we'll have to depend on whatever you brought."

After applying night-time lipstick colors at eight in the morning, Pennie and Karolina caught an Uber to the Miami airport where they would catch a shuttle to PortMiami. Waiting in the Festival Cruise area of the airport terminal, Pennie pretended to work a puzzle as Pietra and Chip walked by to check in. They turned in the rental car at the airport to catch the same shuttle to the same cruise ship.

As of last night, Pennie and Karolina wouldn't act like they knew Pietra and Chip. The mission had begun. It was time for the game face. They eventually loaded onto a shuttle bus to head to the ship terminal. From their seats midway through the bus, they watched Chip and Pietra take a seat a few rows in front of them. Rather than focus on them, Pennie gazed out the window and listened to the driver offer interesting facts about the city of Miami during the ride.

Everything went smoothly when they arrived at the Festival Cruise terminal. Pennie and Karolina checked their suitcases with the porters and made their way through the checkpoints. Security scans. Verifying passports… and visa in Karolina's case. Showing their boarding passes and receiving their *SailAway* cards. Usually, Festival took a photo that linked to the *SailAway* card to become their official form of ID on the ship.

When the Festival representative handed them the SailAway cards without taking a picture, Pennie asked her, "Don't you need to get our photo?"

"No, we upload your passport picture as your identification. And most of the checkpoints use facial recognition, so you won't have to show any official ID to get through."

"What checkpoints?" Pennie asked, slightly fearing what her answer would be.

"The itinerary for your trip doesn't look like it has any international checkpoints until you get back to Miami. The customs team will wave you through with only facial recognition. It makes the process so much faster and easier."

"Great!" Pennie said. That wasn't what she was thinking, though. Fear seeped into her bones, and she tried to not let it reach her facial expression. There was no turning back now.

Pennie and Karolina went through all the lines and stops and finally boarded the ship by noon. The muster station safety drill was checked off quickly so the ladies could find some lunch. The pasta bar on the top deck even had a gluten-free option for Karolina. After eating, they moved to the deck for a few minutes to soak up the sun and feel the warm breeze. They needed to find momentary peace as their part of the mission grew nearer.

"Hey, ladies. Are these chairs taken?" a man asked expectantly. He indicated the two chairs on the other side of the seating area currently occupied by Pennie and Karolina. There were plenty of empty chairs on the deck, and they weren't occupying any seats close to the pool. Why did the guys want to sit here?

While Pennie contemplated their motive, Karolina answered him, "They're not taken."

"We're taking a cruise to celebrate my little brother's college graduation."

Their uninvited company wanted to start a conversation. Pennie had already put on her game face. Even if these guys were worth meeting, it wasn't like she would ever see them again after this cruise.

"Where did you graduate from?" Karolina asked politely, carrying the conversation for both of them.

The younger brother, who was cute in his own college boy kind of way, eagerly answered. "Tulane. I got my degree in engineering."

Big brother, who was also cute, jumped back in. "Is that an accent? Where are you from?"

"I'm from Brazil. My host mom is from Tennessee."

Extending a hand, little brother said, "It's nice to meet you, Brazil. I'm JJ. This is my big brother Nick."

Karolina never smiled fully in her attempt to prevent premature smile lines. JJ must have interpreted her little grin as flirting and leaned back in his seat to keep chatting.

"I'm Karolina, this is my host mom Pennie. We're just taking vacation while I'm out of school for the semester. I'll graduate next May. I'm hoping we get to take an Australian cruise for that celebration!"

Both boys grinned in return, displaying dimples. They reminded Pennie of Mario Lopez. Wavy, dark hair, sparkling dark eyes. They may not be of Hispanic descent, but they had perfect tans that could pass for some kind of Latino heritage. After yesterday, Pennie wouldn't be making any assumptions about anyone's heritage from now on. Both guys also had what she would consider *runners' bodies*. Toned muscles without being bulky. They also both wore tank tops, displaying a handful of colorful tattoos on their arms. And one big Green Wave tattoo on Nick's leg.

Even though Memphis and Tulane weren't quite rivals, they always had competitive games. What was a Green Wave anyway? A real university deserved a real mascot. Her internal monologue prevented Pennie from hearing any of the conversation taking place in front of her.

Big brother was in the middle of a story, "...so he left us plenty of money to get our education and get established. I finished my master's a few years ago, and now I work as a speech pathologist in New Orleans." He beamed with pride.

"When I finish my doctoral program, I want to teach quantum physics at the university level."

It sounded like little brother had good plans too. Cute and educated. If their quiet time had to be invaded, at least these two had potential. Not actual potential after this week, but it made her hesitate to dismiss them after two minutes of conversation.

Pennie slowly stood. "Guys, I'm sorry, I'm a little tired from our long drive yesterday. Karolina, do you wanna go with me to the stateroom to see if our luggage arrived?"

JJ quickly stood. "Maybe we'll see you later at the shove-off party?"

"Maybe," Karolina and Pennie said in unison.

In the hallway outside the stateroom, they met their room steward Edgar. After cursory greetings, they ducked inside the sanctuary of their room.

"How do the stewards always remember everyone's name? And the names change every week for them."

"It's impressive, but they've trained themselves for it. That's why I always leave a good tip in the room," Pennie responded as she applied fresh lipstick in the mirror.

"Why didn't you want me talking to JJ?" Karolina asked from her bed.

Pennie had a seat and thought about the best way to respond. She wanted to let her daughter have a few fun days, but she didn't want her focus to waver. "You'll only be on the boat for a few days. I don't think you should be making any friends to hang out with. Let's relax without finding you a boyfriend."

"I don't care about finding me a boyfriend. I was trying to get you to talk to Nick."

"I don't need any boyfriend either, Karolina. For real. No connections with new people, okay?"

The conversation came to an end when their luggage arrived. Unpacking was easy enough. But now Pennie's outfits were out of whack since she wore her Saturday dress today. Tomorrow would be a day at sea, and she anticipated wearing shorts and a tank top, but Karolina might not allow that either. She had just finished unloading all her bathroom supplies when a knock came from the door that adjoined their stateroom to the next one.

Pennie and Karolina exchanged a glance before approaching the door. "Who is it?" Pennie asked with a singsong tone.

"Open the door, Skipper," Chip answered without bothering to identify himself.

As she fiddled with the locks, Pennie tried to decide whether she liked his use of her nickname from their time on the yacht. Even more so, she wondered if his use of her nickname made Pietra jealous. It wasn't like she would say anything about it, so she just opened the door and greeted them with a smile.

Chip and Pietra moved into their stateroom and plopped down onto the small couch. "From here on out, our job is just to watch out for Karolina. No one needs to know our group's here together, but we'll want to keep a visual on y'all whenever we leave the ship. Other than that, just relax for a few days. Ambassador Hernandez will send us updates if anything comes up."

"Is there anything we need to discuss?" Pietra asked the rest of the group.

With a little trepidation, Pennie mentioned the facial recognition concern. "They've never done this before. So, when Francelia gets back to Miami, her face might not get a green light."

Chip nodded. "I'm sure the customs officials will scrutinize her passport and visa paperwork. She just needs to be ready for any kind of inquiry and hope for the best. Anything else?"

Pennie shook her head, "Nope. I guess we'll just plan on having our last pow wow on Sunday before we port in La Romana."

"If anything unusual happens on the ship, send me a message, and we'll meet back here," Chip said as he got up to leave. Pietra offered a condescending smile as she followed him back to their own stateroom.

Pennie tried not to fixate on the fact that Pietra and Chip were sharing a bed. A year ago, Pennie and Chip shared a bed on a cruise ship, but they worked out a way to keep a blanket between them. Strictly platonic bed-sharing for undercover work. In her mind, the same thing was happening next door this week.

"We have a few hours before dinner. You wanna go to the pool? I can read a book," Pennie offered, knowing how much her daughter loved to spend time in the sun.

With a generous layer of sunscreen applied, Pennie lounged in a chair near the pool. Karolina floated and chatted with a few children who laughed and played. Eventually, her Brazilian daughter stretched out in the adjacent chair to get a sip of water.

"Are you making friends with the neighborhood kids?" Pennie asked with a smile.

"They think I'm younger than I am."

A flashback from her dream the night before flitted through Pennie's brain. "What's on that boy's swim trunks that looks like a red wasp?"

"The new *Thunder Swarm* movie is coming out. That's the red jacket silhouette on the superhero's uniform."

"Shouldn't it be a yellow jacket and not a red jacket?" Pennie asked.

"Um, no. In the movie, the yellow jackets are the good guys, and red jackets are the bad guys, but the bad guys must save the earth. Like anti-heroes."

At least Pennie identified where the red wasp silhouette came from in her subconscious. She must've seen an advertisement for the movie at some point.

"Can we go to the slides next?" her daughter asked, not wanting to waste a single minute on the ship.

Pennie followed Karolina up a deck where the tall slides started. While the excited girl got in line, Pennie found a seat in the shade to keep up with their pool bags.

A voice interrupted the climax of the book Pennie was reading. "Do we have to be enemies because you're a Tiger fan?"

Nick sat in the chair across from her without waiting for an invitation.

"I'm not a Tiger fan. I *am* a Tiger. My daughter is too," Pennie answered, realizing her pool bag displayed the University of Memphis logo.

"Your daughter and my brother seem to be getting along really well."

Pennie looked up to see Karolina chatting with JJ in the line. She had never seen this side of her daughter. Karolina twirled her hair and tilted her head to the side in a flirty manner. It was hard to believe she was twenty years old. Since she never allowed boys to distract her from her education, Pennie wasn't prepared to see Karolina acting interested in a boy now.

"She's got a tough school schedule, so dating's never been a priority for her."

"What about you?"

Pennie turned her head to look at Nick, but she left her Oakleys in place. "What about me?"

"Is dating a priority for you?" He offered a tiny smile with the inquiry, just enough to display the dimple on his left cheek.

"No, Nick. I'm a widow, and I ain't worried about dating. Karolina's my only concern these days. Maybe after she graduates, I'll dip my toe in the dating pool."

"Okay, Tiger. I hope we'll see you around the ship though."

Finally finishing the book, Pennie only had to wait another minute for a soaking-wet Karolina to show up.

"Mom, let's get showers and get ready for dinner."

Dining on a cruise ship was the way to go. The diverse menu. The amazing service. The entertaining crew. Best of all, no dishes to wash afterwards. After being shown to their assigned table, Karolina managed to find some kind of mushroom wellington dish for vegans. On the other end of the spectrum, Pennie ordered a surf and turf meal. Their waiter Henry brought warm bread, which only Pennie could enjoy.

As they sipped water, Pennie started a conversation that she never truly anticipated having with her daughter. "So, what're you thinking about JJ? Do you want to date him?"

Karolina's wide eyes and flared nostrils indicated she didn't appreciate the question. "I'm old enough to date who I want, Mom. You don't have to worry about me."

Pennie made a quick look around and turned back to Karolina, keeping her voice low. "Yes, I do have to worry about you. When you get off the ship Monday, JJ might be looking for you, but he's gonna find Francelia instead. We don't need that kind of attention on this mission."

Now a furrowed brow joined Karolina's facial

expression. "What do you know about missions? I'm just talking to a boy I'll never see again. Like I said earlier, I'm more interested in you talking to Nick than me talking to JJ."

Karolina settled back in her chair as the food was served. They said grace and dug in. "After dinner, can we go to the dance club?"

At that moment, Chip and Pietra were seated at their assigned table on the opposite side of the restaurant, looking like a couple in love. Pennie tried to quell the lingering jealousy. All men were off limits. She couldn't see if there was a spark with Nick thanks to their mission. She couldn't follow through on her ridiculous sentiments for Chip thanks to his own ridiculous sentiments for Pietra.

She needed to get out of her own head in a bad way. "You know what, Karolina? I think the nightclub might be a good way to end the evening."

The nightclub was crowded with adults who wanted to get their vacation started. Karolina and Pennie sat at a table sipping virgin Piña Coladas, watching all the cruisers dance along to the latest mainstream hip-hop song. Eventually, JJ and Nick entered the club. Karolina immediately joined JJ on the floor, easily outdancing everyone else in the room as only a Brazilian can do. Nick ordered a beer and joined Pennie at the table.

"Don't you want to dance?"

Choosing not to answer immediately, Pennie remembered the last time she danced with a man. Chip had some good moves, and she almost flushed thinking about their visits to a couple of nightclubs.

"Not right now," Pennie said, still lost in thought.

Nick stayed at the table. He managed to draw Pennie into a conversation about the value of college education. She refused to be rude, so she chatted with him even though she kept an eye on the younger couple on the dance floor. If JJ made one wrong move, Pennie wouldn't hesitate to punch him in the throat.

"Why do you look like you want to pummel someone?" Nick asked.

Her face was more expressive than she realized. Trying to replace her scowl with something more pleasant, Pennie answered with honesty. "Karolina's never dated anyone. I'm fretting over her ability to make good decisions, and I'm worried about the intentions of your brother." She held her hand up to cut off Nick before he could jump to JJ's defense. "Nothing against your brother. That's a general concern, and I've never had to worry about this before."

"JJ's a good kid. He won't do anything to sully the reputation of your precious Karolina."

What the heck? Pennie thought as Pietra and Chip entered the nightclub. Can't she just wind down for a couple of hours without Nick pestering her and Chip invading her space?

"What's wrong? I promise, JJ won't take advantage of her."

Adjusting her gaze back to her table companion, Pennie responded, "I'm sure he's a perfectly respectable young man. This is just new for me."

Her teammates went to the bar area to order a couple of glasses of wine before they occupied the table next to her. *What the heck again?* Pennie thought. *Can't they just go away?*

"I understand, Tiger. Come on and dance with me. You

look like you need a mental break."

Reluctantly, Pennie allowed Nick to lead her to the floor. They moved with the music for only two songs before Karolina indicated she was ready to go.

Pennie and Karolina lay in bed in their pajamas, both needing some real sleep. They managed to turn off the lights, but neither of them could turn off their brains.

"Mom, you're right. JJ acts like he wants us to hang out every night. The last couple of days of this cruise, I won't be here. I see how that's a problem. Which means you can't get to know Nick either."

"I'll be okay. Let's just lay low for the next few days and chill out." Internally, Pennie felt relief. Relief about Karolina's focus on the mission, and that she wouldn't be forced to get to know someone new. A little time alone, no men at all, would allow Pennie's heart and mind to find a peaceful place again.

A knock from the adjoining room interrupted their exchange. Pennie got up to open the door, allowing Pietra and Chip to enter, still dressed in their sexy nightclub clothes.

Pietra had a seat on the edge of Karolina's bed, while Chip remained standing near the doorway. She addressed Pennie first, "I can't believe I even have to tell you this, Pennie, but you don't need to be finding any hook-ups or boyfriends on this cruise." She turned to face the Brazilian, her profile only illuminated from the light coming through the doorway. "Karolina, you need to remain low key. Don't form any relationships or friendships."

Chip spoke up at that point, "I really thought this went

without saying, so I'm glad that Pietra wanted to shadow y'all tonight. I didn't realize either of you would do anything to compromise this mission."

Pennie didn't like the disappointed tone that Chip spoke with. She also hated that Pietra planted these seeds of distrust, as if Pennie and Karolina were loose cannons on this mission. While contemplating the best way to respond, she was surprised that Karolina answered first.

"Those boys are stalking us. I only realized it tonight when I was dancing with JJ, but they fixated on us because we're not here with any men. I let JJ know that I'm not looking to hang out with him again, and Mom and I just had this conversation about laying low and avoiding them. You don't have to worry about us."

"I hope you mean that," Pietra replied. Then she got up and returned to her own stateroom with Chip.

THURSDAY, JULY 7

Karolina and Pennie spent the first half of the day at sea in peace. They visited the gym for a good workout. They visited the spa for relaxing facials. They ate an amazing brunch in the restaurant.

No sign of Nick and JJ. If Chip and Pietra followed them, they did so stealthily.

By mid-afternoon, they found quiet lounging chairs on deck six, away from any crowd, to read books for a couple of hours. This was Pennie's kind of cruise. At Karolina's request, they went for a walk around the ship before it was time to get ready for dinner.

On the tenth deck, they rounded a corner to find an oversized chess board. Pietra and Chip had just started a game. Pennie pulled Karolina to some nearby chairs to watch the match. Another handful of cruisers had gathered to watch, but the match wasn't very competitive. Pietra must've known the rules of chess, but she hadn't played enough to develop strategies and plan moves in advance. Within five minutes, Chip had Pietra's king trapped. Checkmate.

Chip looked at the small group who watched and said, "Who wants to play the winner?"

Karolina nudged Pennie. She hesitated a moment before getting up to help Chip finish resetting the chess board. Chip started a quiet conversation, partially with the guise that they didn't know each other.

"Have you played much chess?" he asked with a smirk.

"I've played here and there, but it's been a long time since I've had a worthy opponent."

"Do we need to place a little wager here?"

Pennie laughed. "No, this isn't Vegas. No wagers. Just bragging rights, okay?"

A half hour later, they were equally matched in the game. Pennie felt the heat of the Caribbean sun beating down on her back, but that wasn't the only reason she was sweating. The silly smack talk and banter she shared with Chip lulled her back into that daydream where they were the only two people who existed in the Gulf of Mexico.

Until freaking Pietra interrupted her thoughts.

"Ma'am, I think your daughter's getting seasick. You should check on her."

Pennie looked over to see JJ talking to Karolina, but Karolina was holding her stomach like she was sick. Abandoning the game, she immediately rushed to her daughter's side. Karolina said she felt queasy, so together, they slowly made their way to their stateroom.

"Tell me what you need, honey. I have Dramamine pills and patches. I have Sprite even if you don't like carbonated drinks. I have some saltines, but you can't eat them." Pennie was steadily pulling things out of the closet to heal her ailing daughter when Karolina laughed from behind her. She was glad she stocked up on everything for this occasion, but she didn't understand her daughter's amusement.

"I'm fine, Mom. JJ was trying to make plans with me for tonight. He's visiting the comedy show later and asked me to go. That's when I started acting sick, and I kept up the act all the way here."

"Well, you certainly had me fooled," Pennie said,

simultaneously relieved and impressed at Karolina's acting skills.

"Let's just get ready for dinner. We have a couple of hours, so we don't have to be rushed."

Back at their assigned table, Henry quickly brought them water and salads. He let Karolina know about the vegan specials for the evening. She decided on a tofu steak, while Pennie chose the smothered fried chicken. She tried not to notice when Chip and Pietra sat at their table and sipped on wine.

"I get it, Mom."

Karolina's words interrupted Pennie's thoughts. "What do you get, sweetheart?"

"Chip is competitive. You need someone to challenge you like he does."

"Maybe Pietra needs that too."

Karolina shook her head. "No, she wasn't any good at chess."

"That doesn't mean she isn't good at other things. Just eat your fake steak and quit worrying about my dating life."

They managed to make small talk throughout dinner without any intrusions or disruptions. After they ate, they walked around the ship to see storm clouds in the distance and breathe in the cool night air.

By bedtime, they were tucked in and ready for some good sleep. Flashes of lightning pierced the curtains as they approached the storm. The ship rolled just slightly with the rougher waters, but that didn't bother either of the ladies in this stateroom.

Too bad the adjacent stateroom couldn't be unaffected as well. The knock on the door roused Pennie before she fully fell asleep.

She opened the door to find Pietra wearing a silk nightie that bordered on being lingerie. Pennie glanced down at her own pajama top. *ZZZs on the High Seas* across the shirt matched the fleecy pajama bottoms. It was obvious which of the two ladies shared a stateroom with a man.

"Chip asked me to get you."

"What's going on?" Pennie asked as she entered their stateroom. As her eyes adjusted to the light, she found Chip sitting up on the couch.

"Skipper, do you have something for motion sickness?"

"Yea, let me get it."

Pennie returned a minute later to place a transdermal motion sickness patch behind his ear and open a bottle of Sprite. She sat next to him on the couch. So close to his beautiful bare chest. Rather than get distracted, she asked, "Are you just dizzy? Or do you feel nauseated?"

"Just dizzy."

"Do you want to take a Dramamine now? It's chewable so it'll start working faster than the patch."

"Sure," he answered as he accepted a tablet from her.

"I'll just leave these saltines and Sprite here in case you

need them later. You might feel better sitting up until the dizziness passes." Then Pennie turned to face Pietra. "He'll be fine. I'm next door if you need me."

FRIDAY, JULY 8

Sea day brunch was a wonderful follow-up to their morning exercise. After breakfast, they moved to the adults only area of the top deck to lay out. Not that Pennie's Irish genes could tolerate much sun, but she enjoyed the quiet time with her daughter. Since Karolina started college two years ago, they didn't get much quality time anymore.

The deck was crowded, but it was blessedly serene. Pennie had just closed her eyes for a minute when a voice asked, "Are these two chairs available?"

Pennie opened her eyes to find Pietra standing over her. She glanced around. No other chairs were open. "Sure, you can have them."

Chip removed his shirt and laid back immediately to get comfortable. Pietra spoke to him, "I'm going to get a drink. Do you want something?"

"No, thanks," he told her.

After Pietra moved to the bar area, Pennie realized that Karolina had inserted her AirPods to drown out the quiet conversations around them.

Pennie leaned towards Chip, who sat with one chair between them, and asked, "Are you feeling better?"

Chip raised his sunglasses to glance at her. Then he glanced back at Pietra who waited on her cocktail out of earshot. "I wasn't sick. She was moving too fast, and I wanted to slow her down. But I appreciate you being my Florence

Nightingale again." He added a wink before pulling his glasses back down and resuming his relaxed position.

With that bit of information, Pennie's brain went haywire. Was Chip keeping Pietra at a distance? Or was he just trying to manage the pace of their relationship better? Were they dating at all? These questions plagued Pennie for the next half hour. By then, her skin protested louder than the questions in her head.

"Karolina," she said as she touched her daughter's arm. "Can we find some shade?"

They abandoned their chairs to find another secluded set on another deck. They had barely started reading when Nick and JJ showed up.

"Where've you been? We've been looking for you," JJ said as they took the remaining two seats next to the women.

"Karolina hasn't been feeling well, so we're just taking it easy."

Flopping her book down in her lap, Karolina added, "I think the fresh air helps, but reading on a boat is making it worse."

"Do you want to lie down?"

"I think so."

Pennie stood and helped Karolina to her feet. "Sorry, guys. She's prone to seasickness."

"I guess a nap works just fine," Karolina said after she dried her hair. "Rest is the most important factor in our anti-aging process."

Pennie took her turn drying her hair. Showers always refreshed Pennie after a sweaty day. "I hate that you've gotta be holed up in here. After dinner, we can watch the live musical, if you're up for it. Then tomorrow, we can walk around Curacao. Are you okay with that?"

"Yes. It's been a tough semester at school, and I only wanted to take it easy this week anyway. After a few days of rest, helping Francelia is a great way to focus on something bigger than myself, and I think it's going to be more like an adventure for me."

"I'm so glad that's how you see it. Honey, let's enjoy these couple of days."

SATURDAY, JULY 9

It was nice to stretch their legs in the sunshine of Curacao for a spell that morning. Karolina arranged her hair in a bun and wore a ballcap to give herself a little anonymity. Pennie mimicked her tactics. They just wanted to shop for a few souvenirs without any stalky guys following them. Of course, Pietra and Chip kept an eye on them in port. But no sign of JJ or Nick.

This was their first visit to Curacao. Without booking an excursion, they were limited to walking through the port area, but it wasn't disappointing in the least. All the brightly painted buildings as far as the eye could see mesmerized the tourists. Pennie was more impressed with the mall that had been constructed inside a fort. They took a few pictures of the cannons, then a selfie from the top of the fort before returning to the shops below.

Pennie allowed herself to relax for a few minutes as Karolina took pictures with different wooden masks inside one of the trinket stores.

"Are you posting that on social media?" Pennie asked.

"Just on my *ReelLife* app."

"What's that? Is it like Facebook?"

"No, you make different groups of friends or family, then a timer goes off a few random times during the day. You have to post a picture to the group, but it must be a live photo of what you're doing at that exact time. Not something already stored on your phone. It creates a *reel* that shows your group what your *real life* looks like since you never know when the timer will go off. At the end of every week and month, the app gives you a highlight reel of your recent experiences."

As Karolina explained the latest trend in social media ridiculousness, Pennie rolled her eyes. She never got on board with creating any accounts or displaying any part of her life for the internet to witness.

They purchased a few souvenirs and headed back to the ship. Karolina presented her *SailAway* card to the ship attendant who scanned the barcode and matched her with the photo associated with the card. This would be the process each time they boarded the ship. Karolina would be hard to recognize with the ballcap and sunglasses, but the attendant didn't seem to care that much as he waved them past.

Their tote bags were put through a scanner for security to check in case they brought back forbidden fruits or alcohol or something. Pennie had never seen security confiscate anything, so she wasn't exactly sure what they checked for.

At the lunch buffet onboard, JJ and Nick surprised them by sitting at their table. Instead of enjoying their hot sandwiches in peace, they listened to the boys jabber on about their adventures on the ship so far. They talked about their beach excursion that morning, but it didn't last long with the sea gulls dive-bombing them the whole time.

Pennie and Karolina managed to listen without being rude, but they didn't want to prolong any interaction with them. Karolina asked if she could go back to the stateroom to get some aspirin and take a nap.

Nick tried to prolong the company. "Come on, Tiger. You don't have to hold her hand. Mabye you'd like to join me for some mini golf?"

"No, thanks. I need to tend to my daughter, but I really do appreciate the invitation."

In the four years that Karolina had been her daughter, she'd never witnessed her take an aspirin. One time, Karolina sprained her ankle in a relay race at school but refused to take anything for the pain or swelling. Now, she wanted the aspirin.

"What's going on, honey?" Pennie asked as she dropped two capsules in her daughter's hand.

"What if something goes wrong? I'm just getting worried."

They had a seat on the couch in the stateroom. Pennie sighed heavily. "You're my daughter, Karolina. Francelia isn't. So, if you want to back out right now, I'll put a stop to this plan, and I'll let everyone know it's my decision. Just say the word."

"Francelia is someone's daughter too. Can we pray about this? Not for a way out, but a prayer for safety?"

Using Pennie's Bible App, the ladies focused on a few verses that applied to their situation. Karolina felt like she was in the valley of the shadow of death. Pennie needed the reminder that worrying wouldn't add one minute to her life. They both wanted God's will to be done. After a prayer, they took a peaceful nap before dinner.

SUNDAY, JULY 10

Aruba was beautiful. Pennie could see why people wrote songs about the gorgeous island. Too bad the rain interfered with them spending much time in port. With only a few trinkets purchased, they hurried back to the ship for the remainder of the day.

After changing into dry clothes, they found lunch in the sushi shop where Karolina ordered cucumber rolls with gluten free soy sauce. "This might be my last good meal."

"Cucumber sushi is a good meal? Oh please, Karolina. Try this deep-fried tempura shrimp roll." Pennie waved the bite of sushi in front of her daughter, only to have the roll swatted from her chopsticks. Picking the morsel back up from her plate, she asked a real question before popping it into her mouth. "Seriously, Karolina. Are you feeling some kind of impending doom?"

"We can talk later. Let me just enjoy this meal."

In the privacy of their stateroom, Karolina flopped down on her bed. She never had a flair for the dramatic, so the exaggerated display of trepidation had Pennie concerned.

"Honey, please talk to me. Do you want to back out? Do

you want us to finish this cruise without any talk of missions or death threats or anything else?"

"No. I don't know," Karolina whispered.

"Is there something else going on?"

"Kind of. When Ambassador Vale spoke to me in Portuguese at our meeting, she told me she was concerned about the protective detail they're assigning to Francelia once you get her back to Miami. She's worried that somewhere in the government, someone will leak some information. Then Francelia will be in trouble thousands of miles from home."

"Is that what has you worried? For Francelia's safety and not for yours? Who're you worried about?" Pennie asked, sitting on the bed next to her daughter.

"I'm worried about her. I know that Pietra's sister will take care of me. Mom, please promise me that you'll watch over Francelia and keep her safe, just like she's your own daughter."

"I promise, Karolina. It's just like when your international friends come to my house. Anyone in my custody is treated like my daughter. You know that."

MONDAY, JULY 11

The ship docked in La Romana—the stop they'd been waiting for. Karolina and Pennie spent all the extra time they needed getting ready that morning. Karolina curled her long, newly colored hair in a style showcased by AmberLou in her most recent music video. She topped it with a white visor. Her flowy summer dress featured a colorful tie-dye design. Flip flops and a straw tote bag completed her look.

Pennie pulled her own auburn hair into a ponytail and donned an AmberLou concert t-shirt with denim shorts. Knowing the excursion for the day featured some walking, she wore sneakers instead of flip flops. It was time to meet their group for today's adventure.

Once they loaded onto the bus that would take them into town for a sightseeing tour, Karolina and Pennie put on sunglasses and looked around the bus nonchalantly. Pietra and Chip were among the other fifty cruisers joining them on this five-hour excursion.

The bus drove them through the town of La Romana, past the beautiful Church of Saint Rosa de Lima, and through the extravagant neighborhood of Altos de Chavon.

The cruisers got to walk around the postcard-worthy streets of the Mediterranean-inspired village for a few minutes. The church in this neighborhood had been used for more than one celebrity wedding. Jennifer Lopez married Marc Anthony there. With the same marital luck, Michael Jackson and Lisa Marie Presley got hitched there as well. As stunning as the church might be, Pennie made a mental note that the nuptial location had nothing to do with the success of the marriage. A gorgeous Caribbean church or a neon steeple in Vegas. It didn't really matter.

Overall, her impression of the island was pleasant. What did she really expect to see? Did she think she would witness a murder or an acid attack? Did she think anything *machismo* would slap her in the face? Not at all. Everything seemed laid back and welcoming. That got Pennie thinking. What if the machismo culture wasn't as bad as everyone made it out to be? What if one hot-headed gang made threats loud enough to capture everyone's attention even though they didn't represent any number of Dominican residents?

As she soaked up the beautiful scenery from Altos de Chavon, Pennie changed her way of thinking. The danger couldn't be that bad if life went on as normal here. President Vasquez wanted to exercise an abundance of caution by sending her daughter out of the country. She walked along with the group towards their waiting bus, inhaling deeply to calm her nerves.

The next stop was a relaxing boat ride down the Chavon River. Surrounded by pristine nature, Pennie found herself only partially listening to their tour guide. This river was used to film part of the movie *Anaconda*, as well as various other reality television shows. Instead of being placated by the scenery, Pennie's nerves felt more fraught with every moment that passed.

Despite her momentary calm a half hour ago, she

realized that her own daughter would soon be trading places with Francelia. Karolina would be the one in danger. That fact made Pennie more pensive than she had been up until now.

They arrived at the chocolate-making factory stop of the tour. The factory was in the middle of a strip mall with a variety of stores. The tour guide gave them a quick lecture about cacao trees before leading the group through the factory where visitors could see the process from the raw cacao bean to the assortment of final products. On the other side of the factory, they ended up in a small shop selling chocolates, lotions, coffees, and teas all made from cacao beans. The group was given enough time to do some shopping or visit the restroom if they needed it.

Pennie and Karolina moved outside to get out of the way of the serious shoppers. Once they found a bench, the Brazilian leaned over to whisper, "I need to use the restroom. Please hold my bag and water bottle."

Holding the bag, Pennie noticed Pietra and Chip hanging out close by.

A few minutes later, the tie-dye dress joined Pennie back at the bench. Keeping her voice even, Pennie asked, "Was the restroom clean?"

"Yes, can I have my water back now?" The voice was soft like Karolina's, but the accent was slightly off. Pennie thought she was prepared but knowing her daughter was gone made her heart heavy with dread. She handed the girl the water bottle and glanced around, looking for the denim shorts and white tank top that Karolina had on under the tie-dye dress that Francelia now wore. She looked for the pink ballcap that Francelia traded with Karolina for the white visor that now perched on the head of her substitute daughter.

But there was no sign of her. Karolina must've gotten out of the area quickly. Francelia needed Pennie to be her mother now, and she wouldn't succumb to the panic that rose in her chest.

The fifteen-minute bus ride back to the cruise ship passed with more interesting facts shared by their tour guide. Pennie and Francelia didn't try to speak to each other, but they held hands. They knew the next obstacle would be pivotal to the success of the extraction.

The line to get back onto the ship after an excursion required a little patience. They also felt a little fear when the attendant scanned the *SailAway* card that belonged to Karolina. Francelia sure resembled the Brazilian, but the swap made them nervous.

The nervousness was wasted as the attendant scanned and ushered them onto the boat without a second glance. Pennie released the breath she didn't realize she'd been holding. As their bags went through the security scanner, an officer with a drug-sniffing dog passed by.

"Ma'am, I need you to wait right here please." The thick accent instructed Francelia to stand to the side while he searched through her bag.

Pennie's heart stopped beating in that moment, and Francelia appeared frozen in place. She tried to get her nerves under control enough to encourage her new refugee. "Honey, move over here. You must've accidentally put something in your bag."

Since the bag was Karolina's, neither of them had a clue what caught the attention of the security team. The armed officer removed a few expected items… sunscreen, extra bottle of water, lip balm… then the prohibited item—an apple. The forbidden fruit.

"Ma'am, you can't bring fruit onto the ship," the officer instructed as he handed the bag back to Francelia, tossing the apple into a bucket behind his table.

"Sorry, I thought I might need a snack," she responded.

Chip and Pietra waited in the lobby to see what the holdup might be, but they moved on after seeing Pennie and Francelia pass the checkpoint.

When they finally made it to the stateroom, Pennie knew it was time to have a talk with Francelia.

"You're safe now, sweetie. The last obstacle is getting you back into PortMiami, but you really do look enough like Karolina that I don't foresee a problem. You'll just want to remember the small details like your visa type and the name of your school. We have a few days to go over all that. Until we get off this boat, you're my daughter. You call me Mom, not Pennie. Are you good with that?"

"Yes, Mom." The girl smiled as she had a seat on her bed. "Is this my bed?"

"It is your bed." Pennie took a few minutes to show Francelia all the possessions that became hers in Karolina's absence. Clothes in the closet, hair supplies, makeup, and toiletries.

"Mom, I've been living in the National Palace for eight months now, but I feel like this little room is more luxurious than anything I've ever experienced before."

"It's amazing how a little security can make everything seem better," Pennie replied.

Francelia physically jumped when a knock came from the stateroom door.

Pennie greeted their room steward who offered to turn down their beds. Pennie declined, saying they would be getting ready for dinner now.

The next knock made them both jump. This time, it came from the door to the adjoining room.

Pietra rushed into the room to wrap Pennie in an unexpected hug. "I know how hard that was for you. Bianca has Karolina now, and they're headed for the yacht. As soon as they make it out of the country, my sister will let me know."

"Thank you, Pietra. I'm feeling a bit beside myself right now."

"Francelia, I'm Pietra. This is Chip. We're police officers from Tennessee, and we're going to be watching over you until we get you into the hands of the security team in Miami."

"Muchas gracias en realidad estoy muy aliviada en poder estar aquí en el crusero! ¡Nunca había estado en un cruser entonces de paso voy a poder relajarme por primera vez en un ano!"

"I don't speak Spanish," Pietra replied, slowly shaking her head.

Pennie laughed aloud. "See? I'm not the only one who thinks you look Latina, Pietra."

Plans were made to get ready for dinner. Nothing out of routine as far as anything on the ship was concerned. After

Francelia's shower, Pennie braided her hair at her request. One of Karolina's rompers fit her perfectly. They moved onto the dining room without any delay.

"Oh, Karolina, I have a treat for you! Tonight, we have a special vegan dish inspired by the Dominican culture," their ever-grinning waiter Henry said as he poured glasses of water for them.

Francelia glanced at Pennie before saying anything. "Um, I want to try something different tonight. How about the steak? And can I have a Coke to drink?"

Henry looked at her quizzically. Pennie decided to intervene. "I had a long talk with her earlier about trying new things. She hasn't eaten meat since she was six, but she's going to choose something different every night we're on the cruise."

At that time, Francelia took a bite from a warm dinner roll.

"So, you aren't allergic to gluten?" Henry asked.

"No, I... um... only choose to be healthy. What I eat on the cruise is all vacation food. It doesn't count."

Shaking his head, the waiter walked back to the kitchen with their orders.

"I guess I should've warned you that Karolina is gluten intolerant, lactose intolerant, and vegetarian."

"I'm sorry, Mom. What else do I need to know?"

"Nothing really. Enjoy your steak, and we'll just try to stay under the radar for the rest of the cruise."

"Can I ask a question?" Francelia prodded.

"Ask me anything, sweetie."

"Are you an AmberLou fan?"

Of all the questions… "Oh, not really. I had to borrow that t-shirt to wear earlier. Karolina is a huge fan, and she traveled to Chicago to see her in concert a few months ago. I've already bought tickets for when AmberLou comes to Memphis in October. Karolina and my nieces will go along with another couple of adults. I bought tickets for them, but I don't care to see the show."

"Did it disappoint you when Karolina had her hair styled like AmberLou's?"

"Absolutely not. Karolina is beautiful no matter how she does her hair, and so are you."

In the meantime, Pietra and Chip occupied their table in the dining room. Pennie immediately felt that every eye in the dining room was watching them. That all the staff watched their every move. She mentally willed herself to calm down.

After they both dug into their steaks, Pennie couldn't enjoy hers. Pietra hadn't let her know that Bianca and Archie had gotten Karolina safely out of the country yet. It should've taken less than an hour, but that passed over an hour ago. She watched as Francelia enjoyed her first meal without worry in months. The girl managed to finish the entire steak and top it off with some chocolate lava cake.

Back in the stateroom, Francelia asked if they could go to bed early.

"You can go ahead to bed. I'm just going to play a game on my phone until I'm tired."

"Are you nervous, Mom?"

Pennie kicked her shoes off and moved to the bed to sit next to Francelia.

"Of course, I am. I have no idea where my daughter is, and I just left her in a country that's looking to murder someone who looks like her. And now I'm scared for your family, because even though we got you out of the Dominican Republic, your own mother doesn't know where you are. No one knows what your protection detail will look like when we get to Miami, so all the unknowns have me on edge. For your safety and for Karolina's. And for your mother's peace of mind as well as mine." Pennie wiped an unexpected tear from her cheek. Hearing Francelia call her *Mom* in Karolina's absence was bittersweet among the feelings of dread that tightened her chest and restricted her breathing.

"Thank you, Pennie. Mom. You have no idea how much I appreciate your help. My mom knows that you host exchange students, and she read all your blogs from when Karolina lived at home in high school. She has peace of mind right now knowing that I'm with you instead of on lockdown in my own country."

Pennie almost forgot about the blogs. It had been two years since she made daily posts for Karolina's family in Brazil to follow along with, and for Mako's family in Japan before that. The blogs weren't publicized, but anyone could follow the page and read the archives if they wanted to.

"Obviously, I have a history of welcoming internationals into my home. So, you're my daughter now. I can't pause that part of me that wants to protect anyone in my custody. I'll watch over you, defend you, and shield you as long as you're here with me."

A few tears in Francelia's eyes threatened to fall, but their emotional moment was cut short when a knock came from the door of the adjacent room.

Pietra rushed in with another hug. "Pennie, I know you're worried sick, but Karolina is fine. Bianca ran into some unexpected roadblocks to get back to Santo Domingo. They've sailed off though. Karolina is safely out of the country."

Pietra and Chip got comfortable on the couch, obviously waiting for Pennie to ask a few questions.

"Santo Domingo!? Why were they so far away? Weren't they supposed to be in a marina in La Romana somewhere?" Pennie bordered on having a total freak out. Karolina should've gone straight to a yacht and sailed off without a ninety-minute drive through hostile territory first. Feeling lightheaded, she sat back on the bed before she fell over.

Chip answered, "That was part of our alternate plan for Francelia. If they couldn't get her out of the capital city with all the roadblocks, the driver would bring her straight to the marina where Archie was waiting."

"Why couldn't they just do that to begin with then? Why did we go through all this if she could've just jumped on a private boat to begin with?" Pennie asked harshly, now more confused than ever.

"The marinas here are severely strict. They have facial recognition cameras. It would've been difficult to get Francelia past them. They were prepared to hide her in a box to get her on the boat, but they still might've had to abort depending on how diligent the guards were being. If they had to abort from that plan, she would've tried to get back to the presidential home until another plan could be formed. And then hope she could get back into the palace without being caught there."

Pennie sucked in a lungful of air. If they would've told her the plan included Karolina traveling in a car to the capital city, she would've never allowed it. Only knowing that Karolina was safe in international waters right now prevented a panic attack.

That spurred another question. "Okay, so how did you get past the roadblocks, Francelia? How did you get out of the city?"

With only the hint of a grin, much like Karolina would do, Francelia said, "I left with the housekeepers. They were going to buy supplies and groceries. My hair looks different now that we've colored it, and I did my makeup to have thick eyebrows and freckles. Facial recognition would've still caught me, but the roadblocks don't pay much attention to housekeeping crews in work vans. Then one of the housekeepers took me to La Romana in her personal vehicle. She could've gotten killed too if they found me with her. So many people worked together to get me to safety today."

"Did Karolina know the plan? Did she know about the road trip?"

"Yes," Chip said. He sounded sympathetic. "Her cooperation was necessary, and we wouldn't have tried to surprise her with anything like that. I'm sorry we didn't tell you to begin with, but we didn't want you to worry unnecessarily."

"Worry unnecessarily?! What do you think I've done for the last few hours?! I just want you to be honest with me, then let me decide whether I want to worry or not."

Pietra moved to the bed and put an arm around Pennie's shoulders. "You're right, Pennie. No more surprises. You'll be informed every step of the way. I promise."

Still feeling like she was missing a few details, Pennie dug a little deeper. "Okay, so when the exchange took place earlier, I asked my *daughter* if the restroom was clean. Her answer would either be yes or no. *Yes* meant everything went smoothly, and we stick to the plan. What would've happened if she said *No*? If Karolina came back to the bench instead of Francelia?"

"Bianca was still nearby. I would've let her know to look for Francelia and get a hotel for the night. Archie would've headed to La Romana and looked for somewhere secluded to moor the yacht for the night and dinghy to shore. There's a lot more risk to sneaking her out of the country on a dinghy since the island security is so strict. That wouldn't have been ideal. And if Bianca didn't find Francelia, I'd send a message to Vale to let her know the extraction didn't happen. This plan we had today was the best one to get Karolina and Francelia to safety. We made it back on this ship, and Karolina is safe with Archie and Bianca on a posh yacht. Let's just get back to Miami so Francelia can get to her safehouse."

Pietra stood, indicating the conversation with Pennie was over. "Come on, Chip. I was going to show you some pictures of their yacht. My parents just got a new one, too. We could plan a vacation, so you can experience what yacht life is really all about."

Pennie watched Chip's back enter their stateroom as Pietra finished that last statement. At least it let her know they were really dating again. The yacht Pennie and Chip used for the mission in February was dated and older—the opposite of posh. The high life that Pietra tantalized him with was more than Pennie had to offer. Back then, Chip told her he could easily retire on a yacht. Could Pietra use that lifestyle to get a real commitment from him?

Rather than stick to that train of thought, Pennie brushed her teeth and washed her face to get ready for bed. Francelia softly snored by the time Pennie finished her bathroom routine. Hopefully, she could fall asleep that quickly also.

TUESDAY, JULY 12

It was almost disconcerting to watch the Karolina lookalike scarfing down bacon with eggs and cheesy hashbrowns. Pennie sat next to her on the balcony of their stateroom eating breakfast that was delivered by room service. Francelia paused to sip her coffee. That was also odd. Karolina only drank water or matcha. No coffee. No sodas. The occasional juices. This alternate reality played games with Pennie's already-frazzled mentality.

Karolina stood about five-foot-three with a toned body from her intensive workouts. Francelia stood the same height, but she was lean without her muscles being defined. She wouldn't have any trouble fitting into her doppelganger's clothes, but Pennie wondered how she stayed so thin with that appetite.

"Do you like to exercise?" Pennie asked.

"Not really," Francelia said as she shoved a whole slice of bacon in her mouth.

"How do you stay so tiny? I'd blow up like a blimp if I didn't exercise every day."

Francelia shrugged her shoulders. "Metabolism, I guess."

"Okay then. If you want to explore the ship today, we'll just have to avoid calling any attention to you."

"Can I do the water slides? I saw them on the top deck. I've never been on a cruise, so I don't know what else we can do."

Even though it was off topic, Pennie had to ask another question. "Why is your English so good?"

"My school taught in English. I'm better in English than in Spanish. My teachers were all missionaries, so the students got to immerse in real English, not just textbook stuff."

"Karolina had a private tutor to learn English before she came to live with me. She used some language apps to teach herself Spanish, French, and Italian. She watches movies in those languages to help learn more conversational lingo and dialect."

"She must be very brave," Francelia said as she set down her cup of coffee. "I'm sad that I won't get to meet her."

"Karolina is one of a kind. You'd like her, but I have to drop you off at the airport before I go pick her up."

Francelia leaned back in her chair and closed her eyes. The ocean breeze and warm temperatures were so refreshing. "I haven't tasted freedom in months."

"Soak it up, sweetie. I don't know where you'll be next, but there's nothing like a cruise."

Francelia peeked open her eyes and cut them towards Pennie. "What's a safehouse like?" she asked.

"I could only tell you what I see in movies or read about in books. It'll be a normal house with reinforced locks and stuff. Security guys will stand guard all the time. I don't know what else you can expect."

"It sounds terrible."

"But it'll be safe," Pennie tried to encourage her. "That's the point. I hate that you're here without your mother, but now she can do her job without having to worry about your safety. She can get rid of the Wasps and make the country safe so you can go home soon."

From Pennie's perch in the shade, Francelia appeared to enjoy the water slides immensely. She kept an eye out for any stalkers. That sounded harsh. JJ and Nick were nice enough and just wanted to meet some new people. Karolina had made friends on their cruises before. She even kept up with a few of them, probably with the help of *ReelLife* or other social media platforms.

Regardless of the motives, Pennie didn't want any suspicion to follow Francelia around the ship. They only had one full day left before they disembarked tomorrow. This might be her only reprieve from lockdown and protective custody, so Pennie would allow her to have fun as long as it seemed safe.

Across the deck, she could see JJ getting in line for a slide on the upper deck. Since children formed most of the line, he was easy to spot. Which meant Francelia would be easy to spot too when she got off the slide. Pennie pulled her floppy hat lower and pretended to be with the group sitting next to her. Nick might not notice her if she wasn't by herself. The new flamingo tote bag didn't broadcast the same beacon as her Memphis Tiger one. She observed Nick having a seat on the other side of the deck, a hundred feet away. He scanned the area, but Pennie wouldn't allow herself to be spotted that easily. As soon as she saw Francelia appear at the bottom of the slide, Pennie made a beeline with a towel so they could vacate the area.

"It's time to find somewhere out of the sun for a few minutes, honey," Pennie said as she led Francelia away.

"Okay, Mom."

With a soft serve ice cream for each of them, Pennie and Francelia found a corner table behind a divider in the food court area. No one would notice them here unless they were specifically looking for an open table. Francelia tucked her hair under her hat, and Pennie kept her floppy hat low. This might be the best they could do without keeping the girl cooped up in the room all day.

"I almost couldn't keep up with you two, good job." Pietra said as she sat at the next table. Chip joined her a minute later with two plates of pulled pork barbecue.

"Mom, can we get some of that?"

Chip answered for her, "I'll go get two more plates. Keep your seats."

Ten minutes later, they all savored the tender pork, macaroni and cheese, and crispy fries.

Francelia relished the food. "This is so delicious."

"To be fair, Memphis is known around the world for its barbecue. This isn't near as good as anything you get in Memphis."

"We don't have food like this in my country at all," Francelia commented before shoveling a forkful of macaroni and cheese into her mouth.

"Karolina said the food is much different in Brazil also. In *São Paulo*, their capital city, you can get a variety of cuisines, but small towns like she's from don't have the big selection of food. She never knew we had meatless substitutes for burgers, chicken, and such. She found out the hard way that some of the meatless products are made with high-protein gluten flour. After eating one fake chicken nugget, she spent two days in the bathroom."

Francelia made eye contact with Pennie for the next question. "How did you start hosting exchange students?"

"My deceased husband and I agreed not to have children until we were thirty years old. It was his idea to host a student as our test run."

"How many students have you hosted?"

"Officially, only two. We hosted Mako from Japan for one year. Then Karolina. We sent her to a private school since public schools don't typically allow exchange students to come back for a second year, and she knew from day one that she wanted to finish high school in the States. She renewed her visa and came back for her senior year, then stayed for college."

Between munching on fries, Francelia kept asking questions. "Did you like having Karolina to stay with you for that long?"

"Of course. My husband died while Karolina was a senior in high school, almost two and half years ago now, and she really helped me through the grief." Pennie's thoughts drifted back to that terrible period. "She swept the floor and made sure I ate. I don't think I could've made it through without Karolina and my mother. We're a close family, and I needed all of them. Having Karolina in my home kept me grounded, though. When she started college, I had to work on finding myself again. Reimagining what my future might be like without Johnny."

"Do you want to get married again?" Francelia asked.

"Yes, and I still want to raise a family. I want to host more exchange students. I might go on a gameshow to find my next husband." Pennie stopped to chuckle so Francelia would know she was kidding. "Seriously, dating is harder than I expected it to be. I don't even know how to meet new men."

"That guy already has a nickname for you, *Tiger*," Chip interjected with a patronizing tone. "It looks like you're meeting new men just fine."

His comment surprised Pennie. First, because they weren't really supposed to be acting like they knew each other. Second, because what business was it of his if she talked to other men anyway?

Pennie glanced around to make sure no one else was within ear shot and stood before responding, "It's no different than you calling me *Skipper*. It doesn't mean anything. Let's go, daughter. I'm tired of sitting still."

They made it to the adult area of the ship where the ladies signed up for facials. This would be Pennie's second one in a few days, but Francelia had never experienced one before. The ninety-minute beauty treatment helped Pennie decompress. They came out of the spa to find Chip and Pietra lounging with drinks. Their chairs gave them a clear view of the spa entrance, so they must seriously be trying to keep an eye on Pennie and her substitute daughter.

Naps and showers preceded dinner time. They changed the dinner plans for tonight. Instead of eating in the main restaurant, they booked spots for a hibachi show on the fifth deck. Pennie kept doing a double take to notice that Francelia sat next to her instead of Karolina. They obviously had their hair cut and colored the same way on purpose, but the button nose, full lips, and large brown eyes were so similar. Karolina had perfectly straight teeth as only braces could provide. Francelia's front two teeth were slightly in front of the rest of the top row, giving her an adorable chipmunk-like smile when she chose to smile.

Karolina and Francelia both maintained stoic expressions most of the time. Karolina wanted to prevent smile lines and wrinkles, and Francelia just hadn't found a reason to smile for a long time.

When the show started, they watched the chef in awe. Flaming onion towers, egg balancing, knife twirling... Then Francelia gobbled down a plate of fried rice with chicken and shrimp. Pennie couldn't bear to make her eat vegetarian food if she didn't want it. Even though Pietra and Chip watched closely from their seats across the table, Pennie didn't feel the same anxiety she felt last night. Despite the worry that remained right under the surface, she managed to enjoy the meal and the show.

Foregoing the plethora of activities they had to choose from, Francelia and Pennie went back to their stateroom after dinner. They used the time to discuss the details of Karolina's visa. She had previously witnessed the guys in customs ask Karolina questions when they arrived in port. From the best Pennie could tell, the questions were more out of curiosity than trying to catch an illegal immigrant.

Now that facial recognition was part of the security process, the details seemed more important than ever. Either way, Francelia would be prepared.

She memorized the name of *her* high school and college since both were listed on *her* visa. Pennie made sure she knew the name of *her* hometown in Brazil and how far it was away from the capital of *São Paulo*. With a few more minutes of practice, they spent the rest of the evening packing bags. Karolina's bags would go with Pennie. Francelia had literally nothing to her name right now. Not even an ID card to prove her identity if anyone asked for it.

At this point, everything came down to the plan. Pennie only had to get Francelia through customs, then to the baggage return area of Miami Airport. Afterwards, Pennie would pick up a rental car so she could drive to Bianca's house to pick up Karolina. She tried to figure out what Francelia's frame of mind was at this point.

The young Dominican sat on her bed and scraped polish off her fingernails. That had to be a sign of nervousness.

"Francelia, can I pray with you?"

The large brown eyes looked up. She nodded slightly and moved back on the bed. Pennie had a seat so they could pray together for safety and blessings. Francelia cried softly, leaning into Pennie's extended arms. They stayed like this for about half an hour.

Pennie couldn't imagine the turmoil this sweet girl was experiencing. Away from her home. Away from her mother. Death threats. Her father had been abducted years ago. And the only thing in her foreseeable future was a sterile safehouse.

A light rapping on the adjoining stateroom door beckoned Pennie to get up and open it. Pietra and Chip walked in to make sure they were packed, and that Francelia had memorized the details for the customs check the next morning. They were as ready as they could ever be.

WEDNESDAY, JULY 13

If the security guys weren't attentive when they scanned guests onto the ship, they sure didn't care as they exited. Francelia scanned Karolina's *SailAway* card for the last time as they stepped off the ship to enter the port.

They grabbed their bags from the carousel where the porters unloaded them. Pennie's heartrate accelerated slightly as she got out her own passport and driver's license in case anyone wanted to see them. The customs line moved quickly. Each person stopped long enough to look at the camera and get a green light to move forward. Pennie got her own green light and tucked her passport back into her bag as she continued walking.

Behind her, Francelia did not get a green light. Pennie paused, still close enough to hear the exchange. The customs official examined the visa and passport. Francelia mentioned the photo was taken almost four years ago when she was sixteen, and she needed to renew it soon. He did ask Francelia how she liked living in Memphis, to which she replied that they have the best barbecue in the world. Pennie smiled at the perfect response.

The short quiz ended with the officer handing back the paperwork and telling Francelia to have a good day. While waiting for her heartrate to return to normal, they followed the flow of people to get on the shuttle back to the airport.

Pietra and Chip occupied seats on the shuttle bus three rows behind Pennie and Francelia. The drop off was the last task of the mission. Getting Francelia into the hands of her protective detail.

“Mom.”

Pennie glanced at the girl sitting next to the window. “Yes, daughter.”

“I’m scared.”

Pennie looked around to see if anyone might be eavesdropping. No one sat on the row across the aisle. Two small boys sat directly behind them with their parents on the row across the aisle behind them. A group of senior citizens occupied the four rows in front of them. Hopefully, no one could listen in as long as they spoke softly.

“What is it, sweetie?”

“Do you know what my plan is today?”

“No. I only know that I’m walking with you towards the baggage claim area, where you’ll stay behind to meet up with your new security team. We’re not supposed to walk together, and I’m not allowed to look back at all. You’ll go with whomever after we’re out of sight.” That would be hard for Pennie. She wanted to watch Francelia be safely delivered, but this part of the plan was out of her hands.

“A guy in a Miami Dolphins t-shirt will be holding a sign like he’s waiting for someone. The name on the sign will be *Paula*. I’m supposed to pick up a green suitcase with a pink ribbon from the conveyor and go to him.”

"You're not supposed to be telling me this," Pennie whispered.

"I want you to go ahead of me and check out this guy. If anything looks suspicious, if he doesn't seem trustworthy in any way, can I stay with you? Can I please go home with you?" Francelia begged in a hushed tone.

"That's not the plan, sweetie." What was Pennie being pulled into? She couldn't leave this girl behind if she were scared to go with the guy.

"My mom said that I should stay with you if I don't want to go with that guy. She doesn't know if she can trust the American government. Please."

"Does this guy know what you look like? Does he even know who you are?"

"I don't know. If we can't trust him, it means he knows exactly who I am, and there are more guys in the airport who're looking for me."

"What am I supposed to notice at a glance that lets me know he's not trustworthy? Why do you think I'll know better?" Pennie pleaded with the girl. She felt like the weight of the world was on her shoulders at that moment.

"Because you trust God. Not the government. If God gives you a sign that I'm not safe, please let me go with you."

"You know that Pietra and Chip will be going in front of us to get their rental car. None of us are supposed to see who you go with. They can't help us if we stay behind and do something different. Do they even know what your plan is?"

"No one knows except for me and you and the guy with a sign."

Feeling the burden of this girl's safety, Pennie leaned her head back against the seat and grasped Francelia's hand. She closed her eyes and willed for God to give her a sign. She didn't want to be flighty or haphazard with this pivotal decision.

"Didn't Karolina ask you to keep me safe? Didn't you promise her you would?"

Pennie shot a sideways look at the girl. "How do you know that?"

"My mother told Ambassador Hernandez to give Karolina that message. To tell her to tell you. If you think I can't trust the guy at baggage claim, please keep me safe with you."

The remaining fifteen minutes of the ride to the airport left Pennie in a state of agitation. If there were a team of bad guys here, they'd be looking for Francelia. Would they think she's coming in on a plane? Would they think she caught a taxi to the airport? Would they suspect she's on a shuttle from a cruise ship?

Regardless, all roads led to baggage claim in the Miami airport. Pennie tried to mentally map out the place. She had only been there on two other occasions, both times she flew into the city for a cruise. Last week, they took an Uber to the airport. The Festival Cruise desk was on the far end of the airport. When they got off this shuttle, they'd have to pass the baggage claim area to get back to the main terminal. Then, they could bypass the terminal to take a tram to the rental cars.

Formulating a plan on the fly proved difficult, but Pennie knew they'd only have one shot to get it right.

"Let me quickly braid your hair. Then you can tuck it under your hat." Pennie pulled out her makeup case from the backpack at her feet. "Can you draw some thicker eyebrows or something to give yourself a different appearance?"

Within five minutes, Francelia had all but created a unibrow and added a few freckles. Her long hair was tucked under her hat. The bus came to a stop. It was showtime.

When they grabbed their luggage, Pennie led the way inside the airport. They entered next to the same Festival desk they exited from a week ago. Francelia followed her to the restroom in that area. Without speaking first, Pietra followed them as well.

"What's going on?" Pietra asked as the three of them stood in the small restroom.

"She's feeling nervous. She needs to use the restroom and make sure her makeup and hair are good for the exchange. Will you stay in here with her for a minute? I'm feeling a leg cramp starting, and I need to walk it off," Pennie insisted as she rushed out of the restroom.

Chip was standing outside the restroom with a quizzical expression.

"Pietra's staying in there with her for a minute while I walk off a leg cramp. I'll be right back."

Pennie didn't wait for a response from him either. She maintained a brisk pace without looking hurried or worried in any way. At least she hoped she didn't look worried. She walked like she had a purpose. The baggage claim conveyors were about five hundred feet ahead. She smiled and nodded at a few people as she made accidental eye contact. At least two young passersby had their hair colored like AmberLou, so the dramatic style wasn't as much of a hindrance as Pennie expected.

There he was. Miami Dolphins shirt. Placard bearing the name *Paula*. The gangly man looked in the direction of the main terminal. What kind of sign was Pennie seeking here? A menacing scowl? A teardrop tattoo? He wasn't even scary looking. The lanky man reminded her of a giraffe. The plan would stay intact or change right now based on whatever she observed.

She didn't break stride as she passed the man. Instead, she ducked out of the airport exit like she might be catching a taxi. But instead of catching a taxi, she hurried on the sidewalk back towards the shuttle area she just entered a few minutes before.

Chip waited in the same spot.

"I'm much better now. Let me see if my girl's ready."

Inside the restroom, Pietra touched up her lipstick in the mirror. Their suitcases remained next to the stall occupied by Francelia. Pennie softly spoke through the door. "Sweetie, are you okay? Are you ready to go?"

Francelia opened the stall door and nodded.

"Here, you might need a neck rest for the next leg of your journey." Pennie pulled out her blue neck pillow and made sure it obscured just a little more of Francelia's face.

"You two give me about thirty seconds so we aren't leaving at the same time. And you," Pietra hesitated before giving Francelia a hug, "You be safe."

"Let's go, sweetie. Follow me."

With a glance to make sure Chip and Pietra were out of

sight, Pennie ushered Francelia out the same door where the shuttle bus still idled, waiting for its next load of cruisers. They passed by the bus and moved along the sidewalk to the waiting line of taxis.

The first taxi driver they came to spoke broken English. His hat read “Safety First.” If she was looking for another sign, that was as good as any. Pennie didn’t hesitate to hand off their luggage and push Francelia into the minivan.

“Where to, ma’am?” the man asked with a toothy grin.

“The Enterprise rental car area please.”

“You know you can get there on the tram without paying for a ride?”

Pennie smiled in response, making eye contact in the rearview mirror. “I get so turned around in airports. If you don’t mind taking me there, I don’t mind paying for the ride.”

He simply nodded and put the van in gear. Pennie felt grateful for the tinted windows when another guy walked past on the sidewalk as they pulled away. She didn’t know the guy, but he gave her the creeps anyway.

Five minutes later, Pennie gave the taxi driver a hefty tip and checked in with Enterprise. Thankfully, her rental car was ready and waiting.

Safely inside the Chevy Malibu, Pennie focused on the road. Navigating the congested streets to get out of the airport area gave her as many nerves as her stowaway in the shotgun seat. Once they made it to the interstate headed north, Pennie let out a breath and tried to calm herself down. She released her tight grip on the steering wheel so she could find a little Jesus music on the radio.

"What did you see?" Francelia asked quietly, as if it still might not be safe to speak.

"The guy was there like you said, holding his *Paula* sign."

"Why didn't you trust him?"

Pennie glanced to her right to see Francelia nervously clutching the neck pillow tightly in her hands. "He wore a *Red Jacket* hat."

"I don't know what that means," Francelia replied softly.

"It's from a new movie called *Thunder Swarm*. The logo is a red wasp."

The girl sucked in her breath. "*Mata Cacatas*. The Wasps."

"When the taxi pulled away, I saw another guy walking around outside wearing a *Red Jacket* hat. You understand this could mean absolutely nothing. I might've just messed up your plan for safety because I had a nightmare about wasps a few nights ago. Plus, we have to explain this to Ambassador Hernandez and to Chip and Pietra. I don't know what we're gonna do."

"Thank you, Mom. Really." Then Francelia adjusted the pillow around her neck to drift off into a peaceful sleep.

The five-hour drive to Bianca's house wasn't relaxing for Pennie like it was for Francelia. She purposely avoided any turnpikes with cameras for the drive north, which meant she couldn't stick to the recommended route on her map app. With a terrible sense of direction, Pennie did the best she could and managed to get to the neighborhood without too many issues.

By the time they arrived, she should've been ready for lunch. Instead, she was ready for some antacids. She followed the map on her phone to the beautiful pink stucco home in a perfectly manicured neighborhood of Homosassa. The city, settled on the Gulf Coast of Florida north of Tampa and southeast of Gainesville, resembled exactly what people pictured when they thought of Florida: palm trees, Spanish moss, and lush vegetation. She parked the Malibu at the end of the long driveway, behind a Volkswagen sedan under the shade.

She knew Chip and Pietra would arrive before them by a few minutes, but she didn't expect to see them just now exiting their own rental car. Pennie hadn't come up with any good excuse as to why Francelia was still with her, and now she had no more time left to come up with something reasonable.

The look of exasperation Chip and Pietra shared was more than Pennie could bear as they watched her passenger exit the car.

"What the hell?" they said in unison.

"Let's just go inside, please. I want to see my daughter."

Karolina greeted Francelia with a hug before she even acknowledged Pennie. The twins embraced for a full minute before they let each other go with tears in their eyes.

"You'll be safer with my mom," Karolina whispered.

Archie and Bianca stood in the crowded entry hall, obviously as confused as everyone else.

Chip almost growled when he demanded an answer. "What did you do, Skipper?"

"Ambassador Hernandez wasn't sure we could trust the

security guys assigned to Francelia. We made a last-minute decision to move on instead of leaving her there. I'm sorry, guys. I couldn't do it. I couldn't leave her, knowing there was any chance her safety was compromised."

"I get it," Pietra said.

"You do?" Pennie asked her unexpected ally.

"Yea." Pietra shrugged her shoulders. "Let's figure out what to do from here."

Everyone gathered in the posh living room where huge windows revealed a screened-in pool and a variety of flowering shrubbery in the backyard. They ate delivery pizza for a late lunch and discussed different variations of how to move forward.

Chip remained mostly quiet. He lacked the maternal instinct that Pietra and Pennie must be trusting in, which was odd since neither of them had ever given birth. After they finished eating, Pietra asked Pennie to follow her outside.

"Look, I had a bad feeling about all of this. I didn't like it when Vale said she involved the government. I thought I had it worked out to get Francelia there safely without one extra person being aware. Originally, I offered for her to stay with me as my niece from Florida, but that wasn't my call once Vale said a security team was set up."

"So, you're really not mad at me for making this decision?" Pennie asked.

"No, quit looking so shellshocked. You trusted your gut, and your only goal is to keep her safe. We might have our differences here and there, but I'd never doubt your motive. You have a pure soul, Pennie, and Francelia trusted you too. We're all still on the same team."

The ladies re-entered the home to find Bianca cleaning the kitchen and chatting with the girls. Pietra and Karolina took Francelia to a bathroom to remove the drawn-on unibrow and add some more flattering makeup. It was Chip's turn to pull Pennie outside for a private conversation.

"Do you really feel like abandoning her original plan was the best idea?" he asked with a tone somewhere closer to curious than frustrated.

"Yes. I couldn't leave her there, Chip. I promised her that I'd keep her safe. I don't know how this is gonna play out, but I plan to keep my promise."

"Do you understand that your own safety is compromised now? Assuming the security team in Miami was breached in some way, you've created enemies who are now looking for Francelia. They might find her, and you, and your family. This is a big deal."

"Chip, over the years, I've had lots of international girls stay in my home when Karolina invites them from her school for holidays and stuff. These girls always had one thing in common— they're all in a foreign land with no family, with no home base. Every one of those girls called me *Momma Pennie*. Every one of them found a safe and secure haven under my roof. You know why? Because I treat them all like my daughter. Every single girl who spends the night under my roof will know she's loved and safe before she goes to sleep each night. I care about every one of these girls, and Francelia is no exception. She knows that anyone who comes for her will find the fight of their life against me. She trusts that, and I'll never regret any decision to keep one of my girls safe."

Chip nodded slowly. "Okay. You keep her safe, and I'll keep you safe."

Before they left Bianca and Archie's home, they made plans to follow Chip to a hotel in Birmingham, Alabama for the night. They wanted as much distance between Francelia and Miami as they could get before bedtime. Pennie took the interstate north for the seven-hour journey with two girls in tow. The girls had a never-ending conversation in Spanish, leaving Pennie completely excluded from any of the chatter. Karolina must be happy to have someone new to practice her Spanish with. When they arrived at the hotel, Pietra and Chip each booked a room in their own names, but Pietra gave her room key to Pennie. She assumed they didn't want Pennie's name on any registration as long as she had a Dominican refugee in her company. The sun had long since set, and the hours had zapped Pennie of any remaining energy.

Pietra went to pick up a late dinner Taco Bell for everyone, leaving Chip to keep watch. Their rooms were on the same hall, but Pennie wasn't sure how Chip was watching anything. She knew that Chip would keep them safe if he could, so she allowed herself to decompress for the rest of the evening.

Now that the girls were both in the room with her, Pennie felt a lot like she was in the *Twilight Zone*. The girls continued chatting in Spanish. She understood a few words and phrases, but she purposely avoided eavesdropping on them. Instead, she turned on the television to find the evening news. When she flipped through enough stations to find a national network, Pennie set the remote down with intentions of mentally zoning out.

A meteorologist spoke about developing storms off the Atlantic Coast. Just when the monotonous voice lulled Pennie into a trance, the face of Adolfo Cabral appeared on the screen. She sucked in a sharp breath and grabbed the remote to turn up the volume. Karolina and Francelia stopped chatting to listen as the reporter spoke solemnly about the leader of the Wasps and some of the recent political changes in the Dominican.

"In the wake of the threats made against President Vasquez and her daughter, the elder Cabral brother just issued this recorded message. Let's listen to the video."

The face that had been hovering on a screen behind the reporter now filled the television. Cold snake-like eyes stared a hole straight through Pennie's soul. She needed no help deciphering his evil sneer, but the closed captioning translated his message into English.

"It's come to my attention that little Francelia is planning to travel. Beware that I have eyes all over the place. If you run, I will track you down. You can't interrupt the big plans I have for the Dominican people, and I'm a peaceful man. If the president and her daughter vacate the National Palace, I'll allow them to return to their civilian lives—to go back home where the women belong. Then I can take my rightful position as the leader for our nation."

Before the news anchors could discuss the video at length, a knock on the door startled everyone in the room. Signaling for the girls to stay back, Pennie peered through the peephole. It was only Pietra.

Pietra pushed her way inside and had a seat on the bed with the girls. After confirming that everyone saw the message from Cabral, she said, "We spoke to our boss at the police station earlier. He got in touch with Vale, and she knows you're safe with us."

"Who's Vale?" Francelia asked.

"Valentina Hernandez. She's the Dominican ambassador. The one who coordinated everything for you."

"Oh. *Señora* Hernandez. I've never met her in person."

Pietra nodded. "Well, she seemed relieved that you

stayed with us. She told her contact with the secretary of state that our plans to get you out of the country failed. It sounds like the Wasps were looking for you in Miami, and we hope that bit of misinformation may deter their efforts. A few trusted members of our police department will take shifts at Pennie's house to offer some extra security until we figure out something for the long term. Get some sleep tonight, *amigas*."

"*Buenas noches*, Pietra," Pennie said with a smile.

"Bunches of nachos to you too, Pennie," she replied with a snicker as she exited the room.

Relying on tactics Pennie had seen in movies, she balanced a glass on the handle of the door. They would hear it break if someone tried to enter their room during the night. Not sure what she would do if it woke her, but Pennie would attack with her two bare hands if she had to.

THURSDAY, JULY 14

The last leg of the journey home took four hours, two pee breaks, two drive-thrus, and one massive case of heartburn for Pennie. They arrived at her house by lunchtime. Pietra stayed at the house with the girls so that Pennie and Chip could return their rental cars to the Enterprise location at the Memphis International Airport where Chip left his personal truck the week before.

After returning the vehicle, Pennie climbed in the cab to catch a ride home with Chip, but he turned to her before starting the truck.

"You okay, Skipper?"

"Sure. Why wouldn't I be?" Pennie asked in reply even though she had at least one big reason to not be okay.

He smiled. He already knew her state of mind. They pulled out of the airport property to get back to her house. "Tony wasn't surprised at all when we called him. We don't want Francelia to feel like she's in jail at your house. Do you have a cover story for any of your neighbors and family who might encounter her?"

"Yea. We had a conversation and created a little backstory on the drive home. We're going to call her Maria since that's such a common Latina name. We'll tell people that she's an international student at the University of Memphis, but she didn't get to go back to her home country of Honduras for the summer, so she's staying with us. Karolina had to move out of her campus apartment for the summer, so this coincides with her moving back home for the next month. Since this has happened before, I doubt anyone will question us."

"Since what's happened before?" Chip asked.

"Karolina has brought home friends from school plenty of times before. Even in high school. She had a Brazilian friend who didn't have a good host family. Ana spent more time with us than at her host home during their junior year. Then her senior year of high school, she made friends with a South Korean girl. Ji-Ahn spent quite a bit of time at our house too. Her host parents had good intentions, but they were older. They couldn't keep up with teenage get-togethers, sports schedules, and musical competitions. Ji-Ahn and Karolina were joined at the hip that year. I even drove them to South Carolina for a national music competition where Ji-Ahn played the piano accompaniment to Karolina's flute performance. We had so much fun on that trip."

Chip smiled but didn't try to interrupt the pleasant memory. Pennie averted her gaze to watch the scenery pass by from her side of the truck. The good memories introduced a smidge of peace to the turmoil that had taken up residence in her soul.

"Then, in college, Karolina met so many internationals. Most of them didn't have any kind of host family at all. That first Thanksgiving she was in college, six girls stayed the weekend at my house. They helped put up a Christmas tree and decorate. A few of them came back to stay with me for the entire six weeks of winter break. You never know how many lives you might touch when you host one international student."

Chip asked, "So, this happens over and over again?"

"Yeah. Different students have spent long weekends, winter breaks, and holidays with us. Karolina went home to Brazil last summer, so I didn't have her then. But it makes sense that she's spending this summer with me along with a tagalong friend. It might even be more odd if Karolina came home without an extra foreigner."

"She's okay with you calling her Maria?"

"Yeah, and that even goes along with an inside joke I share with Karolina. Every time we ate dinner during her first year, I'd make jokes about her being vegetarian. Johnny would join in too. We'd tell her our next exchange student will be Maria from Mexico, and she'll eat real tacos and bacon and steak. So, her fake enemy for the last four years has been a fictitious Maria. Now I'll have my Maria, and we'll eat tacos and bacon and steak in front of Karolina."

"Okay. Maria from Honduras. Got it. Just so you know, we aren't leaving a vehicle at your house during our watches. Pietra will take my truck home with her while I take the first watch. Cole, Tony, and Pietra will be the only other officers in rotation for your security. When Tony comes to relieve me in the morning, I'll take his car home. Maybe no one will notice you have a 24/7 bodyguard. That'll be harder to explain than Maria from Honduras."

Pietra had already ordered Japanese food to be delivered for dinner. Pennie went next door to let her neighbor know she made it home and to retrieve her Golden Retriever mix from Kennedy's care. After some delicious yakisoba noodles, Pietra went home, the girls went to bed, and Chip got comfortable on the couch. He planned to stay awake all night, and he gladly accepted a semi-automatic rifle from Pennie's arsenal. She had never shot the AR herself, but once upon a time, her husband told her it was the ultimate home defense weapon.

Her own Glock sat on the nightstand, and a shotgun waited behind the bedroom door in case she needed it. The state-of-the-art security system would alert the entire town of Bartlett if someone so much as cracked a window. They were as secure as they could be.

FRIDAY, JULY 15

The changing of the guards happened seamlessly that morning. Chip took Tony's truck home. Pennie made pancakes for everyone, including a gluten-free batch for Karolina.

"Are you mad at me, Chief?" Pennie asked as they sipped coffee on the back porch.

Karolina and Francelia sunbathed in the middle of the yard, out of earshot of their keepers.

"Mad? No. I'm not even surprised. In fact, I won the bet."

"What bet?" Pennie asked.

Tony turned his gorgeous smile towards Pennie. "We had a pool going. All of us believed you'd bring her back to Bartlett, so it wasn't really a bet. It was the scenario we put money on. I bet that you'd rent the car and drive back, surprising everyone at Bianca's house. Chip bet that you'd change the plans while still on the cruise and ask them how to move forward. Pietra bet that you'd freak out at the airport and ride with them from Miami without renting a car yourself."

"So, I'm really that predictable? Why'd you let me do this if you knew this is how it'd go?"

"It wasn't up to us. Vale Hernandez put the plan in motion. I think by the time she met all of us, she trusted us more than her contact at the State Department."

"Is she coming here to check on us?"

"No. She doesn't want to make any more trips to

Memphis, so she doesn't draw any attention to the area. You need to get Francelia a phone so she can get a message to her mom's private number. And she's going to need clothes of her own. I'd prefer to wait until Pietra is back with you to go clothes shopping, but you can go get the phone today if you want."

"I can do that. Let me ask a question though," Pennie asked.

"Hmmm," Tony muttered as if he wasn't sure he wanted to hear Pennie's question.

"Why didn't you put my brother on the rotation of officers coming here?"

Tony leaned back and rubbed his forehead with his fingertips. "Think about it, Pennie. How mad would James be if he found out after the fact that we sent you and Karolina on an assignment like this?"

"I guess that wouldn't go over well." Pennie wondered how James would be kept out of the loop for the remainder of the unexpected part two of the mission.

"Has anyone reached out to you now that you're home? We need to limit the people who come by here in the meantime."

Pennie glanced at her phone. "Not really. My mom and sister both made sure I got home safely, and I already talked to Kennedy next door when I picked up my dog. Other than that, only my boss has reached out to me. Her daughter is home now, and she wanted to make sure I was coming back to work this week."

"Where has Cynthia been?" Karolina asked. Cynthia and Karolina were the same age, and they enjoyed chatting over the past few years. Of course, Cynthia was born here, but she felt like an outsider enough to form a bond with the Brazilian.

"When she got out of college for the semester, she

stayed in Alabama to do some intern work at a bank. She'll still have a month at home before she moves back to campus."

Interrupting the chit-chat of the women, Tony interrupted, "Pennie, are you really planning to go to work with the extra company under your roof?"

"Well, Chief, I thought we needed to keep up the guise that everything was normal. If I'm personally on some kind of lockdown, that would do nothing but call attention to us. Going to church and going to work is routine for me."

The annoyed huff surprised Pennie. "I suppose that's true to an extent. I'll speak to Vale and make sure everyone is on board. Let me add you to my *Life 360* app so I can keep tabs on you."

One brand-new iPhone later, Pennie spent the afternoon being ignored by the twin amigas as they set up the new device.

"Mom, her camera is better than mine. I need a new phone too." Karolina commented here and there about other new features she wanted since her poor phone was sixteen months old now.

Pennie used her own phone to create a grocery list to be delivered. Karolina added her vegan options, and Francelia added a few specific things like Fresca drinks and plantains. Tony made multiple laps inside the house, making sure the windows were still locked, and nothing seemed amiss.

When they finally sat down for dinner, Pennie tried to drum up some conversation with her new, mismatched family for the day.

"So, Tony… is this the most boring security detail you've ever done?"

"Yes, but that's likely because I don't usually do security detail." He turned to Francelia, "Have you been to the United States before?"

"No, sir, but I've seen a lot of movies."

Stifling a laugh, Tony replied, "Don't believe everything you see in movies. What do you think in just the little you've seen so far?"

Francelia pursed her lips and considered what to say. "Well. I think the heat surprised me. It's a different kind of hot. There's no breeze. The air is so heavy."

"Welcome to the Midsouth!" Pennie chuckled.

"But," Francelia said with a brighter expression, "You can drink the water here!"

Karolina changed topics with her next statement. "Mom, we've set up the *ReelLife* app on Francelia's phone. She's connected with her mother. This way they can send pictures a couple of times a day so her mom can know she's safe."

"Is that wise, honey? She doesn't need to be using her name on any apps like that."

"Her mom has a personal phone with the app set up with a fake name. Francelia used her fake name, and she found her mom since she knew the alias she was using."

"Don't post any pictures of Karolina or anyone else on that app."

Tony interjected, "I don't like the idea of all this social media at all. Our priority is to keep you safe, young lady. I thought you were just sending a text to your mom's private phone. After we eat, let me see your phone. I want to see the app for myself."

Pennie decided she liked this side of Tony. The

protective, fatherly type. He'd make a good father one of these days. "How's it going with your lady friend?" she asked him.

"That's not pertinent, Pennie. Let's stay on task."

So much for asking.

After dinner, Tony checked out the *ReelLife* app on Francelia's phone. She used the name Maria Jose Lopez to create an Apple ID and subsequently download the app. The details of the app don't give away any location information, and he made sure all location sharing was turned off within the device. During the day, Francelia had exchanged only one picture with her mother.

In her picture, Francelia proudly posed, displaying AmberLou's hairdo and Karolina's clothes. She took the selfie with only the bricks on the house as her background. The photo that President Vasquez sent back showed a forced smile with worry etched into her face. The plain white wall behind her didn't hint at where she took the picture. Hopefully, the simple picture from her daughter would bring a little joy her way.

Tony handed Francelia her phone back with some instructions. "Don't download any other social media on this phone. Don't make any calls and don't send any messages unless it's to one of the officers I just added to your contacts. Is that clear?"

"Yes, sir. But can I download a music app? I'll use my fake email."

He turned his disappointed father gaze towards Pennie. "Why didn't you get her a burner flip phone or something where she couldn't connect to the internet?"

Defensively, Pennie huffed, "I just got her the newest phone. I don't know. You can still add parental controls if you want to."

"Since you added this phone to your wireless plan, it's better that she isn't sending any kind of text messages from a number that points to you. Anonymous app pictures might be safer, so we'll just trust her for now. She knows what's at stake."

The evening wound down with another news story reiterating the same video Adolfo Cabral released previously. Nothing breaking had been reported, and Pennie considered that a win.

SATURDAY, JULY 16

"Jenna would be so pissed if she knew I was here right now," Cole said as he sipped coffee with Pennie on the back porch. The amigas spent more time soaking up the morning sun in the middle of the yard.

"I've only sent her one message saying I got back safely from the cruise. I'm guessing most of her time has been monopolized by her job and by you, so I'm not pressing her to hang out with me."

As if saying her name too many times prompted some communication, Jenna sent a message to Pennie at that moment.

"Oh Cole, Jenna's pissed anyway. She just said you abandoned her today, and she wants to come over."

"Don't let her come over," he insisted.

Pennie gave him a crazy look. "I'm not stupid. I'm telling her I have Karolina here with one of her friends, and we need to run some errands." She finished pecking out the message, hopefully deterring her best friend from dropping in unannounced.

"What did you even tell her?" Pennie asked.

"I told her I had to do a twenty-four-hour security detail, and I wasn't allowed to give her any information about who I was protecting. She didn't dig for any information, and she didn't act mad."

"That's a side of Jenna I've never seen. She didn't press you for any details at all?" she asked, not believing what she heard.

Cole shook his head, keeping his gaze focused ahead. "No, she's very respectful when it comes to my job. I offer the same respect about her work. Even though I'm a cop, I think her job is more grueling than mine."

"How do you feel about her? Do you think y'all might go the distance?" Pennie asked, wondering how much personal information he'd reveal.

"Why are you asking? So, you can run back and tell her?"

So much for Cole revealing anything. "No. I'm just curious. Jenna has been growing as a person lately, and I think it's because of you."

"I love her. That's no secret. We could go the distance." He almost whispered that last statement.

Her best friend, who had always been one-hundred-percent solitary and self-reliant, had found love. Even if Tony didn't want to talk about it yesterday, he'd found a woman last year, and they seemed to be going strong. Chip and Pietra were figuring out their relationship.

Where was Pennie's love? Instead of finding a man, she found another foreign daughter.

Distracting Pennie from her pity party, Cole dropped a bombshell. "Don't tell her, but I'm shopping for rings now."

With wide eyes, Pennie looked at Cole's profile. "You don't need a diamond. I bet she'd marry you with a bread tie."

Before she could dig any further into the bombshell Cole just dropped, Pennie's phone alerted her that someone was at the front door. "Cole, my neighbor is here. Can you move out of sight while I see what she wants?"

"Hey, Adriana! How's it going at the nursery?" Pennie greeted her with a hug.

"*Hola*, Pennie! Things are okay. You'll be glad to know we're going to tear down that building. You were right. It's a hazard. I have a new portable office being delivered in a few weeks. Are you coming back to work Monday?"

Walking towards the back of the house, Pennie pointed towards the girls through the window. Fortunately, they both lay where Adriana couldn't see their faces. "Karolina is here for the month, and one of her international friends joined her. I just need to make sure they find a good routine, but I'll be back at work on Monday."

"Can I check out your garden? It's looking good."

Adriana exited the back door without waiting for permission. Since her crew constructed the enormous, raised garden, it made sense that she wanted to check its progress.

"Everything is producing perfectly, Pennie. This makes me so happy!" As she continued to touch all the plants and circle around the garden, she asked more about the cruise. "Well, what did you think of my home country?"

"It was beautiful. I did a whole excursion to see the landmarks and some of the natural scenery."

"I've been hearing from my family lately. They have some gang activity right now that's getting worse in Santo Domingo. We talked about how the president's daughter has been receiving death threats. Now everyone thinks President Vasquez is trying to get Francelia out of the country. The gang members are showing up at the airports and marinas around Santo Domingo. It's hell for them right now."

"That's terrible. Are the president and her daughter safe right now?"

Adriana huffed. "I guess for now. But these gangs will eventually take over unless something major happens. They need to get Vasquez and her daughter out of there. I just don't see how they can do it without the *Mata Cacatas* knowing about it."

Pennie grimaced when Francelia rolled over at that time. They were within ten feet of where the girls were laying out. As a perpetually friendly personality, Adriana greeted the girl. "*Hola*! I'm Adriana."

Francelia got up and shook hands with her. "I'm Maria, Karolina's friend from school. I'm here from Honduras. Momma Pennie is letting me stay here until school starts back."

The women continued with a short conversation in Spanish. Why didn't Pennie ever commit to learn Spanish? Other than some conversational phrases, she couldn't follow their fast-paced dialogue. Karolina had taught her some basic Portuguese, but she could only follow when they spoke slowly.

Karolina got up to join in, and Adriana pulled Pennie back into the conversation by switching to English. "Pennie, you know I picked up Cynthia from college. Hopefully, you'll get to see her before she goes back to school." Turning back to the younger ladies, she added, "This hairstyle is so popular; Cynthia had hers done like this too," she said as she tousled Karolina's hair. "It makes you two look like twins. I need to get back to work now. You amigas have fun!"

Pennie walked her back through the house, but Adriana lingered by the front door.

"Pennie, this is not my business, but I don't know if you can trust that girl."

"What do you mean?"

"She said she's from Honduras, but I know the accent. She's from Dominica... from my country. I don't know why she's lying to you but keep an eye on her."

The ominous ending to the visit worried Pennie. She locked the front door and went back to let Cole know it was safe to come out. He had only stepped behind her little shed for concealment.

They resumed their seats under the shade of the porch while the girls turned over to tan their flip sides.

"Cole, Adriana recognized her accent. She just told me not to trust Francelia. Plus, she said the gang activity is getting worse in the Dominican."

Without responding to Pennie, Cole made a phone call. She listened to his side of the conversation as he recounted the news of the day to Tony.

When he hung up the phone, he turned to Pennie. "Nothing changes here. We're still just keeping her under the radar. As of now, your neighbor doesn't know who we have here, and we'll do our best to keep it that way."

"Is there something special I need to do about tomorrow?" Pennie asked.

"What's tomorrow?"

"Church. My family will expect my presence. I already mentioned this to the chief," she answered.

"Let's think about this for a minute. Can you just make an excuse not to go? Or would that be more suspicious than you showing up with an extra kid?"

"I show up at church and other family functions with extra students all the time. My family doesn't even try to keep up with the girls who tag along."

"Pietra has watch tomorrow, but let's verify this with Chief first."

The rest of the day passed with a few movies and a few more conversations with Chief Lawrence. He confirmed the political unrest in the Dominican Republic had escalated over the past few days as Adriana had indicated earlier. They gave Pennie a hall pass to take the girls to church the next morning but not to go to lunch with her family. She had no idea why arbitrary lines were drawn, but she had to play by the rules.

The national news had been playing in the background all day, but a breaking story disrupted Pennie's sulking session.

Everyone gathered in the living room to watch the latest story. They sat down in time to hear the message Adolfo Cabral personally delivered. "The lack of response from the National Palace is a sign of disrespect. A real woman knows her place. Daniela Vasquez is not a real woman; she's nothing but a dog."

Pennie knew the word "*perra*" could be translated into a more derogatory word than "dog," but she appreciated the G-rated version used in the captions.

After a snort, he continued, "If Vasquez isn't willing to step down, I'll be required to take action to bring order back to our country."

The short video ended with no hint as to what action they might expect. When the reporters resumed their discussion of the video, they commented about the state of affairs in the Dominican Republic. Rumors and suppositions were tossed around with little regard for the audience listening in Bartlett, Tennessee.

One anchor mentioned an unofficial report stating that Francelia not only escaped the island, but her mother did too. Another reporter hinted that the Vasquez women were hiding in an undisclosed location within the Dominican borders. The lone female of the group spoke as a mother, stating Daniela likely sent her daughter away to safety, but she wouldn't abandon her country. Overall, they downplayed the level of danger the Wasps were capable of.

The banter continued with the reporters suggesting that neighboring island nations would provide a safe harbor for the threatened women, but the USA was in a prime position to hide and protect Vasquez since Puerto Rico, officially a territory of the United States, could easily be reached by ferry from Santo Domingo. Another reporter implied that Miami presented the best entry point for international visitors of all kinds. One Hispanic lady could easily enter the metropolis by sea or air without anyone batting an eye.

Pennie wondered if all this dialogue on the national news provided ideas for Adolfo Cabral. The original plan to hand Francelia off at Miami Airport had to have been leaked, and all the discussion reinforced the idea that she arrived in Miami as intended. The Wasps had a starting point. Hopefully, Pennie didn't leave a trail that could lead the Wasps to Bartlett.

When the station moved on to another topic, Pennie stood to get ready for bed. Her anxiety was building. What could she do about it? Other than keeping Francelia under cover, how could she bring this situation to a close? She didn't know how to stand idly by while evil reared its ugly head.

SUNDAY, JULY 17

Pietra wore a splendid dress to church with Pennie and the girls that morning. Both women hid guns in their purses. Her family acted happy to see Karolina along with her new friend. Pennie's sister and mother were slightly suspicious of Pietra's attendance this morning.

"She had you arrested last November. Why're you being nice to her?" her sister whispered as they had a seat in their usual row.

"Love your enemies. That's what the Bible says, Alice."

"Is she going to lunch with us? I think Mom still hates her. James isn't a fan of hers either, even though they work on the same police force together."

"We're friends now, and she wanted to come to church. We're going shopping later, so I'm skipping lunch."

Alice cut a sideways glance at her baby sister. "Why would she go shopping with you? What are you shopping for?"

"Karolina likes her style, and both girls want to update their wardrobe," Pennie answered, slightly annoyed that Alice was prying into her business.

"Well, her dress is amazing. Just don't let her bougieness rub off on you."

Fortunately, the praise band started and invited everyone to join in singing. The next hour was spent as a revival for Pennie. The preacher spoke on the peace of God, which transcends all understanding, as if he were speaking directly to Pennie. She needed all the peace she could get these days.

A stop at Marshalls would ensure Francelia could get everything she needed so she wouldn't have to borrow all of Karolina's clothes and toiletries. Nothing seemed amiss during their visit. The girls filled up two baskets of items, including a few new colors of nail polish for Karolina. During one instance, the *ReelLife* timer prompted Francelia to take a picture, which she did in the middle of a clothing aisle. Pennie and Pietra made sure no one else was included in the photo before she submitted it.

This was a couple of thousand dollars Pennie didn't expect to spend. Her intent was to be frugal with the settlement she received after Johnny's death, but the girl needed the personal items more than Pennie needed the money.

By this time, they were starving, so a quick deli stop would take care of a late lunch. While waiting for the food, Pietra received a message from Chief Lawrence to head home and go on lockdown. Taking the sandwiches to go, they headed out in a hurry.

By the time they arrived at Pennie's house, the chief had

already parked in the driveway, still driving Cole's Tesla from the vehicle exchange. Karolina helped Francelia get all the bags into the spare room she'd been occupying. They stayed in the room to eat their lunch and organize things, leaving Tony, Pietra, and Pennie in the living room alone.

Tony got right down to business. "There's been some activity in the Dominican Republic this morning. A new video was released where Cabral is making new threats, mostly aimed at anyone trying to help President Vasquez. He's outright stated that feminism is ruining their country and undermining what makes their nation great."

Pietra snarled her lip. "So, a bunch of machismo propaganda?"

"Yes, and they're calling for President Vasquez to step down."

Pennie shook her head. "They've been doing that. What's different this time?"

Tony cut his eyes back and forth between the ladies. "This time he's suggesting the Wasps storm the palace if she doesn't step down. They'll take over by force."

"Like some kind of political coup? Do they even have enough manpower to accomplish this?" Pietra asked.

"Vasquez has military protection right now, but..."

"But what, Tony?" Pennie asked. Her appetite for the uneaten sandwich was gone now. Pietra wasn't hungry anymore either.

He looked down at his tightly clasped hands before answering. "Ambassador Hernandez thinks that some of her military protection has affiliation with the Wasps. They've only been on the map as organized activists for about two years, so there's a lot no one knows about them. We're just now deciding they might have some technological sophistication with the release of the videos. Before now, they've just been an unruly gang located in loosely associated bands across the country. They appear more cohesive than we expected, and they're gaining momentum."

Pietra and Pennie shared a scowl with clenched teeth and narrowed eyes. The female officer spoke first, "What does this mean now? How do we get President Vasquez out of the country? What do we do?"

With an abrupt shake of his head, Tony said, "Absolutely nothing. None of that is our responsibility, and we don't have time to come up with a plan like we did for Francelia. Nothing can be done under the radar now anyway. Our only goal is keeping Francelia hidden and safe."

"How much time does anyone have?" Pennie implored. "Can't the US military send in a Blackhawk tonight and get Vasquez out? Surely, they have a map of the palace and can figure something out. I've seen *Zero Dark Thirty*; I know they can pull this off."

"This isn't a movie, Pennie, and we aren't making those decisions. In the most recent video, Adolfo Cabral gives Vasquez three days to step down. Of course, they say she can freely leave the palace with her daughter if they do so by Wednesday, but no one believes his intention is to let them live. They'd be assassinated at the first opportunity."

Pennie felt so impotent to help. The Dominican Republic wasn't her country. The battle wasn't hers. But it was Francelia's, and Francelia became her daughter as of last week. Her heart felt so heavy. Just trying to get a better idea of how things might play out, she asked a question she was scared to know the answer to. "We know Vasquez won't step down. Three days from now, what does Cabral say he's gonna do?"

Tony cast his gaze back to the floor. This might be worse than Pennie imagined. When he looked back up, he said, "They're going to take over the presidential palace by force and behead her on a live feed for the world to witness. They also say they're going to take Francelia into their gang and teach her how women are supposed to act."

"What?!"

The screech caused them all to look back simultaneously. Francelia stood in the hallway, privy to the conversation they had just finished. Pennie jumped up to grab her in a fierce embrace. "Honey, shhh," she whispered in the shivering girl's ear. Karolina joined in, making a group hug out of it.

With all five of them seated in the living room, Tony recapped his information with Francelia and assured her that her safety was still the top priority of the team in Bartlett.

Finally calming down, Francelia said, "She sent me a picture around eleven on the *ReelLife* app. As long as she's sending me pictures, I'll know she's safe."

Tony nodded, wanting the refugee to have some peace of mind for the time being. "We're staying in direct contact with Ambassador Hernandez. She's our best source of accurate information unless we see something on the news that's broadcast faster than she can communicate with us. Francelia, let me see your phone. I want to see the pictures you've shared with your mother."

Obediently, she unlocked the phone and handed it over. He scrolled through the ten pictures they had exchanged in the past few days. "Okay, you're doing a good job keeping the pictures anonymous. Remember, no pictures with other people or anything that will give away your location."

"Yes, sir."

"Keep your chin up. Your mother is tough, and so are you. I guarantee, forces all over the world are working on a solution to get your mother out of there." Tony managed to draw a small smile from Francelia, again proving that he would indeed be a good father one of these days. "Ladies, nothing changes right now. Be diligent to stay off anyone's radar. I'm heading back home now, but I'm a call away if you need me."

With Pietra keeping watch, Pennie took her dog for a run through the neighborhood. Peach needed to expend some energy as much as Pennie did. The simple routine brought some welcome relief from the anxiety. Too bad the moment of peace would be short-lived.

Jenna had pulled into Pennie's driveway as she returned to her house. She wasn't expecting any company, and she needed to make sure Jenna didn't notice anything unusual within her home. Giving her best friend a hug, she scrambled to come up with some way to announce her arrival without it seeming suspicious.

As they entered the door, Pennie spoke louder than necessary, "Jenna, I haven't seen you in a month. What's been going on?" She delayed her right inside the front door an extra minute to unclip Peach's leash and hang it up.

Passing through the entry area, Pennie peeked around to see if Pietra was in sight. Since she wasn't visible, Pennie ushered Jenna into the living room.

"I'll tell you what's going on. Cole is a man-whore, and I hate him!" Jenna exclaimed with clenched fists, stomping her foot in the process.

"Oh, what? You don't mean that."

Before the conversation could continue, the two amigas entered the room.

"*Oi*, Tia Jenna!" Karolina greeted her with a sweet hug and introduced her friend Maria. The girls moved outside to work on their tans some more.

"Okay, sit. What in the world are you talking about?"

Pennie patted the seat next to her on the couch, but Jenna paced and stomped circles, shooting daggers with her green eyes.

"I wanted to surprise Cole today, so I went to his house with some rose petals, candles, and wine... You know, to set the mood... But when I got there, do you know what I found?"

She opened her mouth to speak, but before Pennie could utter a syllable, Jenna cut her off.

"I found Pietra Russo's Mustang in his driveway! That ho!"

"Jenna, surely there's a misunderstanding here. Did you go inside and talk to Cole?"

"No. I'm never talking to him again!"

This was a sticky situation for her friend. During the bodyguard-vehicle-exchange, Cole had to take Pietra's car home this morning. Jenna didn't, and couldn't, know anything about this.

Jenna plopped back in a recliner hard enough that it almost flipped back on her. Then, as dramatic as possible, she leaned forward with a groan and placed her head in her hands. Whew, this was more than Pennie wanted to deal with today.

Using the most soothing voice she could muster, Pennie said, "Has Cole ever given you a reason to doubt him? You may want to give him a chance to explain."

The angriest green eyes ever looked up at Pennie. "I can see it all in hindsight, Penn. You should know that we haven't slept together— his idea, not mine. Last night, we should've had a date night, but he suddenly had some kind of emergency shift at work that he couldn't tell me any details about. Now, that tramp's car is at his house. I don't know why he's been stringing me along, but it's over now."

Wow, things didn't look good for Cole. "Jenna, you really need to talk to him before deciding anything rash."

"Don't defend him! And don't put it past Pietra either. She's a homewrecker with no moral boundaries. She messed things up for you and Chip just like she's messing things up for me and Cole. It's a game for women like her."

"Can you please just take a deep breath, Jenna? Please. You're emotionally charged right now, and it's not like you. Cole would never do anything to hurt you. There's gotta be a plausible explanation. She could've given him a ride home or something. Give him the benefit of the doubt."

"So, you think I should just go over there right now like I intended?"

"Did you already have plans with him tonight?" Pennie asked.

"No. He said he wanted to rest after his shift last night. I figured I'd surprise him, and we could stay in together for the evening."

Pennie's curiosity got the better of her, so she asked something she didn't really want the answer to. "If y'all aren't sleeping together, what mood were you trying to set?"

"I planned to take advantage of his exhaustion and seduce him."

Despite herself, Pennie grinned. "Jenna. Have you ever

had to work this hard for a man?" She took stock of Jenna's appearance. Her slinky dress and hooker heels... red lipstick... platinum-blond hair swept up gracefully into a twist.

"No, and it's killing me."

"He wants things to be perfect. He knows you need to start your relationship by getting to know each other and not in the bedroom. Please go talk to him."

"Fine. I'll go see what his excuse is, but you'll have to help me hide a body or two if I walk into anything that remotely looks like cheating."

"I'll definitely help. Now go!"

"You better send Cole a text and warn him," Pietra said as she emerged from Pennie's bedroom.

"Doing it now," she replied, pecking out a quick message.

"I guess I should've brought Chip's truck for Cole to take home instead of my car. Does Jenna really think I messed things up for you and Chip on purpose?"

Pennie set her phone on the coffee table and offered a weak smile. "Jenna thinks a lot of things that aren't based in fact. I'm guessing you didn't start talking to Chip until after we ended things last August. I've never assumed you were trying to mess things up." For the first mission she helped with, even Pietra thought her relationship with Chip was real, and Pennie had to remember these details to keep up with the ruse a year later.

"Seriously, Pennie, do you think I'm capable of being a

homewrecker?"

Not sure how to diplomatically answer, she said, "You're a little ruthless, but I can't imagine you'd purposefully sabotage anyone's relationship for your own benefit."

As if she was offended, Pietra placed her hand over her heart. "Ruthless? Why would you say that?"

"Two months ago, you stood right here in my living room and practically threatened me, telling me to stay away from Chip even though you had no claim to him. That's ruthless."

"I was looking out for his career. He gets careless around you. I'm trying to help him become a better investigator and show him what a sophisticated relationship is supposed to be like."

Exasperated, Pennie rolled her eyes. "So now I'm a bad influence, and I'm unsophisticated?"

Pietra moved to sit next to Pennie on the sofa. "Please don't misunderstand me. You're the girl next door, Pennie. Chip has dreams and goals beyond what you can provide. I'm cut from the same cloth he is. We're compatible in every way. You, on the other hand, need to find a downhome guy who wants to stay in Bartlett forever and raise a bunch of kids."

Pennie couldn't believe what she was hearing. Who was Pietra to put her in a category like that? Before she could reply with anything catty, Karolina and Francelia came back inside the house.

"Mom, that boy JJ is sending me messages on

Instagram."

"Can't you just ignore him?"

"Now that we're home, why can't I chat with him?" Karolina asked with a curious tone.

"Based on how you just asked, I'm guessing y'all are already chatting. Why're you even asking me?"

Karolina scoffed. "It's not like he's going to come here and visit. Plus, his brother wants your phone number."

"Absolutely not, Karolina. Don't you think we have enough going on without you playing matchmaker? He lives in another state, and he's a Tulane fan. It'd never work."

"If you say so, Mom. But we're going to make gluten-free cookies now."

The girls got busy in the kitchen, while Pietra and Pennie continued watching the repeating news stories in tense silence thanks to their earlier bickering.

The ladies left the news playing constantly in case any new messages were broadcast. By the time five rolled around, Adolfo's face filled the screen again. Everyone moved to the couch where Karolina and Francelia listened, and Pennie and Pietra read along with the closed captions.

"I've tried to be patient. I expected a response from the National Palace by now. Blatantly ignoring my generous offer to vacate the palace is a sign of insolence. Daniela Vasquez, you've left me no choice but to impose a deadline. Seventy-two hours from now, the *Mata Cacatas* are taking over. If you choose to still be in the palace at that time, I promise to make an example out of you and your daughter. A beheading will make sure everyone sees what's in store for disrespectful dogs, and Francelia will learn to be a good little servant for the *Mata Cacatas*!"

Karolina and Pennie wrapped the young Dominican in a hug without even waiting for her reaction. Quiet tears slid down her face. Pietra excused herself from the room to call Tony.

"I knew this would happen," Francelia whispered without the hysterics she displayed earlier in the day.

Pennie agreed, "I think we all knew it would get worse before it got better, sweetie."

"My mom should've come with us. Why didn't we get her out at the same time?"

Pietra reentered the room and said, "I actually spoke to Vale about that initially. I wanted to get both of you out of the country, but your mom insisted she needed to stay. She's the president. It would've been a sign of weakness for her to run away."

"It's not a sign of strength to be killed," Francelia muttered, not an ounce of emotion in her voice.

Worried that shock might be a factor, Pennie tried to encourage her. "This isn't over. Your mom has allies all over the world. Good will win in the end. This fight will have a long-lasting impact to show women it's okay to stand up for what's right. Just because something is scary doesn't mean you don't do it. You're safe with us so your mom can fight for justice without any hesitation."

"She's right," Pietra added. "Your mother can't protect you and lead the fight at the same time. There will be a clash of power, but the Wasps will run out of steam before they claim any victory."

Karolina decided to give all the women manicures to ensure a peaceful evening. Tony called on one occasion to let them know the Wasps had taken over the marina where Bianca and Archie normally stay, along with two other marinas near Santo Domingo. It seemed like they were trying to block off methods of escape for President Vasquez.

As she blew on her nails, Pennie asked, "Pietra, do you think the Wasps think that Francelia is still at the palace there? Or do they think she's already escaped?"

"Mom, quit blowing on your nails. That doesn't help," Karolina demanded.

Pietra smiled at the girl before answering, "That's a tough question. This is all supposition anyway. I'd say they think she's still there. That's my opinion."

"Tell me why." Pennie wanted some sense of security. As long as the Wasps were looking for Francelia on their island, they wouldn't be looking for her in the United States.

"For starters, I think the Wasps do have some kind of inside track. Cabral knew there'd be an attempt to get her out of the country, and he thought they were one step ahead of us and planned to take her at the Miami airport, which means they could have a contact within the US government. They had no way of knowing our identities or how she'd get out of the Dominican, much less into the USA. Their assumption had to be that she was flying into the airport, and that's where they'd intercept her."

Francelia's jaw dropped. "You felt certain they'd take me at the airport? But you didn't do anything?"

Pietra smiled in return. "I didn't have to do anything. I knew Pennie would."

"Tony told me you had a bet going. That all of you knew I'd bring her home."

"Yea, that lucky dog. He's the only one who knew you'd wait until you got to Homosassa to let us know, so that it'd be too late to back out. We wouldn't have a choice but to help at that point, but we all knew you'd bring Francelia with you."

Pennie got back to her original question. "If you thought they wanted to intercept her at the airport, they had to know she'd be on the move. Why didn't they have extra security or whatever to catch her before she got off the island?"

"They had their guys all over the Dominican airports, marinas, and major highways near the capital starting two days before her supposed flight to Miami. She got lucky to get through those extra safeguards."

Karolina spoke without disrupting her polishing of Francelia's nails. "That's true, Mom. I had to show my driver's license at one roadblock and at the marina. We had to go through the facial recognition camera at the marina also. The guards knew Bianca and Archie, so they didn't give us a hard time after they did their job."

Pennie felt lightheaded at the thought of Karolina being in danger. She took a deep breath and continued, "Okay, Pietra. In your best interpretation of things, the Wasps think Francelia is still in the palace with her mother?"

"Yes. As far as our government is concerned, the attempt to get her off the island failed. Then she never showed up at the airport. Everyone is left to think she's at the palace. Francelia, what do you think?"

"I agree with you. For the last three months, we've been locked down to one wing of the palace. Only my mom's trusted security team has been in the wing with us. Aside from the security guys, only the trusted housekeepers and cooks have been allowed to enter and exit our area. I'm sure other members of the palace staff or security communicate with the Wasps, but they never got to be in our space."

"How did you manage to sneak out of the palace?" Pennie had been wanting to ask that question for a while now.

"A hairdresser came with the housekeepers last week to do my hair the day before I left. They rolled me out of the palace in a garbage can. Then I sat in the van like I was part of the crew when they drove off. I don't think anyone knew I could escape like that. I haven't talked to my mom since I left, so I don't know if anyone is suspicious that I'm not there. But I think the core security team is keeping that information safe."

Pennie hadn't gotten to know Francelia as a person yet. Only as a target and a refugee. The escape from her home... leaving her mother... That had to be terrifying for her.

"Francelia, now that you're here, how are you handling all this?"

"I feel safe for the first time since I was a kid. After my dad was abducted, my mother became an activist. Then she became a politician. I've been bullied and picked on since I was ten years old. For these few days, I feel like I can breathe. If I weren't worried about my mom, I'd probably feel like I'm on a holiday."

Pennie could see that. But she still wasn't living a normal life for a twenty-year-old. "Did you have plans to go to college? Or start a career? What did your future look like if the Wasps didn't interfere?"

A smile lit up her face. "I wanted to attend school in the United States. The land of the free. Where even women are encouraged to get an education and pursue a profession. My mom wanted me to wait until she made a difference as president, then she would help me get my visa to come here. I wanted to go to MIT to be an engineer."

"Let's keep that dream alive, Francelia. Your mother might need a break in the States when this turmoil comes to an end. Someone else can be president for a while after this."

Lying in the dark, knowing she needed to sleep, Pennie's head swirled with the emotions of the day.

Worry for Francelia's peace of mind.

Fear for Daniela's life.

Torment over Karolina growing up and talking to boys.

Burden over Jenna's relationship, and the inadvertent stress Pennie placed on it.

Discourse with Pietra over some non-existent relationship with Chip.

She wanted nothing more than to revisit her boring life from a few months ago. Pennie channeled the tranquility she felt when the only thing she had planned was a relaxing cruise with her daughter. But great things don't happen from comfort zones. She knew this.

The opportunity to help Francelia was a decision she'd make over and over again. These times of adversity reveal character and strength. Pennie's overall involvement in the adversity was small, but she'd fulfill her role to the best of her ability.

MONDAY, JULY 18

It was Chip's turn to come back for security. Pennie made omelets and tried to not act happy to see him. Pietra had her clutches on Chip, and she shouldn't get distracted with the domestic feelings of having him in her home. She tried to avoid any personal conversations, choosing to focus only on the business at hand.

Despite her commitment to avoiding personal conversations, Chip didn't seem to mind a little idle chit chat. "Karolina, I didn't think you could eat eggs as a vegetarian."

"That's only for vegans. Vegetarian is different. If I weren't lactose intolerant, I'd drink milk and eat cheese. Eggs are a good source of protein for breakfast. If I can get gluten-free bread, I like to make avocado toast with a fried egg on top."

"That's interesting," Chip said. "Francelia, do you normally eat eggs for breakfast?"

The girl acted like she'd been starved the way she shoveled food in her mouth every time they sat down to eat. Swallowing her bite, she said, "Yes. We usually have fried eggs and mashed plantains with some salami or other meat. I've never tried eggs like this before."

After they finished eating, Karolina and Francelia moved to the bunkroom where her young nieces normally stay when they spend the weekend. All of Karolina's instruments were in that room, and the girls found reprieve playing music.

"Did you know Francelia could play the piano?" Chip

asked since they could hear the instrumental duet in the living room.

"No, there's still a lot to learn about her. That's a keyboard in the room, and Karolina never goes far without her flute. She can also play several percussion instruments and the guitar, along with similar instruments like a ukelele and piccolo and stuff. She's like a savant. She can play perfectly by sight."

"You mean she can play by ear?" Chip asked.

"No, it's different. Karolina can look at a sheet of music for a song she's never heard before and play it perfectly without practicing. Don't get me wrong, she can play by ear too. She's extremely talented." Pennie loved bragging about her daughter.

In the next minute, Chip drowned out the music by turning on the national news. Random stories about celebrities that Pennie never kept up with. A few political pieces. A quick mention of the political unrest in the Dominican Republic without anything new. Just a world watching to see what would happen next.

"Chip, how do you see this playing out?"

He cut his eyes around the room while he thought about his response. "I think the US has to intervene for Vasquez to make it out alive. The Wasps are terrorists with nothing to lose."

"If they're making their presence known at the airports and marinas, why aren't they terrorizing the cruise ports?"

"The US Coast Guard protects cruise ships and ports. I think they're mostly safeguarding against pirates, but they have a big presence in the cruise terminals anyway. The Festival Cruise Company provides hefty onboard security as well. The Wasps would have to come out in full force to take over a single cruise ship. Plus, I also don't think the

Wasps want to deter tourism since that's a huge part of their economy."

"Do you want some more coffee?" Pennie didn't wait for his answer. She just grabbed his mug and refilled it along with hers. Settling back down in the living room, she asked a question she seriously did want the answer to. "Are you mad that I did this? You, Tony, and Pietra were automatically tangled up in this mess I created."

"I'm not mad." His words didn't have any inflection, and his eyes didn't leave the television when he answered.

"You can't do your new job as an investigator because you've gotta babysit us. It's messing up your personal life too."

"I'm part of an operation that's protecting an international political refugee. And I was part of the mission that successfully extracted her from the Dominican. This is better for my resumé than arresting the latest meth dealer in Bartlett, Skipper."

At that time, Karolina rushed into the room. "I need a picture for *ReelLife*, Mom. Pose with me." She snapped a picture and moved back to the bunkroom to continue the two-girl-band concert with Francelia.

"What's she up to?"

"She twenty. How would I know? Kids these days." Pennie finished the statement with a shake of her head. "I guess it's the social media thing to do right now. I'm just glad my fifteen minutes of social media fame is over."

Chip's mouth curled up in a playful smile. "The *Don't Litter Lady* would've thrown that building in the trash."

"What building? The one at the nursery?"

"Yea. That thing's atrocious. It's not safe at all."

"Adriana came by the other day and said they plan to tear it down. She's moving in a trailer or something to be the office. That building has some old chairs and desks in it. I hope she lets me get rid of those rickety things and buy new office furniture. Speaking of the nursery, I need to head to work now. I'll be home after five."

"I'll holler if anything changes here."

During the short drive to work, Pennie contemplated how she could learn more about the threat against the Vasquez women. Without any resources, how could she find out if any Wasps were actively searching for Francelia on US soil? Any insight she could gather against the Wasps could aid her efforts in keeping her refugee safe. She pulled into the driveway of Avocado Farms without determining any course of action.

Pennie opened the nursery gates at nine. Monday mornings were only busy for the drivers and landscape crews who arrived right behind her to get their day started. The crews wasted no time leaving to make deliveries, cut grass, and tend lawns, leaving only Lupe with Pennie. She instructed the young worker to water all the annuals so she could check out the progress on the old house.

Fortunately, a peek from the front door revealed that most of the old furniture had been cleared out. The racoon with her ever-growing babies peered down from above. Pennie backed away slowly, but nearly jumped out of her skin when a voice surprised her from behind.

"Penelope Nichols, I have some questions for you."

Pennie turned to find Judy Thomas standing with a hand on her hip and an impatient expression on her face.

She'd almost forgotten about the reporter's visit a couple of weeks ago, and now she wondered what was uncovered about a historic cemetery.

"What questions do you have for me? I just work here."

Judy glanced around suspiciously. Lupe remained a hundred yards away. Only the three women were in the vicinity. No customers or cameraman. Pennie noticed Judy wasn't wearing her typical suit. Instead, she wore cargo pants and a fitted knit top. Pennie hoped she could age gracefully and dress with style like the local reporter.

"I'm investigating a story. You've known the Acevedos for a couple of years, personally and professionally. Is that correct?"

"Yea, but I don't know anything about this new property they bought or any supposed cemetery."

Judy shook her head. "The cemetery's been hidden for over a hundred years. It'll wait. There's a bigger story here, but I'm researching it completely under the radar."

"What kind of story?" Pennie asked cautiously.

With narrowed eyes, Judy implored, "I need you to promise that what I share with you today will be held in the strictest of confidence."

In her recent history, Pennie had gotten good at keeping secrets. "Cross my heart, Ms. Thomas."

Something in her demeanor must've been interpreted as sincere, causing the reporter to visibly relax. "You can call me Judy. Are you at all aware of the uproar in the Dominican Republic?"

This might hit closer to home than Pennie anticipated. "Sure, the terrorists and all. They've threatened the president and her daughter."

Nodding, Judy continued, "There've been reports that

the daughter managed to sneak out of the country. Given the facts I've collected, I think she's hiding in our city."

Acting dumbfounded—or maybe not entirely acting—Pennie asked, "But how did she get out?"

"According to my sources, the American government arranged to get Francelia Vasquez safe passage into our country, but she shook the security team that was supposed to take her to a safehouse in Florida. I'm putting the pieces together as we speak."

"What pieces?"

"When I came here last week to speak to Adriana Acevedo, she insisted she didn't have time for me because she had to pick up her daughter from college. That didn't immediately alert me, but I'm sure you know the Acevedos are Dominican. Ever since they returned from their road trip last week, they've acted fishy. My attempts to visit and call have been blatantly ignored. I think they're hiding something... or someone."

As much as Pennie wanted the attention somewhere aside from herself, she didn't necessarily want it on her boss, who was also her neighbor and friend. "Judy, are you sure? They have a daughter. They might be spending quality time as a family without outside interference."

"Cynthia Acevedo is currently working as an intern for a bank in Birmingham, Alabama. I verified that myself this morning. So, who would they be hiding in their home?"

"That is bizarre," Pennie responded truthfully. "Even if they're hiding the Dominican president's daughter, I'd assume you don't want to call attention to her or jeopardize her safety. What are you hoping to find out?"

"I'm hoping to trap a Wasp or two," Judy declared.

"You mean the terrorists? How will you catch them?" Pennie asked, seriously intrigued.

Taking another glance around to make sure no one could eavesdrop, Judy explained, “It’s only a matter of time before the Wasps find out she’s here. I want to find out who and where the Wasps are and plan an ambush for them. I want to single-handedly take down a terrorist on US soil. Opportunities like this only fall in a reporter’s lap once in a lifetime. I’ve already gotten a credible tip that at least two members of the Wasps arrived in Florida last week.”

“Are you asking me to help you locate the terrorists and take them down? Won’t there be some federal task force already assigned to this?”

“There’s a lot of misinformation being distributed throughout the government right now. I have a few sources deep in the political arena, but my instincts are all I trust right now. The Wasps are the only ones looking for Francelia Vasquez, and no one is looking for these Wasps. No one except for me—and you if you agree to help.”

Before Pennie could grasp the situation, Judy looked at her phone. “Oh, breaking news. I’m gonna run, but text me if you want to help.”

Judy shoved a business card in Pennie’s hand and hurried back to her car.

Pennie spent the next several hours transplanting seedlings and taking inventory of the garden statues. Lupe checked out the few customers and handled the phone orders requesting mulch and sand deliveries. The conversation with Judy mulled around in her head. Whatever happened in the Caribbean was out of Pennie’s control. But Wasps on US soil—

Pennie could help with that. In fact, she'd love to help. Nothing would please her more than to take down a terrorist who posed a threat to Francelia.

Close to one, Oscar Acevedo showed up. "Hola, Pennie. I can stay until closing so you can leave if you want to. Adriana and Cynthia are having a girl's day. I know you want to spend time with Karolina since she's home from college, too. We'll take turns relieving you after lunch every day."

"Thanks, Oscar." Then out of curiosity, Pennie added a question, "When did Cynthia get home from Alabama?"

"Last week. We picked her up in Birmingham on Wednesday."

"Okay. Thanks, again. I'll be back in the morning."

Pennie retrieved her bag from the cashier's shack. She pecked out a quick text message and headed out.

Fifteen minutes later, Pennie found a table at JoJo's Espresso in Germantown. Knowing she should've gone home, she felt uneasy meeting with the reporter. Being on lockdown didn't put her in a good position to investigate anything, so she had to use whatever unencumbered time that became available.

A text came through as Judy ordered a coffee.

Pennie, Life360 shows you speeding in Germantown. Why did you leave work?

Dang it. Tony was tracking her, and her speeding alerted him.

She pecked out a quick reply. *I'm making a delivery for*

work, then I am getting off early.

He didn't immediately reply, so she hoped that was a good cover. About that time, Judy joined her at the table.

"I got off work early, so I thought we could discuss how you want me to help."

Judy glanced around, verifying they were the only two people sitting at an outside table. Feeling free to speak, she said, "I don't think I've slept a wink in the past seven days. Since I got a hint about this story, I've devoted every waking hour to the situation in the Dominican and the possibility that our country aided Francelia Vasquez. I've researched the Cabral brothers and tried to narrow down who the enemy on US soil could be."

Pennie simply nodded.

Pulling an iPad from her purse, she flipped through some pictures to help paint the picture. "I've gone back to the beginning to find out what made them who they are today. Julio and Adolfo were the only children of Francois and Natacha Cabral. They were still young when their father relocated the family from Haiti to the Pedarnales province of the Dominican Republic. Their immigration to the Dominican was undocumented, which was typical thirty years ago. Francois found a manual labor job with a telecommunications company. Using his interpersonal skills, he worked his way up to a supervisor, eventually transferring to the capital city of Santo Domingo."

From the screen a grainy photo of two teenage boys with their mother and father showed smiling faces. Judy continued, "You can see the family had a light complexion, so they didn't look like other Haitian immigrants. Based on what I understand about the Dominican culture, this gave them a better opportunity to blend in without becoming victims of discrimination."

Pennie asked, "What happened to their mother?"

Judy zoomed in on the smiling face of Natacha. "Shortly after settling in Santo Domingo, first responders were called to their home and found her in critical condition. According to the accounts of all family members, while cooking dinner, Natacha accidentally spilled hot grease over most of her body. She died three days later from her wounds."

Flipping through the photos on her tablet, she stopped on one to show Pennie. The grotesque body of Natacha Cabral lying in a hospital bed, never to wake again. "No one believed the grease-spilling incident was an accident."

"Oh my. Now I'm scared to ask what happened to their father?"

"Within ten years of this incident, Francois was killed in a hit-and-run incident outside a bar. The woman charged with his death turned out to be one of his lovers who acted out of revenge when he broke up with her. By this time, Adolfo was twenty-two. The brothers were already working for the same telecommunications company and learning how to promote the toxic masculinity they learned from their father."

"So, all the hate-filled propaganda started with the dad. How did the brothers go from telecommunication jobs to terrorism?"

Judy swiped to find another photo of the young men outside a rally of some sort. "They just became unreserved in their efforts to restore male power to the nation, repeatedly crashing protests like these to break up women's attempts for equality. Enough men joined the efforts to create a movement. Social media helped spread their message across the nation."

Huffing, Pennie asked, "How do we use this information to help Francelia now?"

"First, I'd like to confirm that Francelia is here in Bartlett. Since you're friends with the Acevedos, I need you to visit their home and get a visual. Here's some current photos of her..."

The pictures on her iPad showed Francelia with long locks of solid black hair, a far cry from the layered, two-toned style she sported these days. Another big difference was her facial expression. In photos, Francelia could've been at a funeral based on her sullen appearance.

Judy resumed her plan. "I'm using my connections in the government to identify anyone within the US who has possible terrorist ties. They won't give me any complete manifest or other documents to see who all entered Miami around the day of July thirteenth, but I have a friend at Border Patrol who shared a filtered list of names."

"Why July thirteenth?" Pennie asked, halfway impressed by how fast Judy nailed down the date Francelia arrived, and halfway fearful of what else might be discovered. Judy could easily uncover Pennie's own trip to the Dominican Republic and arrival back in the States on that date.

"That's the day Adolfo released his first public message on the topic, and it coincides with rumors about Francelia entering the country. Anyway, about fifty thousand people enter Miami from international flights and cruises every single day. That doesn't even include numbers from nearby airports. My contact provided a list of about ten thousand people, and I've narrowed the list down further by crosschecking it to the terrorist watch list and eliminating based on age and other factors. I've added a few names that have piqued my interest otherwise. Only a handful of them are local, and I'll need your help finding out more about these people."

"How in the world did you cull down a list of ten thousand people into something manageable?" Pennie asked.

"Basic statistics mostly. My original list of people with ties to terrorism was limited to people geographically located between here and Miami. That accounted for about fifty names. The list of ten thousand names were already filtered by my friend at Border Control. He eliminated people who immediately flew out of the area. He broke out the families with small kids into another list, which I won't do anything with unless I strike out everywhere else. Women traveling together… Men and couples over sixty… I had to exclude based on specific parameters to get a manageable list."

A young couple came outside to find an empty table, interrupting their conversation, so Judy took a hint to wrap up. "I'm not emailing this list of names because I'm concerned with leaks in my own office." She handed Pennie a few pieces of folded paper from her bag. "Just take a look later, and I'll check back tomorrow to compare notes on how we should proceed."

"I got off a little early. How's Francelia?" Pennie asked as soon as she walked through the door.

Chip motioned for her to come sit on the couch. "Another video was released. Francelia hasn't seen it. Other than a quick break for a snack, they've been practicing music all day. I didn't want to upset her, so I just had the video ready for you to see when you got here."

The face of Adolfo Cabral filled the TV. She didn't see the intro to the story, but Cabral's message was clear thanks to the closed-captioned translation rolling across the bottom of the screen. The video was released at ten a.m., reminding President Vasquez of her impending deadline to step down. Cabral reiterated his intent to take over the palace to start a new era for the country—an era led by real men. His words said he intended to let Vasquez step down voluntarily and move on to safety. His eyes though… they said Vasquez, along with all her supporters, were already dead.

The message finished in less than a minute, but the news anchor took over speaking. Chip allowed the news to continue playing. With her face aghast with horror, she talked about thoughts and prayers for the Vasquez family. She had no new communication from the US government about their intentions to intervene. Then the story moved on to cover the latest off-season professional basketball trades.

"Is this what the US is all about?!" Pennie jumped up and exclaimed. "A woman's life is on the line, and without even a commercial break, we're talking about where Tal Kadyrov might play basketball next year? Like these stories are equal?"

"Have a seat, Pennie. You already know that's what every country is all about. The woman in danger is two thousand miles away. That's far enough away for us to feel bad for a minute without becoming all consumed. Since you're wearing a Memphis Grizzlies shirt instead of a 'Save Vasquez' shirt, I'd say the news has it spot on."

"Really? You think I'm that shallow?" Pennie implored without sitting.

"No, I know you're not. You're the one with a Vasquez under your roof right now. But most Americans would help if they were given an opportunity like you were. I'm law enforcement, and there's nothing I can do to help President Vasquez right now, so why would I fixate on something I can't help with? I can only send up a prayer and focus on what I do have control over, and that's what we're doing here."

Resigned, Pennie resumed her seat on the couch.

"Don't look defeated, Skipper. You're the one who picks up a stray napkin on the sidewalk. By itself, that doesn't save the earth, but you did your part. The next person doesn't use a straw to save the turtles. The next person drives an electric car to minimize his carbon footprint. Don't be mad at the world because you can't see how all the pieces fit into place."

The unexpected pep talk helped. Everyone was doing what they could within their power. "I get it. I guess I'm personally invested in this one, so I want everyone to give it their full attention."

"The right people are giving it the attention it deserves. We're only guessing that someone in the US government might not be trustworthy, and that's why you brought Francelia home. The truth is, we don't know the truth. Francelia could've gone straight to a safehouse from Miami without being in danger. How did she convince you that she couldn't trust the team in Miami anyway?"

Pennie felt embarrassed thinking back to that day. "She asked me to check out the guy to see if he looked trustworthy. That's why I made a lap before we went to get the rental car. I didn't like the way he looked, so we made our own plan."

"You didn't like how he looked? What? Did he have a peg leg, an eye patch, and a hook for a hand? Or did he dress in all black with a scar across his face while stroking his hairless cat? Did he—"

"Stop it, Chip. You think that's funny, but the only thing I didn't like was his hat. He wore one of those *Thunder Swarm* hats with a red wasp on it. That was my sign that Francelia needed to stay with me. Even if he were trustworthy, and their plan was on the up-and-up, I'd venture to say she's safer and happier here than in a safehouse."

"His hat? That's it?"

"I prayed for a sign, and that's all I needed. I'm not second-guessing myself."

"That's bold, but I'm not even disagreeing with you. Ambassador Hernandez knew you'd treat her like a daughter, and that's what she needs right now."

Eventually, Karolina and Francelia brought the keyboard to the living room so they could put on a concert. They combined classic songs with popular hits, including one AmberLou tune about puppy love.

The concert was disrupted when a breaking news story flashed across the screen. An anchor gave a quick intro to the latest video.

Cabral's face appeared on the television with his usual sneer. The entire message was delivered in five seconds. "*Cuarenta y ocho horas.*"

Forty-eight hours.

The reporters rehashed information without knowing anything. Francelia didn't want to listen to it any longer, and asked Karolina if they could cook dinner. Francelia wanted to make empanadas from scratch, and Karolina wanted to see if she could make them with gluten-free flour. The kitchen became their laboratory for the next couple of hours, while Pennie and Chip watched the news. No updates came from anyone else on the team except a message from Tony to make sure they saw the video.

Chip was still committed to staying awake all night. After the girls went to bed, Pennie cleaned the kitchen and brewed a fresh pot of coffee.

Moving to the recliner, she said, "I can stay awake for a few hours if you want to take a nap first."

Only television illuminated the living room. In the soft glow of the screen, Chip gave her a sideways glance. "I'm okay, Skipper. It's my job to protect."

"Do you need anything before I hit the hay?"

"Nope. I'm just going to watch the news and a little ESPN."

Before Pennie could say anything else, Chip's phone lit up on the coffee table. Pietra was calling.

"I guess I'll leave you to it then," Pennie said as she headed to her bedroom. She could hear him speaking quietly on the phone, and she sure didn't want to hear anything he had to say to Pietra.

Pennie lay in bed with her loyal dog snuggled close. What a day. Judy Thomas wanted to investigate the Wasps thinking Cynthia was the Dominican refugee. But where was Cynthia? Was she still working in Birmingham? Was she at home in Bartlett? She couldn't come up with a single reason the Acevedos would lie about it, but something was screwy.

Ideas swirled through her head, preventing any sleep, but the train of thought kept derailing. Wasps in Florida. Wasps in Alabama. Pennie stopped in Birmingham on the way home Wednesday. Apparently, the Acevedos covered the same stretch of highway on the same day. If they didn't pick up Cynthia, what purpose did they have in Alabama? Or did they even go?

Pennie felt wired. Nervous energy coursed through her. Instead of attempting to rest, she decided to get a head start on the list that burned a hole in her pocket all afternoon. In the privacy of her own room, she retrieved the list. A quick tally revealed almost two hundred names with corresponding ages and addresses. A few names were already marked off. A few names were linked as being married or in a relationship. Two names stood out—brothers James Jackson "JJ" and Nicolas "Nick" Lee Bell of New Orleans. She expected Adriana and Oscar Acevedo. She didn't expect Charles "Chip" Jordan and Pietra Russo.

Most of the names appeared to be of Hispanic descent. Pennie didn't anticipate knowing any of them, and she had no idea how to research the list. More than half of the list had home addresses in various Caribbean Island nations. One address though… It was in her neighborhood, belonging to Frank "Bone" Fox. The name didn't ring a bell, but he only lived several blocks away. How did Judy Thomas even come up with this list? It was time to find out.

A year ago, she had purchased a laptop for a little amateur detective-work. She retrieved the laptop from a dresser drawer and found a VPN service to do some incognito research. After subscribing to a bank-grade encryption network, Pennie started the task of going through names. Simple internet searches didn't reveal much on the Hispanic names except for a few with LinkedIn profiles, assuming these corporate guys were the same people on Judy's list. No news stories or anything exposing a threat to Francelia.

Switching to some local, American names, fifty-year-old Frank "Bone" Fox and the brothers she met on the cruise were also a bust on the internet. Finally, the name Richard Ewers prompted multiple articles. Ewers, who was forty-two and living in the midtown area, currently held the position of head coach for the University of Memphis baseball team. A quick perusal of the articles didn't shed any light as to why he was on this list though. Moving on, it took a few more names to get another promising hit.

LaToya Gunn, thirty-three from Corpus Christi, Texas. Why did that name sound familiar? Her LinkedIn profile listed her profession as the chief marketing officer of Grandfather General Contractors—the same company where her best friend worked. *That's right...* LaToya was the corporate bigwig helping Jenna organize the national construction convention in Vegas next year. How did her name wind up on this list?

Determined to do a preliminary search on everyone listed, Pennie kept pounding the keyboard. Two of the names appeared Hispanic, but married, forty-five-year-old couple Thomas Juan and Jamie Sarai Reyes had a Memphis address, only about ten minutes away from Pennie's house. For some reason, their names sounded familiar. They both worked nearby also, Jamie for a tool company and Thomas as an AC repair man. Even with that information, she couldn't place them, and the internet wouldn't assist in jogging her memory.

The last name she wanted to check out belonged to Diego Castellanos. The twenty-three-year-old resided in Southaven, Mississippi according to the list, and his Instagram page popped up immediately. Since she didn't have an account herself, Pennie couldn't log in to see much. His profile picture could be mistaken for a young Johnny Depp, except Diego had bright blue eyes. She couldn't see where he worked or who his friends were since his details were private. Oh well.

Without much to show for two hours of researching, Pennie shut down the laptop. Tomorrow, Judy could provide some clarity on these names and how they ended up on her not-so-short list. For tonight, she needed some rest.

TUESDAY, JULY 19

Tony returned to take his shift at Pennie's house. Despite being allowed to leave the house for her shift at work, she still felt like she was in lockdown. The boring days of being cooped up had to be getting to the girls as well.

On the back porch, Pennie asked Tony if she could attend her Krav Maga class that night. Without hesitation, he shot down that idea. He suggested she go for a run through her neighborhood with Peach before she left for work.

A run sounded great. She loved her settled neighborhood in the working-class area of Bartlett. Large trees and spacious yards. For this morning though, she was on a Fox hunt. Whoever Frank Fox was, she wanted to get a visual on his house. Leading Peach several streets over, she kept her eyes open. As it were, Pennie didn't even know what he looked like.

Until she saw him. Dang. For eight in the morning, she didn't expect to see Frank in his driveway wiping down his Harley. With his garage open, she got a peek at a side-by-side and a four-wheeler in addition to his jacked-up Chevy truck. Frank appeared to have the redneck machismo starter set.

'Wiping down the Harley' wasn't a clear depiction of what was happening. Frank used a cloth to lovingly caress and stroke the motorcycle. And Frank himself... He clearly had Native American in his gene pool. The facial stubble didn't hide his high cheekbones, and his long, dark hair exuded strength and power. His tanned arms with wiry muscles were on display thanks to the tank top. Pennie didn't realize she had slowed down until his mesmerizing blue eyes looked up at her.

"Can I help you?" his velvety voice asked. A few lines in his forehead and around his eyes substantiated that he was fifty, but he wasn't the least bit geriatric. In fact, time made his magnetism stronger. Women of any age group would swoon around this guy.

Finding her composure, Pennie answered, "I've lived in this neighborhood for a couple of years, and I've never met you."

Rising from his crouched position, Frank stood six foot three. His long tresses hung halfway down his back. He could easily star in a shampoo commercial. He was old enough to be her dad—why was she so fascinated by him? Oh, and he was potentially sympathetic to terrorists. She regained her focus in time to hear his response.

"I've been here for thirty years, but I recently retired. I'm at home more these days."

"What kind of work did you do?" she asked.

Wiping his hands on the rag, he extended one for Pennie to shake. "How about a proper introduction before you question me? I'm Frank, but my friends call me Bone."

"I'm Pennie. It's nice to meet you."

"Likewise, I'm sure. I was an aircraft mechanic at the Air National Guard for the past two decades. I had some cryptocurrency investments pay off, so I decided to retire. Enjoy life a little more. This is the same collection of toys I've had for years, but now they're paid off." The husky laugh was alluring.

"I quit my corporate job after my husband died a couple of years ago. Now I'm working for a landscape company, and I certainly prefer the stress-free job of tending plants and selling dirt."

The slightest of movements in one of the windows behind him caught Pennie's eye. She quickly added, "So, do you live here alone?"

"Yep. It's just me and the dogs. In fact, I need to let them back inside the house before they overheat. My dogs don't like to be outside for very long. Enjoy your run."

During the trek back to her house, Pennie contemplated what would happen in the future. By tomorrow, the Wasps would attempt a political coup. President Vasquez could be murdered. Francelia could become an orphan.

What could Pennie do? Work with Judy to identify any nearby threats. Was Bone a threat? What caused the movement in his window after he admitted to being at home alone? Could a terrorist be hiding a mere three blocks from her home?

Sipping some water in the kitchen, Pennie considered the effects of being on lockdown. But she was mostly worried about the girls. She approached Tony again. "I've gotta head to work, but do you think you can take the girls to get some kind of drive-thru lunch and eat in a park later? They're not used to being confined like this."

"Pennie, have a seat." He paused so she could perch on the arm of the couch. "We're in lockdown. You're maintaining your work schedule, and that's on you. I'm here to protect Francelia and her twin. Aside from that, we're all taking a personal toll. My fiancé is mad that I won't tell her about this assignment, so there's no way I'm going to get caught having a picnic with a couple of international girls."

"Hear me out... Let Karolina drive y'all to my work. No one will see you leave the house because you can load up in the garage, and her Camaro has super dark tint. You can even sit in the backseat, so no one sees you and gets suspicious when you get to my work. Avocado Farms only has one way in and one way out. I need some new flowers to replace the ones that died out front on the porch. The girls can pick out a few flowers and help me pot them later when I get home. You can stay in the car the whole time and keep an eye on them."

His response was summed up by another disappointing expression. Knowing the girls needed a mental reprieve, she pleaded once again.

"Adriana's already met 'Maria,' and the nursery will be abandoned at lunch time on a Tuesday. We're not that busy now that the spring rush is over. Come up there around noon. If you see any other vehicles in the lot other than mine and Lupe's, just keep going. Otherwise, I'll take lunch when they finish shopping for flowers, so we can eat together at Freeman Park. Please?"

"I'll think about it," he conceded as Pennie grabbed her keys.

The drive to work gave Pennie a few minutes to sort out the crazy thoughts. Could Bone Fox be hiding someone? Aside from him, could Adriana and Oscar be hiding someone? Surely, there was a plausible explanation. The one thing Pennie knew for a fact: they weren't hiding Francelia.

As she unlocked the gate to the nursery, she put the suspicious thoughts to the back of her mind. Whatever Judy thought the Acevedos were up to, it had nothing to do with Francelia. Pennie just needed to capitalize on this opportunity to be proactive against the credible threats against Francelia. While logging into the computer at the cashier station, a flash of AmberLou-colored hair passed by the window of the little shack. Fearful that Karolina or Francelia showed up unexpectedly, Pennie quickly opened the door to find another lookalike.

"Lupe! What did you do?"

"You like? The hairstyle looked so good on Karolina, I wanted it for myself!" She flounced around, modeling the new style. Now, Pennie had three Latinas in her life with this two-toned hair.

Ignoring the hair, Pennie responded, "I really like that shirt. Where did you get it?"

"My mom made us some new work shirts." Again, Lupe flounced around, this time showing off the mint-colored shirt with "Avocado Farms" pressed across the front. "I have some for you. She made them all with ice cream colors."

"Very nice, but it's time to get to work. You wanna get to watering while I get the delivery driver laid out?"

By the time the driver came and left, along with the landscape crews who managed their own schedule, Pennie sent a message to Judy. She was eager to find out more about the Wasps and what she could do to help.

Judy Thomas pulled into the parking lot a few minutes later. No cameraman arrived with her, but she was dressed in her typical tailored suit. For the sake of this visit to the nursery,

Judy traded heels for sneakers. She joined Pennie at the cashier shack to get down to business.

With no customers in sight and Lupe watering the annuals, Pennie felt free to speak. "I did a preliminary search for these names you gave me, but I didn't find out much."

Judy pulled out her iPad to go over the names. "I've reorganized the names to group them based on where the people are staying. We have ten who are nearby. Since I'm a familiar face around here, I need you to find out more about them without any of them realizing we're investigating."

Retrieving the list from her pocket, Pennie made notes next to the ones Judy indicated. "I noticed nine names with local addresses, and a few names I recognize otherwise. Can you tell me why these names are the list to begin with? That way I know what I'm walking in to."

"You already know about Adriana and Oscar Acevedo. Adriana has multiple family members in the Dominican who openly support the Wasps. Her allegiance could go either way. The trip to Birmingham on the thirteenth potentially put them on the path to pick someone up who arrived in Florida, but that would assume someone else helped get Francelia to Birmingham. I'm not getting a sinister vibe from them, but I need to know how they got involved."

Pennie wrote down a few notes, knowing she didn't need to research the Acevedos. "Okay, who's next?"

"The next two are a couple. Charles 'Chip' Jordan and Pietra Russo. They—"

Holding her hand up to speak, Pennie interrupted, "Full disclosure, Judy. I know them. My brother works on the police force with them, and I briefly dated Chip a year ago. I know they were on a cruise that got back on the thirteenth because I was on the same cruise."

"I know all that. I got your name from the original list,

but your background is squeaky clean. You took your exchange student on the cruise. I don't really know how your ex-boyfriend ended up on the same trip, but I'm curious if he and Pietra aided Francelia. Can you shed any light on this?"

"Not really," Pennie responded with a quick head shake. "I've become friends with Pietra and recommended the cruise to her. They just happened to book the same itinerary, but I didn't spend any time with them on the ship."

"You should know they booked two rooms in Birmingham the same night that the Acevedos were there. It's odd for a couple to book two rooms, leading me to suspect they had Francelia in tow. One possibility is that they handed Francelia off to the Acevedos that night. Can you use your friendship to see what you can find out?"

It took a great deal of effort to hide her surprise. Judy's investigative skills were off the charts. "I sure can. Who's next on the list?"

"Frank 'Bone' Fox. He lives in your neighborhood by coincidence. He flew round trip to Puerto Rico on the eleventh, returning on the twelfth with a layover in Miami. Not long after he checked into the airport in San Juan, the police issued an arrest warrant for him. I can't get complete information, but it appears he assaulted someone, then he picked up a second person for the return flight."

"How would you know that?" Pennie asked, wondering how Judy got all this information.

"The TSA flagged a passenger flying one way from Puerto Rico on the same flight. It's common to pay cash at the airport if you want to book something anonymously. Whoever he was used an ID belonging to Diego Castellanos. I've found Diego locally, and I know he used to work with Frank Fox at the Tennessee Air National Guard. As it turns out, I covered a story there last year where I got to know the guy at the base entrance. A quick phone call to him uncovered that Diego hasn't missed a single day of work."

Shaking her head, Pennie asked, "How was he in Puerto Rico last week without missing work?"

"Good question," Judy said with a smile. "I think Frank borrowed Diego's ID to get someone through security in Puerto Rico. Someone who looks enough like him that no one noticed."

"But you said TSA flagged the ticket. How did he get past TSA?"

"That doesn't always mean much. Sometimes, they just get their luggage searched or their hands swabbed for explosives. Maybe an extensive pat down. In this case, I don't know what the TSA did, but they didn't prevent Diego's stand-in from flying back to Miami, and eventually to Memphis."

Pennie's imagination went haywire. Bone was very likely hiding a young man in his home. "Do you think he's harboring a terrorist?"

"All signs point to yes. I don't like to accuse people of terrorism so lightly, but this situation calls for a closer look. Do you think you can check out his house? Observe his comings and goings?"

"I made it a point to jog by his house this morning. I'll try to observe more without ending up on his radar, especially if he's into something dangerous."

"Please be careful, Pennie. I don't know anything more about his pending assault charges. Don't draw any attention to yourself or do anything to lead him to Francelia."

"Of course, Judy," Pennie responded as she jotted down a few notes. "Now, tell me about Richard Ewers. All I know about him is that he coaches baseball at the University of Memphis."

"You should know he recruits players from all over the world. Thanks to Sammy Sosa and Albert Pujols, teams have been looking to the Dominican Republic for their next superstar. The Memphis baseball team currently has one Dominican player who joined the team a few years ago. Ewers has flown back and forth to the Caribbean several times since then, including one trip two weeks ago. On his return flight, nothing was out of the ordinary, except that a man and his son joined him on the flight to Memphis. Their tickets were purchased with Ewers' credit card."

"What are their names? I don't have any notes on them."

"Ricky and Manny Guzman. I haven't learned anything about them yet. I don't even know where they're staying. I've met Richard Ewers a couple of times over the years when I've covered his sporting events, and I never really liked him. I don't have the credentials to see his banking or credit card history, so I can't determine whether he's paying for a hotel or anything on their behalf. According to my research, these two are potentially involved with the Wasps."

"I'll see what I can find out. Who's next on the list?" Pennie asked.

Pulling up a picture on her iPad, the face of a stunning woman filled the screen. "This is LaToya Gunn. She's from Texas, but she's been staying in the Bartlett area for the past several months."

Pennie needed more details. "Why is she on your list? I've heard her name because she works with my friend."

"LaToya, or 'Toy' Gunn, as she prefers to be called, is a world traveler. In the past year, she's visited the Dominican twice. A group of Dominican businessmen followed her back to the States on both occasions, but I can't track their whereabouts after they arrive here. Specifically, two men flew back to Texas with her in June."

"How does June fit into your timeline?"

Judy scanned the nursery for a moment before

responding. "The Wasps' movement started a couple of years ago. Since the male supremacy tendencies are a factor all around the world, I wouldn't be surprised to see some of the Wasp members visiting other countries to spread their beliefs."

"I'm sure that's true, but why would LaToya be helping them?"

"I haven't figured that out, yet. I need to you find out more about Ms. Gunn, while I'm tracking down the men who traveled with her. I don't know whether they're still in Texas or they came to Memphis. Ms. Gunn is staying in an apartment complex called Bartlett Fairways adjacent to the Bartlett Country Club. The men haven't rented any apartment that I can find, but if they're part of the machismo pandemic, they could easily be on the move to find Francelia."

"Which men are these? Are they on the list?"

"Omar Mendez and Joel Batista. Let's not focus on them right now since I don't know if they're truly in our area. Plus, my research hasn't substantiated any affiliation with the Wasps."

"Okay, tell me Thomas and Jamie Reyes are concerning to you."

Judy swiped until she found a picture of the handsome couple. "The Reyes family hails from Guam. Both have full-time jobs, and nothing stands out in their daily activities currently. In their younger years, they racked up a few drug charges. They only made it to my list because they flew to the Dominican earlier this month. They only stayed one day, then flew back to Miami and rented a fifteen-passenger van for the drive back to Memphis. Nothing has stood out other than the quick turnaround and the van rental. That's not an ideal vehicle for a road trip, and it would've been cheaper and quicker to fly home. I'm concerned they were initiated into the Wasps, and they gave a group of them a ride back to Memphis last month."

Exactly a month ago, Pennie met with Vale Hernandez and the rest of the crew to nail down the details of Francelia's extraction. Could the Wasps have been tipped off that far in advance? Without sharing her own involvement in the plan, Pennie couldn't get Judy's perspective, so she left it alone.

"I'll dig into these local people as best I can, but I gotta tell you something else, Judy."

"What's that?"

"You have the Bell brothers on your list. They live in Louisiana, but I met them on the cruise ship. JJ and Nick seemed nice enough. Are you really concerned about them?"

"Homegrown terrorists are a real thing. They were raised by their grandfather who supported a similar male-dominance movement in Mexico years ago before he relocated to the States. The grandfather died about a decade ago, leaving the boys on their own. Nicolas was eighteen at the time and took custody of his little brother. I don't know much else about them, but their grandfather was on a terrorist watch list."

Folding the paper to put back into her pocket, Pennie assured Judy she'd do her best to find out more information. Some customers had pulled in to do some shopping, so they finished their meeting just in time. Judy moved on, allowing Pennie to tend to the clients.

After selling loads of shrubbery to the customers, Pennie spent the next hour wondering about all the names on the list. To keep her hands busy, she cleaned the koi pond and arranged all the stones for a better display in front of the cashier shack.

Eventually, Pennie noticed Karolina's black Camaro pull into the parking lot. The dark tinted windows concealed Tony in the backseat, and he gave the girls space to peruse the colorful flowers. As expected, aside from Lupe's car, only one other truck was parked, belonging to an older couple who checked out the clearance vegetables. Other than the hoop greenhouses on the back of the property, the cashier shack, and the old house that was slated for demolition across the way, Tony had a clear view of everywhere the ladies could shop for plants.

As the clock approached one, Pennie observed Adriana's truck pull into the lot not too far from the Camaro. She expected one of the Acevedos to show up, but she didn't expect her heartrate to elevate as it did. The last thing she wanted was to put Francelia in danger. Moving closer to Francelia, Pennie opted to stick by her side until it was time to go.

"*Hola*, Pennie! *¿Como estas, Maria?* Karolina?" Adriana gave everyone a hug. After a quick greeting, the women brought all the new flowers to the cashier shack where Lupe could check them out.

Adriana offered a parting hug and said, "Pennie, I came so you can take the rest of the day off. I know you want to spend time with Karolina this month. I'm giving Oscar a little daddy-daughter time with Cynthia today."

That got Pennie wondering about the elusive Acevedo daughter. "Adriana, I haven't seen Cynthia at all. What's she been up to since she's been home?"

"Her internship isn't over. Cynthia has to work remotely for a few weeks as part of her training with the online banking department. She clocks in every day, and we plan activities after her shift. Oscar is taking her to look for a new car today."

That explained why Judy verified Cynthia's ongoing

employment in Birmingham. She didn't account for the ability to work remotely. Still, Pennie hadn't laid eyes on the girl. She would need to keep her mind open until then.

Pennie accepted the offer and the stack of t-shirts in a variety of ice cream colors. She tossed them in the cab of her truck before loading the flats of flowers in the back. Then she drove through Chick-fil-A to get lunch and meet them at Freeman Park.

Switching back to family mode, Pennie pulled next to Karolina under the shade trees, all the way in the back of the park near the baseball fields. Pennie exited the truck and relocated next to Tony in the backseat of the Camaro to dine with the group. Karolina left the car running and AC on full blast as everyone dug into their chicken nuggets and veggie wrap.

"So, Karolina already knows this, but I used to play softball on these fields when I was younger." Pennie hoped a little conversation would keep the mood light and make the most of the girl's excursion.

"That's so cool. Did you play in college?" Francelia asked.

"No, I wasn't that good. I played all the sports in high school, but volleyball was my favorite. During the summer, I played for some recreational softball leagues on these fields."

"What about basketball?" Francelia was the only one interested in conversing.

"I played basketball, but I didn't enjoy it like I should have. The first year I played, my older sister Alice was on the same team. She was so good. She's not very tall, but dang, she was an amazing shooting guard. She wasn't a ball-hog either. Alice had as many assists as anything else. No wonder she was my dad's favorite," Pennie trailed off remembering how her dad cheered them on at all their games. Such wonderful memories. So bittersweet today.

"My dad taught me about baseball when I was little."

Pennie looked up to make eye contact with Francelia through the rearview mirror. "What else did your dad teach you?"

Francelia placed her Coke in the cupholder. "He taught me how to play piano. He said I should learn many things so I could get a scholarship to college. He wanted me to have a different life here in your country."

Tony joined the dialogue. "Francelia, your father would be proud if he could see how brave you are right now."

Pennie had to fight a few tears. This poor girl lost her dad at age ten. Not to cancer or something tangible. Not with an opportunity to say goodbye at a memorial service. Her father disappeared thanks to a hate-filled terrorist group —possibly the same group who now threatened to kill her mother. Pennie had the most amazing and involved father in the world. He gave her away at her wedding. He showed her what the leader of a home should look like. Pennie wasn't sad for herself right now. All the emotions were for Francelia.

Francelia used a napkin to soak up a tear before it fell. "I wish I could see my dad again, but now, I doubt I'll get to see my mom ever again either."

"Honey, don't think like that. Your mother was elected president of your country. How likely was that?"

"Not likely."

"So, your mom has a history of beating the odds. And she has more to fight for… now more than ever. We're going to keep praying, okay?"

"Yes, ma'am," Francelia said without sounding like she meant it.

"You know what, Francie?" Karolina turned in her seat to speak to the girl, using a nickname Pennie hadn't heard before. "You gained a sister in the process. And a second mother."

The adorable chipmunk smile lit up Francelia's face. "*Gracias, Karolzinha, mi hermosa hermanita.*" Pennie understood the *beautiful little sister* comment, and she noticed *Francie* gave Karolina a nickname as well.

"Okay, I'm going to get a treat for everyone before I go home," Pennie declared as she opened an app to order treats from a new local coffee shop.

Iced coffees would be the pick-me-up everyone needed. Karolina selected her crazy matcha-oat milk-vanilla-creation. Pennie and Tony stuck to basic iced lattes. Francelia struggled with indecision before finally deciding on the cold coco loco cappuccino.

Karolina giggled at the drink her sister chose. "Cold coco cappuccino! That's too many alliteratives!" Pennie smiled as well with this being one of the few times Karolina pronounced something incorrectly.

Pleased with the uplifted moods, Pennie detoured to the coffee shop while Karolina pointed her Camaro towards home. The one thing that didn't please her was the disruption in her plans. If she hadn't insisted that Tony get the girls out for lunch, Pennie could've used the afternoon to drive by some of the addresses on her list. She purposely hadn't mentioned that the Acevedos were letting her work four-hour shifts for the time being because she wanted to use that time for investigation. But if she had to do anything aside from investigating, staying close to her girls was the next best option.

With the fresh air and iced beverages, everyone's mood had elevated by the time they arrived back at Pennie's house. Tony sat inside at the breakfast table with a clear view of the back porch. He also kept Pennie's iPad handy so he could see the multiple camera angles offered by her security system.

The girls donned gardening gloves and pastel-colored Avocado Farms t-shirts to play in the dirt for the next hour, creating gorgeous summertime flowerpots and hanging baskets.

"That girl Lupe is from Dominica," Francelia said as she arranged some petunias.

"I know," Pennie said. "She's the daughter of one of Adriana's friends. They asked Adriana to give her a job as a favor."

"Why a favor? Is she not a good worker?" This time, Francelia turned her head to speak to Pennie.

"Not really. She's sweet, but she's twenty-five cents short of a taco."

"What does that mean?"

"That was tacky of me to say," Pennie said as she shook her head. "She's not a hard worker. Maybe when she finds something she loves to do, it'll be different. But right now, she's only working because her mom makes her."

Francelia looked genuinely upset. "She has an opportunity to live here and work here. Why would she waste it by being lazy?"

"I wish I could tell you. Karolina works on campus at

school, and she's such an awesome barista at the campus coffee shop, they named a drink after her. It's called the *Catalina*, since that's how her name sounds when us Americans pronounce it quickly without rolling the R."

Francelia adjusted her eye contact to her new sister. "You don't drink coffee, *hermana*. Why do you work in a coffee shop?"

"I must work to earn my spending money. It was the only job available for my work study. I won't work in the coffee shop next semester though."

That was the first time Pennie had heard of these plans. "Where will you work then, *chica*?"

"In the international office. That guy Brandon just graduated. I've been waiting for him to leave because he's been in my way for the last two years. I'm ready to really help the international students. I don't even work in that office yet, and I help more students than he does."

Francelia lit up with excitement for her sister. "That'll be a good job for you. Especially since you know so many languages."

"Speaking of international students," Pennie broached the subject as nonchalantly as she could, "Don't the Memphis Tigers have a baseball player from the Dominican Republic?"

"Yesss," Karolina sighed. "Mateo is so handsome."

Pennie still couldn't wrap her mind around Karolina becoming boy-crazy, but she had to see where this conversation would lead. "Is he now? How does he like being in Memphis?"

"He doesn't like playing for Memphis, but it's the only school that gave him a scholarship."

"What does he not like?"

Karolina rolled her eyes and filled them in, "The coach is

a jerk. He's like a dictator, controlling everyone's time. Mateo, along with the few other foreign players, haven't been to one single international event in the last year."

"Coach Ewers? Is that his name?" Pennie hoped she played that off good enough.

"Yes. I've seen him on campus, always scowling. His players aren't happy, but Mateo wanted the chance to play ball in the States. He thinks he can play professionally when he graduates."

Without adding anything else, the gardeners finished their masterpieces and moved inside to take showers. Pennie stayed outside to sweep off the patio and water everything before moving the arrangements to the front porch. A rapping on the window caught her attention. Tony beckoned her to come inside.

Pennie locked the door behind her and sat at the dining room table next to Tony.

He wore a grim expression and inhaled deeply before speaking. "I just spoke to Ambassador Hernandez."

"What'd she say?"

"Members of the Wasps are surrounding the National Palace now. They aren't on the property yet. Extra military has formed a perimeter, hoping to keep them outside the fences. I'm guessing we'll really see some kind of skirmish tomorrow."

"Let's see what the world news has to say."

They moved to the living room and watched a few unrelated stories without speaking. The girls eventually joined

Pennie on the couch.

"Momma Pennie, I love your shower. My hair smells like coconuts now!"

Pennie was internally pleased that Francelia found moments of tranquility, even if it was just coconut shampoo and conditioner. She eased closer and placed her arm around the girl's shoulder. "Honey, we're watching the news to keep up with your mother's situation. Some Wasps are around the palace, but some extra military is there to stand guard."

She slightly nodded and leaned into Pennie's embrace. Karolina moved to her other side and held her hand.

Tony spoke up from the recliner, "I wish we knew more about the Wasps. We don't know what their manpower or anything looks like."

Francelia offered what she knew. "During the election, they were just a nuisance. They burned some ballot boxes. One time, they swarmed a hospital and shut it down for two days. Around the country, they have several camps to send boys to. *Matas* training camps. If your son isn't manly enough, they train him for you. My mom wanted to shut down these camps. That was part of her agenda when she campaigned."

Leaning forward, Tony asked, "How did they go from being a nuisance to holding the attention of the country like this?"

Francelia turned her head just enough to address him directly. "Probably because my mom won the election. I don't think anyone expected a woman would ever become president. The machismo groups decided to form an alliance with the Cabral brothers as the leaders."

Pennie had trouble reconciling all this. "When we did the town tour in La Romana, everything seemed so peaceful. Women and men worked together in the markets. It seems surreal that such a hate-motivated group could take control like this."

"You only saw the tourist town near the cruise port. Dominica has made progress lately, but the men still have control. In the rural areas—in the poor counties—women don't stand a chance."

Karolina offered her own viewpoint. "Mom, I rode in the back of a taxi with Bianca to the capital city. The kids begging on the street... the poverty... stray dogs... It's a lot to take in. When you send out a postcard of Memphis, you see Beale Street and Graceland. You don't show the bad areas. The cruise line only shows us the postcard parts of the Dominican Republic."

Halting the conversation, Tony turned the volume up to hear the news. The anchorwoman put on her best stern expression to convey the next story.

"The latest update out of the Dominican Republic has the world on edge. The terrorist group, *Mata Cacatas*, has posted at least fifty men around the palace property. President Daniela Vasquez, along with her daughter Francelia, have been locked down inside the National Palace for months, and it looks like things are on the verge of escalation. Here is the latest message from Adolfo Cabral."

The malevolent expression on the Wasp's face conveyed the message before he opened his mouth. "Twenty-four hours. This isn't a joke, but I'm glad it's coming to this. The Dominica needs to see what the *Mata Cacatas* are capable of. Tomorrow will be a demonstration of our power. But, as a man of my word, I will allow the Vasquez women to vacate the palace if they do so in the next twenty-four hours."

The anchor took over speaking immediately after the video stopped. "What an ominous message. Let's hear from our correspondent in DC. Randall, are you getting any feedback from our own president?"

The screen switched to the suited man who looked

more like a used car salesman than a news anchor. "President Carson's advisor released a statement just moments ago, sending out the thoughts and prayers of the White House to all the Dominican people. She alluded to a meeting among the Commander in Chief and his cabinet on the best way to assist President Vasquez. The US has previously joined the fight on terrorism, and this group, the *Mata Cacatas*, should be no exception. Any word of military assistance has not been confirmed, but we all just heard, the hours are counting down for Vasquez."

The screen split to show both news anchors. The lady took over speaking. "Randall, if our country planned to send any armed forces to aid the Dominican president, they would have to be ready to go by now. Is there any activity around military bases that you know of?"

"Not that I'm aware of, Melissa. We've reached out to the Department of Defense as well as the office of the Joint Chief of Staff to get their input, but they're choosing to withhold any official statements to the media."

"Thank you, Randall. We'll check back later to see if there are any developments to this volatile story."

Once Tony turned the volume back down, Francelia asked why the US government wasn't helping.

Tony took the lead on this inquiry. "The US military doesn't back down from a fight, Francelia. President Carson just took office four months ago when President Crawford stepped down. He's already making strides to improve foreign relations and our domestic economy. He has more balls than Crawford did—he won't let this injustice take place without helping. And why are you snickering, Pennie?"

"You said he has more balls." The laugh bubbled up and prevented Pennie from further explaining why she found that funny.

Tony hung his head and sighed before responding. "Okay, that was a bad choice of words since Crawford had his testicles shot off earlier this year. But my point remains valid. Jerome Carson is the leader we've been needing, and he'll make sure reinforcements are sent without sitting around talking to reporters about it."

In the wake of the gloomy story, Tony managed to fire up everyone in the living room with his little speech.

"Okay. Can we make tostadas for dinner?" Karolina asked. She pulled Francelia into the kitchen without waiting for an answer, knowing the girl would need a distraction.

Over the past few days, Pennie had been kicked out of her own kitchen. She normally enjoyed expressing love through her cooking. Being on the receiving end was odd. Nice, but odd.

With officially nothing to do, Pennie let Tony know she wanted to go for a run to expend her nervous energy. Not that it was completely a lie, but she did have an ulterior motive. She chose to leave Peach at home for this little bit of reconnaissance. Jogging towards the eastern edge of her neighborhood, she rounded the corner in time to see Bone pulling out of his driveway. Excellent.

The sunlight was plenty sufficient to give Pennie a good look at the front of the house while she pretended to tie her shoelaces. No security cameras or doorbell cameras. No one out on the street around her. Without coming up with a complete plan, she went to the front door and knocked. Stepping back, she didn't see any movement in the windows.

The dogs barked profusely from the inside, but the front door didn't have any windows to give her a glimpse of the dogs.

She'd been in enough houses in the area to know the large window next to the door would only reveal a dining room. The living room would be in the back, and those windows would be less likely to have coverings. Easing around the garage, Pennie made her way to the back gate only to find it locked. The six-foot wooden fence didn't pose much of an obstacle since the skeleton of the fence was on the outside. Using the two-by-four posts and runners at footholds, she hoisted herself up and over without a problem. The gate was flush with the back of the house, so she immediately had a view of the entire backyard.

Frank hadn't done any landscaping—a few trees and shed on the front corner of the yard to the right of the gate. With nothing interesting to see back here, she slowly moved to her left. As suspected, the blinds on the back of the house were open. Careful to avoid touching any windows, she peeked inside to see the eat-in kitchen. Squinting to see inside the darkened space, she made out a small table and minimalist kitchen. It didn't take a minute for the dogs to notice movement, and the German Shepherds growled through the window at Pennie.

Moving further along, she peeked through the living room window. The dogs moved with her, but she refused to be distracted by the angry canines. Theater seating recliners faced a large television. Something seemed odd about the scene, but she didn't have time to dwell on it when she noticed the dogs ran to the door leading into the garage.

Oh crap! They must've heard the garage open, and someone was coming in. Pennie dashed towards the gate, barely catching a glimpse of the door opening inside the house. She immediately tried to climb the fence, but the skeleton was now on the opposite side. No footholds presented themselves as she heard the back door opening less than twenty feet away from her. This wasn't good.

The high-pitched barking sounded louder as the door opened, giving Pennie only a split second to make a decision. Regardless of the dogs, she didn't want Frank to witness her trespassing. With adrenaline as her wingman, she bolted in the direction of the shed. She didn't have to turn around to know the shepherds were in pursuit. Their barking turned low and growly, and it got closer as she ducked behind the shed.

The narrow passageway between the shed and the fence only measured about four feet wide, just enough distance to *Spider-Man* her way up. Before she could reach the top, the dogs rounded the corner. Using her left foot, she pushed off the shed to launch her body over the top of the fence, but not before a shepherd bounded up to grab her pants leg. Her abdomen crashed down on the top edge of the fence with a thud, but thankfully her pants ripped, sending the dog back to the ground, and allowing her to swing her legs over the fence.

Tumbling to the ground, Pennie gasped, forcing oxygen into her lungs. After a minute, she could see clearly again and breathe without struggling. Her pounding heart returned closer to a normal rhythm. As she sat there in someone else's backyard, she took stock of herself. Her right pants leg was missing from the calf down. Even worse, she didn't notice that her shoe came off along with her pants leg.

At least the current backyard didn't harbor any vicious dogs, and the gate was easy to open. Minus one right shoe, Pennie trudged home. As she approached her house, she dropped her left shoe and both socks in a garbage can. This was a different kind of barefooted walk of shame, but she entered her front door anyway.

"Pennie, what happened?"

Tony sounded concerned because he didn't know Pennie was the one seeking out trouble.

"I splashed through a puddle where someone had sprinklers on earlier, and my socks and shoes got sloshed. I just dropped them in the garbage can since they were uncomfortable."

His furrowed brow indicated he wasn't buying it. "You're missing part of your pants, and you're completely disheveled. I'll only ask one more time... What happened?"

"Right after I splashed into the water, I tried to jump to the side, you know?" Pennie zigged and zagged in her bare feet to demonstrate her sketchy her encounter with the sidewalk obstacle course. "I didn't notice the garden gnome just inside the yard. It tripped me, causing me to tumble forward where my pants caught on the bumper of a car. They just ripped."

His heavy sigh said it all. Lightly massaging his temples with his fingertips, Tony instructed Pennie to get cleaned up for dinner.

After dinnertime had passed, the ladies decided to stay up late with Tony. They made coffee and played Uno with the news playing in the background. After ten, the stories became repetitive, prompting Pennie to suggest bedtime for the women. Tony assumed his role as guardian of the house and prayed with them as the mismatched family they'd become.

Bedtime didn't mean Pennie's brain was ready to shut

off. Booting up her laptop, she thought about what she saw in Frank's living room earlier. The theater sofa had built in consoles and cupholders, which held, not one, but two take-out cups from Whataburger. Frank was certainly hiding someone, but who? Miami wouldn't require any customs or immigration check on flights from Puerto Rico. Given that the Dominican Republic's east coast was only a hundred miles from Puerto Rico's west coast, anyone could've taken a boat ride to the US territory.

Anyone with nefarious motives.

Anyone trying to get out of a country undetected.

If Pennie wanted to give Frank the benefit of the doubt, she'd say he snuck out Francelia or Daniela Vasquez. She knew for a fact that wasn't the case. Could it be some other illegal immigrant? Could it be a Wasp?

The idea that a terrorist was so close made Pennie more than uneasy. One thing was for sure—she needed to help Judy get through these names. Whatever threat was in their midst needed to be dealt with before they found Francelia.

WEDNESDAY, JULY 20

The deadline drew nearer. Everyone was up early. Cole traded places with Tony for the day. Pennie had trouble putting a coherent thought together. Bowls of cereal weren't her normal offering of comfort food, but she couldn't muster the fortitude to cook anything for breakfast. The crunching of cereal provided the only noise around the table in the breakfast nook.

Deciding chatter might be better than silence, Pennie asked Cole, "How are things with Jenna?"

"Fine," he said without elaborating.

She tried again. "Francelia, did you borrow one of Karolina's shirts or did you get a Memphis Tiger shirt when we were shopping the other day?"

"It's Karolzinha's."

The third time could be the charm. "Where did y'all come up with the nicknames?"

"Mom, please."

Karolina wasn't willing to participate either. Pennie huffed and finished her cereal before it got soggy. She internally mulled over Karolina's new nickname and considered how to spell it. Cad-oh-zeenya is how she heard it, but she knew that wasn't close to how it looked on paper.

In unison, the amigas got up to put their bowls in the sink. The news already played in the living room, but the anchors covered nothing pertinent to their situation. Pennie wanted to take Peach for another run, but she didn't want to miss any updates. She'd have to control the pent-up energy and aggression mentally until she could get back to her Krav Maga classes. Then, she got an idea.

"Cole, I'm taking Peach for a long run before I head to work."

Pennie hoped Peach would help her avoid any unwanted attention on this jog. Following the path like the one she took yesterday, she ended up on Bone's street. Her heartrate jumped up a notch or two. Partly because of the potential danger, and partly because Bone posed like a male model, turning a wrench under the hood of his Chevy.

Mentally shielding herself from his charisma, Pennie slowed enough to say hello to her neighbor.

"Hey, Bone!"

"Hey, Pennie. How's it going?"

"Pretty good. Peach enjoyed the longer run yesterday, so we decided to take the same route. Is something wrong with your truck?"

"No, I'm just changing my oil. Can I ask you something?"

"Sure," she answered, trying to hide the nervousness in her voice.

Bone glanced up and down the street. "Have you seen anything or anyone unusual hanging around?"

"Huh-uh, I run almost every day, and I haven't seen

anything. What's going on?"

"I think someone tried to break into my house yesterday."

"Oh no! Did you see who it was on your camera?"

"I don't have cameras, but I'll be adding them this week."

"But, Bone, if you don't have cameras, why do you suspect an attempted break in?"

"My dogs found a shoe in the backyard. They tore it to shreds, so I can't identify anything about it other than it's a Nike."

From where they stood on the driveway, Pennie heard the dogs behind the fence. She sidestepped to see the gate. Feeling like she was in the clear, she commented, "Even if your gate is locked, someone could easily climb the fence with the two-by-fours on the outside like that."

"I did that on purpose. Shepherds can climb fences too, and I'd rather someone climb in than for BoJack and Elanor to get out."

"Well, I'll keep an eye out for anything fishy." They didn't discuss anything else before Pennie made the trek back home. She hoped to witness Frank's mystery guest, but at least she found out he didn't suspect her of anything.

By nine, Pennie unlocked the gates at Avocado Farms. Crews were sent on their way with deliveries and landscape jobs. Lupe had the day off, so Pennie got to work. She was watering all the annuals when the reporter showed up in her casual clothes.

"Pennie, I guess you know there's an ultimatum in the Dominican Republic. This afternoon, the Wasps will try to take over the National Palace."

"Yea, it's looking grim," she answered, feeling the heat from the July sun and from the anxiety over the Wasps taking over the palace.

"The grim part is twofold. First, they won't let Daniela Vasquez live to see tomorrow. Second, based on my belief that Francelia isn't there, the Wasps will go into a frenzy to find her."

Pennie stretched her hose a little farther and kept watering. Taking a deep breath, she said, "I'm sure they won't stop until they find her. I haven't verified anything at the Acevedos' house, so nothing has been confirmed."

"Look, I know this is a hunch on my part, but I have some trusted sources, and I lucked up on some inside information. I'm certain Francelia is under our noses, and we're going to need a lot more than a can of Raid to take down these Wasps. It's all up to us."

"I've already made contact with Bone Fox, and I believe he does have someone hidden in his house. Is there a reason we don't involve the police or some other investigative agency? This is a big deal." Pennie wanted to make a difference, but she wanted to go about it the right way.

Shaking her head with tightened lips, Judy pushed her hair behind her ears before responding. "I've already spoken to Homeland Security, but they'll only investigate suspicious incidents. They don't operate on hunches and instincts. As soon as we have a credible lead on any one terrorist, I want to set a trap and have him arrested. The proper authorities will be involved by the time we narrow this down."

"I'm planning to make contact with LaToya Gunn when

I leave here today. Have you learned anything new?"

"Mostly, I'm ruling people out, but that's still progress. My biggest concern is that some people entered the country using fake documents, and I won't be able to track them. That doesn't mean we won't try, though. I'm going through my list as quickly as possible. It's taking all my time and resources, but if we can save one girl, it'll be worth it. Not to mention I'll have the story of the year."

Pennie quoted Alexander the Great, "Toil and risk are the price of glory."

Judy finished it, "But it is a lovely thing to live with courage and die leaving an everlasting fame."

Everlasting fame meant nothing to Pennie, but the safety of Francelia Vasquez meant everything. Regardless of Judy's secondary motive, the goal was taking down the bad guys.

When Oscar relieved Pennie at noon, she washed up as best she could in the restroom of the Jaybear Bake Shop. Before she dropped in on Jenna at work, she wanted to be presentable. And since she couldn't go home and shower first, the boxes of cookies and cupcakes from the scratch bakery would be a great distraction from her sweaty state.

Pulling into the parking lot of Grandfather General Contractor, Pennie thought about the brief period she worked here with Jenna. The job wasn't rewarding. At all. She'd had enough of the corporate world. Playing with dirt and watering flowers suited her much better. Taking a deep breath, she carried the boxes of treats through the fancy glass doors.

The receptionist greeted her warmly from behind the large desk. "Hello, Pennie! What're you doing here?"

"Hey, Olga! I wanted to surprise Jenna and bring some treats for all my old friends." Pennie trained Olga to be her replacement as her last assignment before quitting the job.

"You know I can't let you back to see Jenna without an appointment."

"Olga, seriously, I'm just dropping off some treats." She must've done too good of a job training Olga since Jenna would fire someone in a heartbeat for not following instructions.

From somewhere down the hall, a voice called out, "Do I smell cupcakes?"

Pennie looked to her left to find none other than the stunning face of LaToya Gunn coming around the corner. Her warm bronze skin appeared photo-shopped, complete with soft cat eyes, sculpted brows, and red lips. Jet-black, shoulder-length waves complemented LaToya's style—a perfect balance of glamorous and sophisticated.

Holding out the treats, Pennie answered, "Yes, I just picked them up from the bakery. I'm Pennie, Jenna's friend." She set the boxes on the reception desk to accept a firm handshake from LaToya.

"I'm Toy Gunn. You can come on back."

The exquisitely dressed Toy led the way down the hall. No wonder Jenna had been feeling threatened lately. If Toy's work attitude matched her style, she was a force to be reckoned with.

Down the hall on the left, they entered Jenna's office, which had turned into a war room since the last time Pennie saw it. Where there used to be a cushy seating area in the corner, a long conference table covered in papers filled the space. Not just the table, but floorplans and other papers covered the walls. "What all are y'all working on?" Pennie asked as she accepted a quick hug from Jenna.

"We're working on the layout of the companies who paid for an exhibit at GenCo Con. Didn't Jenna tell you about our project?" Toy answered as she selected a cupcake from the bakery box. "All the vendors and contractors who want to attend pay for a table, booth, or section of empty square footage. Eighty percent of the spaces are taken, but we have some companies trying to squeeze in. Our team here is prequalifying those companies, while Jenna and I ensure that everyone has their space. It's a jigsaw puzzle, fitting in as many companies as possible inside the convention center."

Pennie observed other changes to the office. Along with the conference table, a second desk was added in the corner next to the window to make a workstation for Toy. A laptop and a few framed pictures made the space officially hers. If Pennie had to guess, neither Toy nor Jenna ever shared an office with anyone before. Even if the tension wasn't palpable, she knew the two boss ladies had to be locking horns on occasion.

Jenna approached the ten-foot-long blueprint on the wall to add a sticky note. "It's coming together nicely. What brings you here, Penn?"

"I only saw you briefly on Sunday, so I wanted to check on you. And you said Toy was here from Texas, so I wanted to offer some Southern hospitality to her as well."

Jenna shrugged her shoulders, still facing the print on the wall. "We've got a lot to accomplish, but it's getting there."

"Toy, how are you handling it all? Are you staying in a B&B or something?" Pennie asked, as she picked up one of the pictures of Toy, who proudly wore a Houston Cougar hoodie.

She licked some vanilla icing off her finger before saying, "I got an apartment. In fact, I overlook the eighteenth green on the Bartlett golf course."

"That does sound sweet, but isn't it tough leaving your home like that? Do you have to travel a lot for work?" Pennie hoped that would lead into a conversation about her recent travels to the Dominican.

Both women were engrossed in their work. Toy had already given her attention to a legal pad. "Jenna, I think the GPS companies should be grouped with the software providers," she mentioned before she addressed Pennie. "I travel when I need to. I don't have a lot of family in Texas, so it's not a big deal. I just settled there after college and never left."

"Well, I love to travel. I just got back from a cruise. We visited several Caribbean islands, and my favorite stop was in the Dominican. I can't believe the turmoil that's going on there now."

"I've been to the Dominican," Toy offered without elaborating.

"Did you take a cruise or stay in a resort?" Pennie asked. Not that Toy would just admit to conspiring with terrorists, but whatever she had to say about her visit would let Pennie know if there was some reason to suspect her.

"Nope, just business."

Now she felt like she was pulling teeth to get information. "Was it something to do with this convention in Vegas?"

Toy set down the notepad and turned to face Pennie. "No, I'm leveraging a partnership with an electrical manufacturer in the Dominican. If we can buy electrical supplies and gear packages directly from the manufacturer, we don't have to pay mark up to our subcontractors."

"Really, tell me about that? I worked for an electrical subcontractor for a few years, and we shopped out vendors to get the best pricing."

"Then you already know the general contractor pays

mark up to the electrical subcontractor, who pays mark up to the supply house, who pays mark up to the manufacturer. This way, we're buying direct and cutting out quite a bit of that cost. One of the biggest electrical plants is in the Dominican. Two of the executives came back to Texas with me not long ago. They're working with our legal team to put the deal in place."

That didn't sound sinister at all. "Have you talked to them this week? With all the drama going on in the Dominican, I hope their families are safe."

"I haven't talked to them, and that's not my problem anyway. My job was to entice them to come to Texas."

Toy didn't appear to be entertaining any further communication on the matter, Pennie didn't feel like she needed to do any more snooping here. She'd have to figure out some other way to get an inside scoop about Toy and the guys she brought back to the States with her. "It sounds like you've been busy. Leveraging deals, planning this convention, relocation. If you need a home cooked meal or anything, I'll give you my number. Any friend of Jenna's is a friend of mine."

A glance at the clock let Pennie know she had about three hours before Cole expected her to be home from work. And about four hours until Adolfo Cabral planned to storm the National Palace. Could she get a look at Toy's apartment without anyone noticing?

Within a few minutes, she pulled into the entrance of the Bartlett Fairways next to the new country club. The gate effectively stopped her progress. A woman's voice came through the speaker to find out what Pennie wanted.

"I'm shopping for an apartment, and I wanted to look around please."

The robotic voice answered, "I don't show any appointments for this afternoon. Did you book something?"

"No, ma'am, I just thought I'd come by."

"You'll need to go online and book an appointment before we can show you any available apartments."

With nothing accomplished, Pennie turned around to approach things from another angle. Meandering through the side roads, she made her way to the entrance of the Bartlett Country Club. She wasn't quite dressed in golfing attire, but she hoped confidence would carry her through this part of the mission. She walked straight into the lobby. After spending a few weeks on the golf course in May, Pennie knew the first hole was right on the other side of the door, making the eighteenth hole not far away either.

"Ma'am, you can't come through here."

She should've known the security guard would stop her. "I don't want to play golf, I just want to take a walk on the course."

"Members only beyond this point. You'll need to leave."

That was a waste of fifteen minutes. She pointed her truck towards the University of Memphis. Maybe a visit with Richard Ewers would reveal something useful.

Thanks to the university website, she had already found the location of his office on campus along with his office hours. When she found parking near the athletic building, Pennie jumped out and soaked up the scene. College was one of her favorite times in life. Being here on campus revived her in a way she couldn't put into words. She inhaled a lungful of hot July air and entered the building.

She could hear Richard Ewers before she made it down the corridor. He was yelling at someone about dedication to the program and putting in one hundred percent. She stopped short of entering the office even though the door sat wide open. A sniveling female voice answered, "Yes, sir," before the young woman bolted from the office and ran off without noticing Pennie.

Pennie tried not to make too much of the scene. Mustering her own confidence, she stepped inside, lightly rapping on the door to make her presence known.

Ewers' official photo online depicted a smiling face—a man who could be a role model and friend to the young athletes. In person, not so much. The angry eyes barely noticed Pennie before he averted his attention to his desk drawers. She watched him slam a few drawers, muttering about a pencil. That was a lot of aggression over a writing utensil.

He eventually pulled out a yellow pencil and switched his muttering about how dull the tip was. Pennie remained frozen. This guy appeared unapproachable as he reached into another drawer. When he pulled out a large knife, Pennie backed up a few paces. The scowl on his face transformed into a creepy smile. He reminded Pennie of the Joker, played by Heath Ledger. Mental instability was a definite factor here. Then he attacked the pencil, using the blade to sharpen the lead.

Only after he returned the knife to the drawer did Pennie feel safe to take a breath. No longer feeling the need to bolt from the office, she took a step forward, towards the crazy coach. Then she almost peed in her pants when he finally addressed her directly.

"Are you just gonna stand there like a knot on a log? Are you the new intern from the nutrition department? All you have to do is stay out of my way, and you'll do better than that girl I just fired. Honestly, I wish they would do away with this darn intern program."

"Um, no. Coach Ewers, I'm not part of any program. I do know a bunch of the international students here on campus, and I'm here to speak to you on their behalf."

He grunted in acknowledgement to her statement, but his attention was on the notebook in front of him. She recognized the scorekeeping notebook they used in her high school softball games. It was amazing that this university-level program still used old-school recordkeeping.

"Well, Coach. I wanted to do a little get-together for the international students, but I've been told you don't allow your student athletes to attend social events. Is that true?"

Ewers abruptly stood, forcing his chair to roll back and crash into the wall. He placed his fists on the desk and hunched forward to give her an evil glare. "How I manage my program is none of your business. Who do you think you are, coming here and questioning me like this?"

Feeling quite a bit on the defensive, she changed her tone, like how she might speak to an angry Rottweiler. "I'm not questioning you; I'm just trying to make sure the internationals have a chance to make friends and get assimilated to our culture."

"I have five internationals on my team, and they're making friends with fellow players. They don't need you."

"But Coach—"

"No buts about it. I hand select every player, and I watch out for their well-being."

"I've hosted students for years, Coach. The social interaction helps their well-being."

Pulling his chair back to its place, Ewers had a seat and pulled his knife back out. He whittled the pencil furiously over the garbage can without saying a word. Intimidated didn't begin to describe her state. She just stood there. Petrified. But if this guy was trying to harbor terrorists, she needed to find out what she could.

Quietly sitting in the chair in front of his desk, she said, "Coach, I respect your position, and I understand you're watching out for the kids. How do I gain your trust so the students can attend a little get together at my house?"

He sized Pennie up, reading her intentions, as he growled and tightened his lips. "Do you know what goes on at frat parties and other social events?"

"Um socializing, food, games…"

"NO! Drugs, drinking, and sex happen. I run a tight ship here to keep my athletes out of trouble. Every one of these young men come from poverty and situations they need to escape. I purposely recruit players who need an opportunity to rise above what life has thrown at them. And they come here with the agreement that they follow my rules. No parties. No social events. No tolerance for missing classes and failing grades. It's all on me. Not you. I look out for their well-being, and I make sure they have a future beyond college without drugs, alcohol, or accidental pregnancies."

Pennie didn't quite expect that fatherly speech from the crotchety man in front of her. "I'm sure these young men appreciate everything you do. I just want to come alongside you to help. These internationals are thousands of miles from home, away from their family and friends. Away from their culture and comforts. A little social interaction makes the transition easier."

She came here with intentions of figuring out how Ewers might be involved with terrorists, but now she felt like she needed to be an advocate for his international students.

This meeting might be fruitful for two reasons.

"You don't think I know about the importance of family? I get to know my players and find out what parts of their life they need to leave behind. Sometimes family is what they're escaping. In other cases, the friends and culture need to be left in the past."

"I understand, and I'm trying to offer clean fun and good influence by organizing an event—"

"We don't need your event!" He slammed his fist down to punctuate the outburst. "I have it all under control. I organize events all the time for my team. They become a family on their own."

"That doesn't replace moms and dads. They need nurturing."

"Do you know another coach who paid for airfare so parents from Italy could come here last year to visit their son for two weeks? They stayed in my house."

"No, I don't—"

"I'm not done. Every August, the immediate family of every new international student is invited to come here and set up their son's dorm. I pay for their hotel rooms, airfare, and food. This year, I pushed for my Dominican player to get an apartment on campus as part of his scholarship so his family could move here."

"Coach Ewers, I had no idea. Is the family even allowed to live in a campus apartment?"

"No, but Mateo needed his family here more than I needed to follow the rules. Like I said, I know what's best for my kids."

"Does that happen regularly? You help families move here?"

His scowl softened a little. "It's never happened before.

Mateo only had his mom growing up, but the violence towards women in the Dominican Republic has gotten worse lately. When he was only fifteen, he watched his mom get murdered by her boyfriend. Mateo had no other family. The father of one of his high school friends took Mateo under his wing. For two years, he had a father and brother he'd never had before, then he escaped to find a new life here. Knowing his surrogate father and brother were suffering back home was taking an emotional toll on Mateo. I got the folks in the international department here to help me get visas for them, and last week, I flew down there and got them. Ricky and Manny are staying in a B&B with Mateo until they can move into the apartment next month."

Pennie had to fight a few unexpected tears. This coach wasn't a terrible person. He was salt of the earth with a crusty exterior. "Coach Ewers, can I help your efforts in any way?"

"You can stay out of my way."

"I'm going to write my name and number here," Pennie said, picking up the nub of a pencil sitting on the desk. "If you'll allow me to help monetarily, or if I can arrange a social event that I promise to be family friendly, please don't hesitate to reach out to me."

The drive home left Pennie in a state of confusion. She felt better about humanity, but she didn't determine anything to locate potential terrorists. Even Judy mentioned earlier that much of their work entailed ruling people out. That was all she could do.

She walked through the door at home to find Cole

watching the news.

"The girls have been playing music since we finished lunch. Nothing else is going on so far."

"Okay, I'm going to take a shower before our deadline approaches and breaking news starts."

After a quick shower, she rummaged through the kitchen to find a snack.

"Pennie!" Cole hollered from the living room. She looked up to see a news alert. Rushing to the couch, she sat in time for the anchor to speak.

"Breaking news out of Santo Domingo, the capital city of the Dominican Republic, this afternoon. All eyes are on the *Mata Cacatas* around the National Palace as the impeding deadline grows closer for President Vasquez..."

Nothing new was happening. The anchor took a few minutes to talk about this history of the island nation and the unlikely rise of a woman to the office of president. The view on the TV panned in and out of live shots around the palace. The red roof, majestic dome, and double columns gave the marble building more charm and character than the White House in Washington DC. It was surrounded by an expansive lawn, palm trees, meticulously maintained gardens, and a wrought-iron perimeter fence. Pennie wondered what the interior looked like.

Cole and Pennie stared at the TV without speaking. The story covered the instability of Haiti, just across the border from the Dominican. They talked about how little anyone knew about the Wasps. Just from the footage shown around the palace, there appeared to be a hundred Wasps buzzing around the perimeter fence, dressed in all black with a red band fastened around each of their left biceps. The scene was daunting. The city streets surrounding the palace had been shut down with the expectation of imminent fighting.

A drone must've provided the footage. It zoomed in here and there. The Wasps each had a pistol fastened around his thigh. Pennie couldn't see any other heavy artillery or weapons of any sort. The military members stood guard inside the fence, wearing drab green camo uniforms and helmets, not showing any fear. They had bigger guns and more manpower on that side of the fence.

"Get the girls. It's starting," Cole said without taking his eyes off the screen.

Pennie didn't see any flinch or movement otherwise, but she went to the bunkroom to interrupt the girls' latest music practice. They got to the living room in time to see smoke obscure a portion of the palace. The melee that ensued was hard to follow. The camera became shaky. Pennie and Karolina encompassed Francelia in a hug on the couch as the reporter spurted out incomplete sentences trying to keep up with the action.

"They're using smoke bombs," Cole said, again not looking away from the TV screen.

More smoke billowed around the front of the palace, closer to the building itself. On the east side of the building, a military-looking vehicle rammed straight through the fence, taking out a portion and allowing the Wasps to rush in. By the time the camera focused on this action, another larger truck took out a section of fence in front of the palace. The screen split so viewers could see the skirmish on the perimeter of the property along with the current message being broadcast by Adolfo Cabral. The sinister expression gave Pennie the chills.

"That's inside the palace!" Francelia said. "It's the housekeeper's storage on the bottom level."

For the benefit of Cole and Pennie, the current message was translated in the closed captions.

"Did you think I was bluffing? Our country is ready for a revolution. Now I just need to find the ladies of the house. Don't go far... this shouldn't take long."

The screen blacked out on the left half of the television. The reporter came back, promising to stick with the developing story.

"Why is all the fighting in the front when he went in through the back?" Francelia asked.

"Honey, are you sure that's current footage? Do you really think he's inside the palace right now? He could've taken that video a long time ago."

Cole shook his head. "Pennie, we appreciate you trying to be optimistic, but that was a live feed. He's inside. We just don't know how many Wasps are in there with him."

They sat, watching the screen as if a train wreck were being broadcast. The smoke bombs, the sound of gunfire, the shaking drone camera... And next to Pennie, the trembling daughter of President Vasquez.

The *ReelLife* timer prompted Francelia to take a picture. She asked Karolina to take the photo while Francelia made a heart with her hands. Sending love to her mother.

A moment later, the return picture froze them in place. Adolfo Cabral sat next to a crying Daniela Vasquez, holding his own heart hands.

Francelia immediately broke down and slumped to the floor into uncontrollable hysterics. Nothing in Pennie's tenure as an international mom prepared her for this. She joined the sobbing girl on the floor, keeping her tightly wrapped in the arms of her substitute mother. Karolina followed suit, joining them on the floor. Cole did the same, forming a protective cocoon around the girl.

It took a full fifteen minutes for Francelia to get it together, enough to breathe without gasping. Cole retrieved a wet washcloth for her to wipe her face with. When everyone gave her room to breathe, Peach moved in to lie on the floor against Francelia. Nothing new was shown on the television. Just more fighting outside the building and endless historical facts from the anchor reading the teleprompter.

Within another five minutes, Cabral broadcast another live feed. Pennie wondered how his messages made it straight to the television but realized he was better with technology than she was. They all read his words as they filled the bottom of the screen.

"The games have begun. I'm trying to convince our president to tell me where her daughter is, but she won't say. It's clear that Francelia has fled the palace, possibly even the country. But there's nowhere safe for her now. As soon as we find her, we'll make sure she watches us kill her mother before we kill her. I hope you're ready for what's next, Maria. I'm the president now. No one can save you."

"He knows my alias," Francelia whispered, clinging tightly to the wet rag in her hands.

Cole sat on the couch and placed a comforting hand on her shoulder. "Your alias was only used for that app. It's not like there's an address or anything associated with that name."

Her phone still sat face up on the coffee table. A *ReelLife* alert lit up the screen. “Does the timer usually go off that close together?" Pennie asked.

Karolina grabbed the phone and opened the app. “It’s the timer for our group with JJ. Not the one with her mother.”

Pennie felt her chest tighten. “Why did you set up more groups? This phone was for minimal communication with your mother only.”

“She needed some friends, and it’s not like they can see the pictures in our group,” Karolina spouted out in Francelia’s defense.

“Just cool it, ladies,” Cole intervened. “What’s done is done, but let’s hope like hell they can’t find the other pictures you’ve sent on this app. Pennie, what credit card did you give her to create an Apple ID?”

It was Francelia’s turn to spout off. “She didn’t give me a credit card. I skipped that part. I made up a new email address, and I didn’t use any information that would give away our location. I’m not dumb.”

“No one thinks you’re dumb. We’re all just on edge, sweetie,” Pennie tried to soothe the girl, who was processing every emotion from frightened to angry.

Switching her view back to the television, Francelia yelled at the screen, “Where’s our military now? Where’s the US military? Who’s going to help my mother?”

No one in this room knew how to answer that. The alarm on Pennie’s iPad notified them of activity outside before the doorbell rang. Cole ushered in Chip, who arrived in Cole’s car thanks to the constant vehicle rotation. They locked the door and rearmed the security system.

Chip crowded in on the couch to sit next to Pennie, right above Francelia who remained on the floor. “Your mom’s intelligent. If there’s a game being played, she’s going to win.”

"How would you know that?" she asked as if she might believe whatever he said.

"I can tell by how smart you are. And I've read a lot about your mother. She's playing chess while Cabral is playing checkers. He can't match wits with her. Trust me."

This was the side of Chip that Pennie adored. The Chip who offered strength for weakness. The Chip who showed up without having to be asked. The Chip who spoke genuinely, exuding comfort and encouragement. Those few words even got a small smile out of Francelia. The girl leaned her head against Chip's leg, and he stroked her hair in return. Cole resumed his spot on the couch on her other side with a hand on her shoulder. If Pennie had to guess, Francelia was the safest girl in the world right now.

The news anchor eventually took over speaking with the drone coverage playing behind her. "It appears that the *Mata Cacatas* have breached security and infiltrated the wing occupied by President Daniela Vasquez. Our team is working on who Maria might be as he referenced in the latest video. According to our records, Vasquez only has one daughter, Francelia, who lives at the palace with her."

The reporter paused to listen to her earpiece. "I'm being told now that the *Mata Cacatas* have taken complete control of the palace. Several of the palace guards surrendered, some were killed, and some have previous affiliation with the terrorist group. Can we get a better shot of what's going on around the property?" she asked some unknown cameraman.

The action around the palace filled the screen. A

handful of dead bodies lay on the ground. Dozens sat with their hands cuffed to the fence. Dozens more had added a red band to their left bicep, indicating their affiliation with the Wasps.

"This is a dire situation for the president and her associates inside the palace," lamented the reporter. The look of disgust she wore had to be a genuine expression this time. "Is there any update from DC? Randall, what do you know?"

This time, the screen displayed two reporters in the foreground with the drone footage in the background. "Melissa, President Carson is keeping any potential plans to intervene close to the vest. I know all our viewers hoped that someone would save the day before this happened, but all hope is not lost. The office of the Joint Chief of Staff has just issued a statement indicating it's not over yet. Obviously, President Vasquez needs a hero to show up and save the day. The world waits on pins and needles until that hero shows up."

The monotonous back and forth of the anchors filled the next half hour. No more updates or live feeds from Cabral. On the bright side, no more hysterics from Francelia. They sat in silence, watching the television—waiting for their worlds to change with any update from the news.

Cole flipped through a variety of news stations, but they all showed the same thing. The waiting game sucked. If Pennie had any pent-up aggression before, it was nothing to how she felt now. If Cabral walked through her door right now, she'd beat the daylights out of him with her bare hands.

Chip moved to the floor, pushing Peach out of the way. He pulled Francelia into a one-armed hug and spoke into her ear. A message he intended for only her to hear. She nodded just slightly in response. Then Chip stood and announced he was leaving. "Cole has it under control here. I just wanted to offer some support for a minute. Y'all holler if you need me to come back."

"Okay, girls. Sitting here watching the news is going to drive us insane. Let's just leave it on in the background for any updates," Pennie said as she rose from the couch.

They all moved to the breakfast table. Pennie identified a variety of birds that flitted around her feeders. Francelia adopted a serene expression, watching the hummingbirds, woodpeckers, and other backyard feathery friends, joined by a fat squirrel or two. Eventually, the deck of Uno cards kept them occupied. The game didn't distract them from the news, but it gave their hands something to do.

The ringing phone on the coffee table forced Pennie to abandon her cards. An unknown number from Atlanta appeared on the caller ID. "Hello?"

"Pennie! This is Vale Hernandez."

"Hello, Vale! Hang on so I can put you on speaker for Francelia to hear..." Pennie fumbled with the screen to press the right button. "Okay, everyone can hear you now. I have Francelia, Karolina, and Officer Cole Mackey here with me." She placed the phone on the middle of the table next to the forgotten deck of Uno cards.

"Hello, everyone. I don't have anything new to share, but I wanted to reach out directly instead of going through Tony this time. Francie, I know your mother very well. *¿Como estas, amorcito?*"

"I'm scared, Señora Hernandez."

"We're all scared right now. But we can have hope, even with fear."

Cole spoke up when Francelia paused without answering. "Ambassador Hernandez, I'd like to ask if you have any information or ideas that might let us know where things stand in the National Palace. The lack of information is the hardest part."

"Yes, Officer. Although I don't have direct contact with anyone inside the palace, I know a few people close to the scene. There's chatter around the palace. Mostly they say that all Dominican armed forces have been removed from the palace except for the ones who joined the *Mata Cacatas*. All the loyal employees of the palace have been detained in one area. We still don't know what to expect next."

"Oh well. Thanks for reaching out to us anyway," Cole said, a little disappointed that they didn't learn anything.

"Of course. I'll reach out directly to Pennie's phone regularly to keep the communication open. Now, may I ask a question?"

"Sure," Cole said even though he didn't know who the question would be aimed at.

"Who is Maria?"

"That's me, *Señora.* I used a fake name on a picture app to send my mom photos. Cabral saw the photos we exchanged and the name I used."

"Thank goodness. I've been trying to figure out if there's another girl who needs protection. Please tell me that the photos don't give away your location."

"No, not at all," Francelia answered, then added, "*Señora*, I'm really scared that I'll never see my mother again. We're waiting for the news to show her dead body." She barely finished the sentence before the tears fell again.

"I wish I had better news for you, *amorcito*, but I don't think Cabral will do anything to your mother until he finds you. As long as we keep you hidden, he'll use her to find you."

The light sobs continued as she asked, "But isn't that worse? He might torture her." Pennie and Karolina moved their chairs around to sandwich the girl with physical support.

Sounding defeated, Hernandez answered, "We can only hope not. My belief is that Cabral won't act on his murderous intentions until he finds Francelia. He might resort to some level of torture, but we don't know enough about his tactics. Even with torture, any delay in his final plans will give other armed forces a chance to move in and take down the *Mata Cacatas*."

The game of Uno kept them occupied for another few minutes with the news in the background. With no updates from the reporters, the foursome played without speaking. Tony called to check on everyone, but no one felt like talking. When the *ReelLife* timer prompted Francelia to take a picture, she offered a fierce expression for the camera. The return picture showed Adolfo Cabral smiling eerily next to Daniela Vasquez. The president appeared exhausted, as if she had aged a decade in the last few hours.

They all studied the picture of Daniela. No signs of torture were obvious, such as acid to the face. No one put their fear into words, but the sigh of relief was audible around the table.

"I can't keep doing this," Francelia said, pushing over the deck of Uno cards. "How am I supposed to sit here and do nothing?"

Pennie was grateful that Cole responded first. "Tell me who all is there with your mother now. What kind of allies does she have in the palace with her?"

Francelia picked up a green *Reverse* card from the table and spoke methodically, turning the card in her hand. "The Presidential Security Corps should be protecting her. *Cuerpo de Seguridad Presidencial.* They protect the president, vice president, their families, and visiting dignitaries. It's a combination of military members and the National Police. The National Police are civilians. Did you know that the Tourism police force is separate from the National Police? They're military."

Figuring the girl was rambling to expend her nervousness, Pennie helped her continue, "So, your mother has some trusted security there with her who are both military and police?"

"We had about twenty men who we truly trusted. They took shifts every eight hours to keep us safe for the past few months. No one was allowed in our private quarters without going through them. I think they were all military. They wore the same camouflage uniform. I wish I got to know them all. I should've learned their names."

"Francelia, you can't worry about something like that right now. Who else stayed in the private quarters with you?" Pennie asked.

Karolina plucked the Uno card from Francelia's hand and shuffled the deck. Francelia looked around the table and elaborated, "Just me and Madre. I slept in her room since I didn't like to be alone. We always had four or five guards at the private quarters, not including all the security around the palace. There would be more uniformed police during ceremonies and executive meetings. But since the end of March, the palace didn't entertain anything that wasn't an important business meeting because of the threats. No more parties or celebrations. Eventually, I started receiving the death threats. By May, we didn't leave the private quarters at all. Even the closest advisors weren't allowed to see us. Madre handled all her meetings virtually."

As Karolina dealt cards to start a new game, she asked, "What about food? How did you eat and get supplies?"

"A team of three housekeepers came every day. They brought food, cooked, cleaned... they were our only friends and company. One crew covered Monday through Thursday, while a second crew worked Friday through Sunday. We only trusted a small group of housekeepers, and they're the ones who helped me escape. One of them colored my hair the day before they snuck me out."

"What's the private quarters decorated like?" Karolina inquired to keep Francelia talking.

"Like a fancy hotel. Statues. Carvings. Heavy furniture. Not comfortable at all. Madre could've decorated it differently, but that wasn't her priority. I didn't sleep in my own room, so I never bothered decorating it. I hated politics. I hated the palace."

After playing a card to get the game started, Cole pushed her to keep sharing. "What was it like to be the daughter of the president? What did you do on a daily basis?"

"Mostly just smile and shake hands. I had to be at all the ceremonies. People told me what to wear. They did my makeup. I had to practice good posture and social etiquette. I was a puppet on a string, but I wanted my mom to succeed, so I did everything I was told."

"What about the last few months? Did you have your own virtual meetings or responsibilities?" Pennie asked.

"No. I didn't interact with anyone who wasn't part of the staff. I practically wore pajamas every day. I read a lot of books and did some practice tests so I could apply for college in the USA."

A tone of depression slipped into Francelia's voice.

Pennie's heart ached to hear defeat in the wake of her recent extraction. Unfortunately, she had no way to fix it. A new direction of conversation to focus on the future might help. "Honey, what all are you looking forward to when you can start your own path in life?"

Francelia inhaled deeply through her nose and stared at the cards she'd been dealt. After a moment to consider her response, she offered a few of her hopes and dreams. "I knew I was getting a late start to college, so I wanted to enroll in some online courses. Then by the time I could get to the States, I might graduate with students close to my age. My mother supported me doing this, and I started applying for schools. Most of them wanted SAT or TOEFL scores, so I was trying to schedule those exams."

"The TOEFL was easy for me," Karolina offered. She elaborated when she saw the confusion on Cole's face. "That's a test of English as a foreign language. International students must score well to get accepted to an American university and qualify for any scholarships. I didn't have any problems with the test, and neither will you," she told Francelia with confidence.

"*Gracias, mi hermanita,*" Francelia said. "It's not just college plans, though. Every year, I get so excited about our *Festival de Merengue*. It's a big celebration in Santo Domingo with parades and music. I wanted to dress in bright colors and dance in the streets like I do every year. But now… It just won't happen."

"When does the festival happen? Hopefully, things will settle down by then."

"Next week," she answered sullenly. "It lasts for two weeks every summer around the last week of July and first week of August. The city of Santo Domingo was founded on the fourth of August, so that's also part of the celebration."

"A two-week celebration? Is it like Mardi Gras?" Cole

asked.

"Kind of. Our Carnaval Dominicano is in February like Mardi Gras, but the Festival de Merengue is a celebration of music, friendship, and culture. I already had all the dresses I planned to wear this year. We had ideas to decorate the National Palace. It doesn't matter now."

So much for trying to cheer her up, Pennie thought. Even though her mood stayed slightly on the despondent side, Francelia spent the next half hour sharing the history of her country. They played Uno without caring who won and without the news sharing any additional breaking updates.

The two amigas decided to make homemade pasta for a late dinner. Karolina couldn't enjoy the cheesy dishes, but she enjoyed hearty marina made from scratch. Pennie was pleased to see the abundance of tomatoes in her garden being put to good use. The salad fixings and herbs came straight from the garden as well.

After dinner, they planned to watch a cozy movie, but Francelia's phone interrupted their indecision on which one to select. The *ReelLife* timer beckoned her to send a picture. She put on her best brave face for the selfie and waited impatiently for the return picture. Cole, Pennie, and Karolina sat around her, waiting as well. It only took a moment for Francelia to gasp and drop the phone.

Karolina picked it up from the floor to look at the picture. Daniela Vasquez stared back at them with a fresh black eye. The *ReelLife* app only allowed photos with no messages, but the message was clear. Adolfo Cabral intended to find

Francelia's location no matter what lengths he had to go to. Francelia must've expected it since she only broke down into quiet sobs and not hysterics.

"Your mother is a strong woman. Cabral can't break her," Cole said. "Cabral only wants to find you, so as long as you're safe and hidden, so is your mother. That black eye won't last a week, and she's more than willing to suffer physically to keep you out of harm's way."

Between sniffles, Francelia challenged his confidence. "How long will it take to rescue her? Cabral will kill her if someone doesn't get her out of there!"

The fresh outpouring of tears broke Pennie's heart. Before she could pull the girl into a hug, Cole continued his optimistic spiel. "You got out of the country just in time to save your life, and your mom's too. If you were there, both of you would already be dead. Now that you're here, Cabral is forced to come up with a new plan, and that delay gives your allies the opportunity to intervene."

"Cole's right, honey. Your mom just needs to hang tough for a short spell. The bullies won't win this one." Pennie supported Cole with a boldness she didn't quite feel.

With a slight nod, Francelia wiped her tears. They finished the evening watching *School of Rock*. Karolina loved any music-themed movie, and Pennie loved any Jack Black movie. It was a good compromise that distracted them from the anxiety in the atmosphere for almost two hours.

THURSDAY, JULY 21

"She's been out of the country for ten days. In Bartlett for a week. Did you think she'd be here this long?" Pietra asked as the women sipped coffee at the breakfast table.

The girls slept late, giving Pennie and Pietra time to talk candidly while the uninformative news continued to play softly on the television. "In all reality, I expected Francelia to be here for the rest of the summer. That would give her country time to get things under control. Then she'd go back home. I didn't anticipate the violence or anything escalating. If any of us saw that coming, we would've come up with a plan to get both of them out of the country."

"I bet we could've. Vale Hernandez is brilliant. If we planned it from the start, both women would be safe right now. We should've been proactive about getting Daniela out of there. Instead, we can't do anything except keep Francelia safe."

"Of all the things in the world, I'd say keeping Francelia safe is the most important right now. Hang on, my nose says the cinnamon rolls are ready." Pennie jumped up to remove the canned delights from the oven. "You know Chip loves these things?"

"You eat too much junk, Pennie. That's something else I have to work on with Chip—his atrocious eating habits."

"So that's another way I'm a bad influence on him?" This might not be the best time to pick a fight with Pietra, but Pennie had so much pent-up energy and aggression… She might explode if she didn't find an outlet soon.

"What's that heavenly smell?" Francelia asked as she emerged from her bedroom and walked towards the kitchen, effectively defusing whatever argument was brewing.

Pennie smiled and offered the girl a freshly frosted cinnamon roll. Behind her, Karolina peered into the kitchen expectantly.

"Mom, I can't eat these," Karolina declared, looking slightly dejected. "What am I supposed to eat for breakfast?"

From the bottom oven, Pennie pulled out another pan of sweets. "I ordered these fifty-dollar vegan, gluten-free cinnamon rolls for you. I don't know if they taste good, but the Etsy seller had hundreds of five-star reviews. Make some matcha and eat your sweets."

With the younger ladies joining them, Pennie and Pietra didn't bother continuing their earlier pettiness. They each ate their own gooey treat and sipped coffee, happy to listen to the girls talk about silly things.

"I bet this icing would be good with Nesquik powder mixed in with it."

"Yessss. We need to try that."

Pennie and Pietra exchanged eye rolls.

"What's the deal with Nesquik? Karolina, you mix it with everything." Pennie didn't realize it was so popular. "Is it a cultural thing? Do all Latin Americans like Nesquik?" At least she knew not to lump Pietra in with the Latina group anymore.

"I can only speak for Brazil, but it's good with everything."

"It really is. Do you have some so I can add it to my coffee?" Francelia asked.

Pennie retrieved the yellow canister from the pantry

but watched as the girl's smile disappeared. It was time for another *ReelLife* update.

Francelia held up her coffee cup to take a selfie with. *Never too old to need your mother.* The mug Pennie gave Karolina when she started college. Everyone held their breath waiting for the return picture.

Daniela Vasquez appeared more haggard, but they didn't see any other injuries. She wore the same green sweater as the previous day. The shiner on her left eye had darkened overnight. By contrast, Cabral sat next to her with his own mug of coffee, freshly shaven with a smirk on his face.

"He's trying to play mind games, Francelia, but this is good for us."

"How is it good, Señora Russo?" At least the girl had a brave façade this time.

"You see how he's responding to your picture? He sent one with a coffee cup since that's what you did. We know in real time that your mother is alive and well."

With an obvious attempt to hold back tears, Francelia asked, "But he hit her. Her face must hurt."

Pennie jumped in, "It's just a black eye. It only hurts for a second. Then it's just embarrassing until you can cover it with makeup."

"How do you know?" Francelia and Karolina asked in unison.

"I take self-defense classes, and we spar all the time. I get a black eye occasionally. Aside from the time I got hit in the face with a softball in high school, Chip gave me the worst black eye I've ever had."

"What? Chip would never hit a woman." Pietra appeared offended that Pennie would even say that.

"We were sparring in my Krav Maga class. It was my

fault for not blocking, and he wasn't wearing padded sparring gear. But seriously, Francelia, it only hurts for that minute you get hit. She isn't hurting right now because of the black eye. He probably did it to get her attention or scare her, but that's not torture."

Pietra cut back in, "Cabral is playing mind games right now. We don't know what his next move will be, but he's biding his time until he finds you," she told Francelia. "So, we're keeping you under the radar long enough for someone to get her out of there."

While the girls went to take long showers after breakfast, Pennie and Pietra moved to the living room in time to see a breaking story on the television. The live video pushed Pennie towards a panic attack. It was only eight in the morning, but Cabral was on his own timeline now.

Adolfo Cabral's face filled the screen with an evil gleam in his eyes. The words across the bottom of the screen displayed his latest threat...

"As the new man of the house, I wanted to ensure all my loyal Dominicans that our country will be stronger than ever. I plan to lead you into a new era where men can protect and defend... An era where women will be women. The Merengue Festival will begin next week, and I want all our citizens to enjoy the activities. Please proceed with the parades and celebrations. I look forward to seeing all the lovely women wearing their costumes."

He stopped speaking long enough for the camera to adjust so everyone could see his captive. Daniela, standing next to him, now wore a red, white, and blue dress with a long, flowy skirt. It must've been a traditional Merengue dancing outfit, but she didn't seem happy to be wearing it.

"I've enjoyed this quality time with Daniela Vasquez, and we shall have our own fun dancing in private, but my patience is wearing thin. It's time to bring Francelia back so I can teach them a lesson... A lesson for all women who refuse to be submissive. Be ready to come home, Francelia. I'm sending a few men to catch a tiger by her toe."

Pennie forgot to breathe after the "Tiger" comment. She stared at the television with a slack jaw, not hearing what the reporter had to say after Cabral's face disappeared.

Pietra scoffed, "Catch a tiger by her toe? Is that a nursery rhyme in their country too?"

Pennie willed herself to inhale and slow down the whirlwind inside her brain. That was just a saying. It didn't necessarily have anything to do with the Memphis Tigers or the fact that she was wearing a Tigers t-shirt at that very moment. The Wasps didn't know who she was... The freak-out was unwarranted. The initial wooziness passed without Pietra noticing her momentary hysteria.

The reporter droned on about the situation in the Caribbean nation without adding anything relevant. When the girls finished their bathroom routines, Pennie replayed the video for them to see. Francelia reacted surprisingly well, feeling reassured that her mother seemed unharmed other than the black eye.

As much as she hated to leave the house, the world

continued to turn. Pennie had to report to work. Flowers needed watering. Lupe needed supervision. Her existence needed to appear normal from the outside. By the time she pulled into the driveway of Avocado Farms, one major thing wasn't normal. If she would've paid attention to her surroundings, she might've noticed a large Chevy truck pulling in right behind her, sandwiching her truck between the gates and his truck.

Her pulse escalated. Did Bone find out about her trespassing incident? Why did he follow her to work? The delivery driver and landscape crews would arrive any minute, so Pennie pushed down her nerves and stepped out of her truck to unlock the gate.

She looked over her shoulder and waved to Bone. From her viewpoint, he had a death grip on the steering wheel, but he raised a few fingers on one hand in response. Carrying on, she unlocked the gates and parked her truck in the lot.

Bone pulled next to her and jumped out. His eyes moved wildly, taking in the surroundings. "Are you alone here?"

She didn't want to say yes, but there was no point in lying. "I am for a minute. The rest of the crew is usually right behind me." Why didn't she bring a gun? Pennie had several concealable guns, but she didn't feel like she was the target. Adriana kept a shotgun hidden in the cashier shack, but she wouldn't be able to get it without Frank observing her every move.

Bone ran a hand across the stubble on his face. As nervous as he appeared, it didn't match Pennie's anxiety. He finally huffed and said, "I need to discuss something with you."

"Okay, what's up?" She eyeballed the highway behind him, hoping to see a work truck or someone pull into the driveway.

"Do you agree that protecting your children is the most

important thing you can do as a parent? No matter what length you must go to? Even if you break a few rules along the way?"

Did Bone know about Pennie's secret? Did he figure out that she was protecting Francelia? Instead of shielding her from danger, Pennie invited it to come nearer. The air had been stolen from her lungs. Breathlessly, she answered, "Sure," without knowing what he had planned.

"Pennie, during the guise of protection, sometimes people get hurt. We betray friendships and do what must be done for the greater good."

She nodded, unsure of what he might say or do next.

"Not everyone agrees with the decisions I've made in my life, but I think the greater good has always been my motive. Even when I've resorted to physical violence."

Did he plan on using physical violence this morning? Pennie's mouth was dry. She opened it to speak, but nothing came out.

"Sometimes, we see loved ones getting involved with people who we can tell are bad news, but adults must figure it out for themselves. They must learn things the hard way. We live in a world where people call bad good, and good bad. On top of that, women are born with the desire for an alpha male to be their protector and leader, but they aren't always smart with how they go about it."

Was this Bone spewing some machismo propaganda? Was he trying to recruit Pennie to the Wasps and ask her to lead Francelia back to the Dominican? She felt dizzy waiting to see what he had planned. The droplet of sweat rolling down her face had nothing to do with the temperature.

"So, when my daughter got involved with her latest boyfriend, I tried to give her space to learn a lesson."

Hang on. His daughter? What was happening?

He continued, "Angel met him in Puerto Rico where she's been working for the past year. She quickly moved in with him. Even though I never met him, I got a bad impression from things she would tell me. A few weeks ago, he hit my daughter. In the face. He apologized and swore it would never happen again, and Angel believed him. What's a dad to do?"

"What, Bone? What did you do?" Domestic abuse couldn't be tolerated, and the thought of a man hitting a woman made her blood boil.

"I came up with a plan and flew to Puerto Rico myself. The next morning, I showed up at Angel's apartment building. The security guard didn't want to let me in the building, so I knocked him out. I'm not proud of that, but I got Angel out of the building. We drove straight to the airport from there."

"Did she not want to go with you? Why did you have to show up like that?"

"Angel was scared to leave him. She's still scared he might follow her."

Pennie was relieved to know Bone wasn't a terrorist, but now, she worried about his daughter. "Is she safe now? Does he know she flew to Memphis?"

"I hope not. Before I left Memphis, I borrowed a driver's license from my buddy Diego; he's kind of a feminine fellow. I paid cash for her ticket using his ID. They're about the same height and size. She changed into some boy's clothes I brought with me, and she tucked her hair under a hat. She walked right through security with only a precheck of her carry-on bag, which I brought for her. I'm not advertising that she's staying with me, but it's a matter of time before he shows up. I think one of his cronies tried to break into my house on Tuesday. I need to find somewhere less obvious for her to stay, and I don't have a lot of friends I can count on."

"Oh. What do you need me to do, Bone?"

"I'll pay for it, but I need you to rent an apartment in your name, so Angel has somewhere safe to live under the radar until this situation is resolved. Somewhere with good security."

This might work out well. "The new apartments on the golf course near here are supposed to be nice. They have security gates, and every apartment has a garage. Do you want me to holler at you after work, and we can get a lease started? Just go online and make an appointment first. Bartlett Fairways."

After Frank left, she got the drivers directed, and Lupe had already started her watering chores. Pennie moved to the annuals to rearrange the displays. It was time for all the remaining flowers and veggies to go on clearance. Before long, they'd be selling mums and pumpkins. A truckload of hay had already been dropped off in preparation for autumn décor. Using a tractor and trailer, Pennie moved all the bales of straw hay closer to the old house on the opposite side of the property.

Oscar must have mowed the property yesterday, getting it ready for the autumn displays and hayrides. If she weren't preoccupied with Francelia, Pennie would be excited about bringing her nieces here for pictures and fall fun. Thanks to the stress of hiding the fugitive, she had trouble being excited about anything these days. The only thing getting her blood pumping was the opportunity to help track down the potential terrorists.

By ten that morning, Judy showed up. "Sorry I keep coming to your work. I have to report for the studio by five, so I don't have time to come by your house in the evenings.

After this story is over, I do need to finish investigating the possibility of a hidden cemetery on the adjacent property here."

The acreage was surrounded by trees. A cemetery might be hidden. That wouldn't distract Pennie from what was going on now. It worked to her favor that Judy never tried to visit her house. She didn't want Judy to find Francelia there, and she didn't want any of the cops to know she was investigating without their knowledge or permission.

"It works better for you to come here. My daughter is home for the summer, so we're using the evenings as our quality time, and she doesn't need to know I'm helping dig into potential terrorists."

Judy pulled out the notebook from her purse. "Your daughter doesn't need to know anything, that's for sure. Since yesterday, I've ruled out a few more names. I tried to find out anything I could on the Bell brothers you met on the cruise, but nothing stands out either way. I was curious if you noticed anything about them that would direct my research."

"Not really." Pennie thought hard. "They seemed pleasant enough, and the younger brother is still sending messages to Karolina on social media. As much as I hate to say it, I think they made a connection."

"Keep on eye on her. Homegrown terrorists like to make connections all over the place so they can stay mobile if the situation calls for it. If they suspect at all that Francelia is hiding in this area, the Bell brothers might be looking for legitimate reasons to travel here. That's how they stay under the radar."

That worried Pennie more than Judy would ever know. "I'll keep tabs on her, but based on what I've learned so far, Bone Fox probably isn't a threat, and neither is Coach Ewers. I need to do a little more research on Toy Gunn. I haven't even started with the Reyes couple, and I haven't learned anything about who the Acevedos might be hiding, assuming it's not their daughter."

Judy briskly shook her head. "I don't know. We need to stay vigilant around the Acevedos. Machismo is deep rooted in the Dominican culture. It wasn't until 2003 that the government tried to correct for the chauvinistic traditions by creating safehouses for women and victims of domestic violence."

Dumbfounded, Pennie asked, "What do you mean? Didn't the government have any safeguards in place to protect victims prior to two decades ago?"

"Practically nothing. It still took until 2010 for them to rewrite the Constitution to *condemn* gender-based violence. You know they've been through thirty-nine constitutions since their independence in 1844?"

"Thirty-nine? Seriously?"

"Yep, and legislature to promote gender equality wasn't introduced until 2019."

"My mom always says, 'The proof is in the pudding.' Did their equality laws materialize into anything substantial?"

A slight laugh preceded Judy's response. "Nope, and my mom used to say, 'Show me your bank account, and I'll show you what you value.' For the Dominicans, only one percent of their national budget is allocated to the ministry of women. Regardless of laws they've passed, the numbers don't lie."

"That's rough, Judy. Okay, I'm keeping an eye on Oscar and Adriana. When I leave here today, I'll dig into Toy Gunn a little more. Then I need to figure out how to get a lead on the Reyes couple."

"Don't forget to talk to Pietra Russo and your ex. Just because they're cops doesn't mean they aren't up to something. Also, be careful with the Reyes. They were never violent offenders, but you don't know what someone's capable of until you back them into a corner."

For the second day in a row, Pennie drove to the Bartlett Fairways to scope out an apartment. Bone met her there this time, and they were permitted access to the leasing office. The lady took one look at Bone and spoke to him as if Pennie weren't in the room. The transition from stuffy administrator to purring kitten was immediate.

Pennie didn't judge. Bone had an undeniable magnetism. She spent the next thirty minutes feigning interest in floorplans and amenities, while another woman came through repeatedly to offer Bone water and refreshments, still not acknowledging Pennie. They toured a model and discussed leasing options. With Bone's input, they decided a twelve-month lease was ideal.

Pennie stayed behind to complete the paperwork so that Bone could view the actual apartment he selected. As soon as he left the room, the leasing manager asked, "So what's the deal with you and Mr. Fox?"

Choosing to have fun with the situation, Pennie waggled her eyebrows and replied, "He's my sugar daddy."

"Is he accepting applications?" she asked dreamily.

"Maybe. After he pays for this lease, I'll be moving on. Let me get my set of keys. When he comes back, he can finish the paperwork, while I take a look around the complex. That'll give you a few minutes alone with him."

Bone came back twenty minutes later, freeing Pennie to walk around on her own. The women in the office practically shooed her out.

Left unsupervised, Pennie didn't bother going to her new apartment on the sixth fairway. The leasing office wasn't far from the start of the golf course, which meant it wasn't far from the end either. Acting nonchalantly on the cart path, she moseyed to the eighteenth green. The buildings were all two stories, and no less than a dozen units had a balcony facing the green. She had no way of determining which apartment belonged to Toy.

That got her thinking, since thinking ahead of time hadn't happened so far. What would she do even if she knew which unit was Toy's? Would she break in and snoop around? Even without a plan, Pennie decided to find out what she could while she was here. A few golfers putted on the green to finish their game, but only the golfing enthusiasts would bother playing in hundred-degree weather. The area wasn't crowded.

Veering off the path, Pennie walked closer to the ground level balconies. The balcony doors featured large windows, and the first couple of apartments she observed left the windows unobstructed. One apartment had children's playthings strewn all over the balcony. The next window revealed an elaborate display of electronics—three televisions, karaoke machine, and video game consoles with controllers perched like precious gems in a museum. She couldn't definitively rule out that this was Toy's apartment, but she felt certain it wasn't.

On one hand, this was better than she expected. Using some personality profiling, she might figure out which apartment was her target. On the other hand, she couldn't get a glimpse of the second story apartments. Pennie glanced up and focused on the balconies across the green. A flash of red caught her eye. Houston Cougar red to be more specific.

One balcony was only adorned by two outdoor chairs, the ones you might use at a tailgate party. The bold "UH" emblazoned on the back gave it away. Now that she knew which apartment to focus on, Pennie had to figure out a way to get a peek inside. The next foursome of men took turns putting, but the area was abandoned otherwise.

Trying to avoid anyone's attention, she walked towards the other side of the green. Upon her arrival at the downstairs unit, she looked up. The posts appeared sturdy. Thanks to the angle of the building, she could approach the balcony from the side and not be in anyone's direct line of sight. Taking a firm grip on a post, Pennie pulled herself up to stand on the top rail of the bottom balcony.

Decorative woodworking around the corners of the frame gave her a solid handhold above her head. With one final glance to ensure no one watched, Pennie scrambled up until she could reach the rail on the upper balcony. Shimmying up a little farther, her head peeked over, providing her with a good view inside the apartment. Something didn't add up.

The comparison to a tailgate went way past collegiate chairs. Beer cans on the counters. A crumpled jersey on the floor. A foosball table was completely wrong for the dining area. Before she could notice any more details, her upper-body strength waned just a little. She tried to regrip it, but her sweaty hands failed.

Next thing she knew, Pennie was flat on her back on the ground, gasping for air. In a moment of panic, her whole body fixated on the pain and forgot how to breathe. Closing her eyes to the blurry trees above her, she tried to force oxygen into her lungs. A mental inventory of her limbs confirmed nothing was broken or paralyzed. She reached a hand out to grab the railing of the adjacent balcony. Realizing how far back she fell, Pennie needed to thank her lucky stars she didn't strike the rails or post on the way down.

Using the railing for support, she managed to pull herself up. Fortunately, no one lingered on the course to witness her tumble. Leaning on the rail for a moment, Pennie allowed her breathing to return to normal. In this same moment, she spotted a magazine on the table inside this balcony. Despite the guns and ammo theme of the magazine, the subscriber's name caught her attention—LaToya Gunn.

In a flash, Pennie remembered her mission. She found Toy's apartment. Raising her gaze to see what lay beyond the backdoor, she found a minimalist dining table. Past that, blank walls and a set of recliners. No décor. A television rested on a console table. Adjusting her view to see inside the kitchen, she noticed a movement from the opposite side of the living area.

She ducked down, hoping the railing and post might hide her well enough. From the shadows, a man emerged. He moved slowly just inside the living room and paused at the coat closet. Pennie couldn't get a good look at him once he opened the closet door, but the *Thunder Swarm* shirt was unmistakable.

Could this be the Wasp who's trying to locate Francelia? Was Toy harboring a terrorist?

Before Pennie's mind came up with a course of action, her phone rang. She ducked between the buildings before pulling the phone from her pocket.

"Pennie, did you already leave?" Bone asked.

"No, I'm just walking around. Do you have everything you need?"

"Yea, it's time to go."

That entire excursion to the Bartlett Fairways took a couple of hours. She didn't have time for much else before heading home. But it did allow for a small detour. Plugging in the address for the Reyes couple, Pennie followed directions to a residential area in East Memphis.

It wasn't really a subdivision, not a typical one with an ornate sign at the entrance. The modest houses were spaced out without any real landscaping in the shade of mature trees. She slowed the truck as it came closer to the address. A brick house with freshly painted trim and a small wooden porch sat on the lot. Some of the yards had chain-link fences, but the backyard of the Reyes family was protected by a wooden privacy fence.

The house had a one-car garage, and no vehicles were parked in the driveway. She assumed they were both at work. After easing into the driveway, Pennie put the truck in park. Could she peek through a window without anyone noticing? After her recent fall, she felt like playing it safe was the smart thing to do. But Francelia's life might be at risk. But they might have cameras. But...

A tapping on her driver's side window brought Pennie back to the present. The boy wore a FedEx hat, and a quick glance in her rearview mirror showed a delivery van on the street. She lowered the window enough to hear the driver ask her to move. She backed out of his way and watched as he unloaded several large boxes on the front porch.

Pennie couldn't help but wonder what she was doing. Just this week, she jumped a fence and almost got eaten alive by vicious dogs. She confronted a cantankerous coach alone in his office knowing he could've been a terrorist. She scaled a balcony to spy on the wrong apartment and almost broke her back when she fell. Now she was planning to get a look inside this house when she didn't have a clue how to proceed.

Some fine line exists between playing it safe and taking a chance. For the sake of Francelia, Pennie just needed to go home. Nothing could be gained here without breaking a law or two. She pulled away just in time to see an AC repair van heading towards her. Thomas sat in the driver's seat, making eye contact with Pennie as she passed. Her elevated heartrate wouldn't return to normal until she returned home.

As a treat for her household, Pennie ordered a bunch of food to go from Chipotle. Plus, she didn't quite feel like cooking, which was a sure sign that anxiety was taking its toll. Karolina looked like a kid at Christmas with her tofu bowl, and Francelia dug into the dinner indiscriminately.

As they finished eating the early dinner, Pietra found a news station that did a feature show dedicated to the crisis in the Dominican. Pennie had never heard of the host, but the sharp-tongued, assertive analyst reminded her of Judge Judy. All four women focused on the show to see what the journalist had to report.

Host Betsy Chase started the show with a few basic statistics. Up to seventy-six percent of the female population in the Dominican Republic had been a victim of some level of gender-based violence in recent years. Up to twenty-five percent had suffered from sexual violence. On top of that, the country existed as a hotspot for sex tourism for decades. Human trafficking and child exploitation were problems that went along with the prevalent sex industry. Betsy Chase practically growled when she shared the next statistic—twenty-five percent of all sex workers in the country were under the age of eighteen. This number made Pennie want to vomit.

Finally, in the post-dictatorship era of the nation, gender equality had become a serious topic within the government. Laws were passed. Their constitution was re-written… again. Equal opportunities were granted to women.

As expected, the overwhelming support of Daniela Vasquez and the Modern Revolutionary Party riled up some of the good ol' boys who weren't ready for a female leader. Protests took place. Misogynists became outspoken. But Vasquez won the election. Even though her transition to power was peaceful, the aftermath of the election results brought a level of hatefulness the country hadn't seen in decades.

Indirect threats from the anti-feminists were originally dismissed as intimidation tactics. Within a few months, things escalated to a new level of danger that the president's security team was forced to take seriously. Very specific death threats aimed at Francelia got everyone's attention. The womanhaters were labeled as terrorists, but they gained their own support from sexist extremists across the country. Adolfo Cabral, along with his brother Julio, managed to organize the *Mata Cacatas* into a cohesive group of machismo advocates.

As the leader of the group, Adolfo contended that his group only worked as activists to protect the core values of their great nation. Betsy Chase offered an exaggerated eye roll before continuing. Threatening to murder the president's daughter didn't line up with any core values she was familiar with. The history lesson provided by Chase ended with the current situation of the militant takeover and a big fat question mark of how this power grab might end.

When the commercials played at the end of the program, Pietra changed the channels. All four females in the living room were familiar with the Dominican history. Karolina encouraged Francelia to join her in the bunkroom for another music session. Within a few minutes, Pennie stared at the television blankly, humming along with the melody in the next room.

Because He lives, I can face tomorrow. Because He lives, all fear is gone.

Pietra continued to flip through stations in her attempt to find reputable news that might shed some light on the current situation at the National Palace. The repetitive stories and prerecorded scenes of Wasps surrounding the capitol building frustrated Pennie.

The ringing phone on the coffee table startled both women. Pennie immediately answered it on speakerphone so Pietra could join in the conversation with Ambassador Hernandez.

"Good evening, Pennie. Who do you have with you today?"

"It's just me and Pietra Russo right now. Francelia and Karolina are in another room."

"They don't necessarily need to hear this bit of news. I've been speaking to Victoria Peele in DC, and she's still under the assumption that our efforts to extract Francelia failed. She asked me about any other ideas to get Daniela and her daughter to safety. Of course, I don't have any ideas, but I was interested to hear what she might have to say on the subject. Aaaand..." Hernandez hesitated, carefully choosing her words.

Pietra jumped in, "What did she say?"

Pennie and Pietra shared a look of anticipation as

Hernandez audibly exhaled before answering.

"I didn't give anything away about Francelia or her location. Victoria called to tell me that she heard chatter about some Wasps being in the United States."

"Where are they? Who are they?" Pennie begged to know. She was already on the hunt for them, and now the government might provide a hint.

"I don't have that information. There is a database of known terrorists, but the Wasps haven't been extensively investigated. We simply don't know a lot about their identities or whereabouts. Some could have easily entered the USA legally without advertising their affiliation with the Wasps. Obviously, people enter the USA illegally every day. This information was gathered through special reconnaissance. We don't know who, where, or how many… I just wanted you to know the threat might be closer to home than we realized."

"Have you already called my boss? Chief Lawrence needs to be informed."

"I'm calling him next. I'm imploring you to be diligent. As soon as I know anything new, you'll be the next to know."

Pennie made sure her security system was armed, which it was. She made sure all the windows and doors were locked, which they were. What else could she do? The girls didn't pay any attention as they performed their instrumental version of the latest AmberLou song. Pietra made a phone call to Tony to see if he could find out anything new.

Eventually, the girls joined Pennie and Pietra in the living room, where they were told about the latest news.

Francelia seemed to handle it well. The thought of Wasps lurking around made everyone uneasy, but their plan of staying undiscovered didn't change. Pennie was the only one assuming any risk outside these four walls.

Earlier, Francelia exchanged *ReelLife* photos with her mother. Karolina took a picture of Francelia playing the piano to send. The return picture showed Daniela still wearing the colorful dress and holding a small drum in her lap. Cabral stood behind her, holding drumsticks in the shape of an "X" in front of her face.

"Is there some significance of the bongo drum?" Pennie asked, hoping to discover a clue.

"Not really. It's a *tambora,* though. That's a typical instrument of a merengue band. When the Merengue Festival starts next week, many performers will play *musica* around the city with this little drum and other small instruments like the accordion and the *güira.*"

Pietra studied the pictures for any insight. "I think Cabral is still reacting to your photos. You sent one with an instrument, so he replied in a similar fashion. We know that your mother still looks unharmed, and that's a current picture. Let's just be grateful for this information."

Before discussing the pictures any further, Pietra's phone rang. Tony was calling her back.

"Hey, Chief. I've got Pennie, Francelia, and Karolina with me."

Tony's rich baritone sounded just as soothing through a speakerphone as it did in real life. "I spoke to my cousin in the CIA after your call earlier. He did confirm that rumors are circulating about several Wasp members on US soil. Without concrete evidence, I can only tell you what the unofficial intelligence is reporting."

"Any heads up on our enemy is better than nothing,"

Pietra lamented. Pennie wanted the heads up more than either of them could fathom at this point.

"Unofficially," he emphasized that word, "the Wasps have sent two to four representatives of their little gang to Florida. They arrived at the same time you all got back from the cruise."

"That's logical," Pennie calculated. "Assuming they were waiting for her at the airport that day, they would've arrived in time to take her."

Tony continued, "We don't know where they've gone since then, but they're staying in the States until they can capture Francelia and take her back to the Dominican."

"Why so few men?" The question Pietra posed got Pennie wondering the same thing.

"Their numbers aren't that extensive, and they've only recently organized. Now this is only my humble opinion, but I think this uprising of the Wasps will burn out quickly. Even if the machismo attitude is still prevalent in the Dominican culture, the people won't tolerate this level of malevolence. The Dominican people are still in shock right now, but they'll get their bearings and get the country on the right track quickly after this situation resolves."

Pennie wanted to believe that. "How can you say that with such confidence?"

"The Dominican armed forces are already in place around the National Palace. They aren't being hasty to take things back by force because they believe Daniela and Francelia will be killed as soon as they make a move. I don't think they have any special forces to attempt this rescue."

"How would a country not have specialized forces? Are we the only ones with Seal Team Six?"

"Pennie, please quit watching military movies." Tony audibly exhaled. "They have specialized teams for border control, tourist protection, anti-terrorism, among other things. A rescue like this… they aren't prepared for it."

Francelia joined in, "We have the Presidential Security Corp to protect the president and her family. Where are they now?"

"It looks like enough of them resented having to protect a woman that they joined forces with the Wasps. As soon as the military gets control of the palace back from Cabral, the Wasps will turn tail and run back to the hills. My only concern is our domestic issue of keeping the younger Vasquez safe from harm. Regaining peace in the Caribbean is someone else's task. As of my most current information, up to four potential terrorists are in the States searching for Francelia. It's our job to make sure they don't find her."

"We're on lockdown, Chief. You know they won't find her because of our actions." Pennie said it like she meant it, but she wondered if her actions would help or hinder the situation.

Just as the women wound down for the evening, the news popped up with another live video from the terrorist who currently held the world's attention. His face filled the screen while the closed captions translated his latest message.

"Even though I've become closely acquainted with our dear President Vasquez, she still won't tell me where to find her daughter. This could all be over so quickly if Francelia would just come home."

The camera angle changed slightly to capture the heinous expression on Adolfo Cabral's face. "Just in case some

Americans are helping hide the first daughter, you might be interested in some bargaining. All the military and police officers who we captured during this takeover... I'm holding them hostage. Over fifty men. Not including the activists I've taken into custody over the years. I have almost one hundred men to trade for one insignificant female tiger. This is my best offer before I start executing people."

After he hissed that last sentence, the live feed was disconnected. All four women remained on the couch to see what might be reported next. The anchor asked questions of an unseen correspondent, seeking more information on Cabral. The screen eventually split so the anchor shared the television with an older man who claimed to be an expert in Dominican history. The two newspeople bantered with each other about the appalling situation before bothering to share any pertinent information.

"Why don't we see Julio Cabral in any of these videos?" Francelia asked, as if Pennie or Pietra might have any knowledge.

Pietra was the first to hazard a guess. "Maybe Julio is one of the Wasps here in our country."

"Based on the pictures I've seen, he isn't the guy who waited at baggage claim at the Miami airport," Pennie offered.

As usual, Pietra never wasted an opportunity to make Pennie feel stupid. "If Wasps intended to intercept Francelia at one of the busiest airports in the world, they wouldn't put Julio Cabral on display like that."

"Pietra, if he's one of only a few Wasps in the States, there's a pretty good chance it would've been him. I'm just saying it wasn't."

Their squabble ended when the self-proclaimed expert on TV shared some history on the Cabral brothers. After discussing their childhood and the death of their parents, the female anchor interrupted the monologue, "What about their current personal lives?"

"Well, Adolfo was briefly married, but his wife was brutally stabbed to death eleven years ago. It's assumed that Adolfo killed her, but charges were never brought against him."

The female again inserted herself, incensed about the treatment of women. "So, his wife became another statistic of femicide? That's it?"

The man held up his hands in surrender to the anchor's indignant tone. "The Dominican culture has made great strides in the past couple of decades, but it remains a work in progress. Neither brother is currently married. They have multiple illegitimate children from a variety of women. Their focus has strictly been on activism against the feminists of the country. Until their recent threats against the president, the men never appeared on the radar of the antiterrorism command. The military is forced to be very reactive instead of proactive with this current situation."

"The nation desperately needs to adopt a zero-tolerance policy against gender-based violence!"

The man responded, "They are constantly updating policy. The nation did just elect a female president."

The back and forth between the reporters didn't share anything else useful. Everyone was on edge. Pennie felt wound up even though it was bedtime.

"Mom," the sweet voice of Karolina halted the voices of vengeance and justice in Pennie's brain. "The issues are being addressed. The world recognizes the problem, and regardless of all the turmoil right now, good will come of this."

Pennie accepted a group hug from the two girls and went to bed to pray herself to sleep.

FRIDAY, JULY 22

Chip and Tony both arrived this Friday morning in Pietra's Ford Mustang. The flip flop of vehicles might never be straightened out. Now that everyone was aware of the Wasps' presence on US soil, the cops decided to tag team the security detail.

Francelia received her first *ReelLife* prompt before she even got out of bed. She showed Pennie and the two officers the photo exchange. First, Francelia's picture showed her resting her head on the pillow with her eye mask pushed up onto her forehead. The return picture showed Adolfo lying in bed also… right next to Daniela.

"Do you think he's forcing my mom to have sex with him?" she asked hesitantly, not really wanting to know the answer.

"No, honey. He's still reacting to your photo, sending similar images of his own," Pennie assured her as she pulled the girl into a hug.

Tony offered his own perspective, "Men like Cabral enjoy seducing women. They don't find any satisfaction in forced sex."

Pennie didn't bother arguing with him since his goal was to quell the disturbed girl. In her own research of machismo attitudes, rape was another form of control that men didn't hesitate to utilize. They would have no way of knowing if Cabral forced himself on Daniela, so there was no sense in spiraling into the worst-case scenario. That wouldn't benefit their situation in the least, and it wouldn't help the situation in the Caribbean either.

Pennie desperately wanted to keep Francelia calm even though there was some unseen timer in the universe... slowly ticking away for whatever dramatic ending this story might have. Thoughts of rape, dominance, violence—they needed to be pushed away.

An expected notification on Pennie's phone distracted her for a minute.

"Adriana just texted me and said she's going to open the nursery this morning. I won't have to go in until noon. It's only eight in the morning, guys. Let's have some coffee and get the day started."

Pennie sat between Chip and Tony on the back porch, watching the girls play fetch and tug with Peach. The dog was accustomed to higher levels of activity, as was Pennie. Her Krav Maga classmates sent several messages over the past week wondering when she would return. She'd only been on a couple of runs through the neighborhood, but Tony didn't allow it this morning after her shenanigans on Tuesday. She didn't have a good outlet for her pent-up aggression these days. And she was certain the girls were feeling pent-up on multiple levels.

"I have a question, guys. Everyone who knows me knows where I live. They know I have international students in and out of my house all the time. I'm not saying the girls should be going out without protection, but how is this better than us going out for lunch or whatever?"

Tony huffed. He appeared exasperated half the time when he answered Pennie's questions these days. "You aren't hiding. Francelia is. If the Wasps have any inside sources within our government, we don't want her parading around where cameras pick up her image. Same with Karolina. They look too much alike to take that risk, and I'd think you want to stay close to them."

He glanced down at the iPad in his lap to check out the front cameras before finishing his spiel. "We don't want to compromise any part of this protection detail by being lax in our day-to-day activities. We took a big enough risk leaving to get fast food last Thursday. Now the threat is closer than we expected, and keeping Francelia hidden is what you signed up for when you committed to keep her with you over a week ago."

Why did he have to make so much sense?

"You're right, Tony. This is about Francelia's safety and nothing else. I'm just feeling stir crazy, and I'm scared things will get worse before they get better. On top of that, I haven't been to Krav in a few weeks, so I'm suffering from hostility."

Tony nodded and rubbed his face with his hands. "We're all feeling some hostility. We're all scared, Pennie."

"Skipper, we've been following all the news coverage and getting updates from Ambassador Hernandez along the way. Let me tell you what scares me. As of yesterday, Cabral has made two separate references to a 'tiger' as if that's what he's chasing. Didn't that guy on the cruise ship call you 'Tiger' as your nickname?"

"Nick was referring to my Tigers tote bag I carried around the boat. It wasn't really a nickname, and he's not really a terrorist." She didn't really know Nick's stance on machismo attitudes, but she couldn't tip off Chip to her investigation with Judy.

"I heard him call you 'Tiger' on two occasions. Homegrown terrorists happen every day. You don't know anything about those guys, so you don't have any way of knowing if they've been radicalized into some extreme terrorist cell. We've already determined that misogyny and chauvinism exist everywhere. It's very plausible that your friend Nick and his brother are the Wasps on US soil. They arrived in Miami the same day we did, and they're the perfect candidates to remain under the radar of any government organization in the USA."

Even though Chip completely summed up her fears and touched on all the reasons she was investigating with Judy, Pennie still felt defensive.

Tony again huffed from his chair on her left. "Pennie. Why would you make friends on the cruise boat?"

"I didn't! Two guys immediately started talking to me and Karolina the first day. After it seemed like they were stalking us, we spent most of the cruise avoiding them. Even more so after we swapped Karolina for Francelia."

"Chip, what's your thinking? Did the men on the cruise ship appear to have any angle beyond socializing? Could they have been on the same cruise to the Dominican Republic for their own mission?"

The men spoke around Pennie as if she weren't there.

"I don't know, Chief. If they were deeply involved in any terrorist activity, they would've mistaken Karolina for Francelia from day one. Then their behavior would've gone beyond what I witnessed. If they're truly homegrown terrorists, they're just starting the radicalization process. They might've been meeting a contact in La Romana to become initiated into the Wasps."

"So, it's a true concern, but maybe not a high risk?" Tony asked.

"The only thing that has me concerned is the reference to her nickname."

Tony tried to make sense of the scenario. "That was almost twenty-four hours ago when he first used a 'tiger' reference. If they knew Pennie's identity, they'd already be here, scoping out her home and her company."

"Guys, I'm sitting right here, and I'd like to offer my own input. If y'all think Nick and JJ pose some kind of threat, you should know that JJ's been in contact with Karolina on her social media. They live in Louisiana, somewhere around New Orleans. See if you can get someone to check on their whereabouts." Pennie would invite some professional help with her little investigation if she could.

While Tony moved inside to call his cousin in the CIA, Chip started a new conversation with Pennie.

"Are either of these girls prepared to defend themselves? Has Karolina ever taken a Krav class with you?"

"No, Karolina likes to lift weights, but she's never done any self-defense training. I don't know anything about Francelia's abilities."

"We could do something about that. Do you have any sparring gear, kick shields, or other padded targets?"

Pennie grinned and made eye contact with Chip. "Of course I have sparring gear. I also have focus mitts, a punching bag, and an amazing kick shield that someone gave me as a Valentine's gift."

He winked in response. "Then let's come up with a self-defense routine starting right now."

They all changed into some workout clothes. Fortunately, Chip brought a gym bag with his own sweats and sneakers. The girls looked excited to take out some nervous energy on the punching bag that Chip moved into the middle of the yard. Pennie was glad for the opportunity to work out the stiffness she felt from her fall off the balcony yesterday.

Tony resumed his seat on the back porch to watch Pennie and Chip teach basic defense moves to the amigas. They covered the correct way to punch, jab, block, duck, and weave. A few kicks were added to the mix. Pennie's personal favorites were knee and elbow strikes. As much as they all needed the workout, the July heat was kicking their butts.

Back inside for a cool down and some water, Tony shared what he learned earlier.

"Without infringing on anyone's privacy, we managed to confirm that JJ and Nick are both at their East Carrollton home in New Orleans. Nicolas Lee Bell and little brother James Jackson Bell have clean background checks."

Karolina seemed upset at this news. "Why are you checking up on them? They didn't do anything wrong."

His baritone cadence calmed the Brazilian before she could get too wound up. "We're just trying to identify all the threats, Karolina. No one has accused them of anything. You didn't hear our discussion earlier about Adolfo Cabral making two references to a tiger. Since Nick used 'Tiger' as a nickname for Pennie, we wanted to rule that out quickly. We just requested that an NOPD officer drive by their house, and they found both men unloading groceries. The officers didn't stop or ask any questions. The background check was a cursory look to make sure nothing stood out. This is all for your protection."

"So, no one questioned them or did anything to embarrass them?" Karolina interrogated the chief.

Pennie resumed her role as Mom and answered instead of the chief, "This isn't a line of questioning you get to ask, Karolina. There is a serious terrorist predicament happening right now in the Dominican Republic, and the threat reaches all the way to our front door. Even if the police chose to detain those boys for the day, it's a small price to pay to keep you safe. When Chief Lawrence entertains you enough to share that kind of information with you, then you need to thank him, not drill him for information to justify his decisions."

"Sorry, Mom. Thank you, Chief Lawrence."

Despite the obedient response, Karolina sulked as she went back outside. Francelia followed her.

"Tony, I'm so sorry for her insolence. She isn't usually like that. I think the anxiety is getting to her."

"I know she's a very respectful young lady, but I appreciate that you took charge of the situation. You'll make a good mother one of these days." His ravishing smile along with the compliment made Pennie a little jealous of whoever his fiancée might be.

Standing, Chip said, "I'm going to give the girls a pep talk, then we can do some grappling. They need to have some kind of defense in case they get taken to the ground."

"The next time I have to send a *ReelLife* picture, can someone get a shot of me punching this bag?" Francelia asked as a scowl took over her face.

"Girl, you don't want to see what Cabral would send in return to that one."

"You're right, Momma Pennie. I just want to do something helpful."

Chip's sexy, Southern drawl gave the girl some direction. "You already snuck out of the National Palace garbage can, made it through checkpoints on a hostile highway, and assumed someone else's identity to get out of your country. Your mother is better off mentally knowing you're safe right now. So, if you want to be helpful, you need to learn some defense tactics to stay safe."

The girl nodded and gritted her teeth. Chip went through a few explanations of escaping from varying holds from the ground. He reiterated a few things to keep in mind. "If you're in a fight for your life, you're gonna get hurt. Fighting through the pain is key. Anything you can do to give yourself an advantage, you need to do it without hesitation. I've said it before, and I'll say it again. If you ain't cheatin', you ain't tryin'."

As the girls watched, Chip had Pennie lie back on the ground so he could instruct them on different escapes. Pennie's brain knew this wasn't the time or place, but the sweat rolling down Chip's strong jawline along with his intense virility... dang it. The butterflies in her belly were sweating bullets. It's a good thing her face was already flushed from the heat, or the blush might've completely embarrassed her.

Karolina insisted that he was teaching them Brazilian Jui-Jitsu, and she was already an expert. Pennie had no idea. She sat up when Chip moved away from her to ask, "Seriously, Karolina, when did you learn Jui-Jitsu?"

"I'm Brazilian, Mom. We did Jui-Jitsu after school every day. It's part of our culture. I went to classes until I came here to live with you."

As a test, Pennie put Karolina in a few compromising positions. She easily rolled out of each hold and counteracted with a submission hold. Impressed, Pennie increased the pressure of her attacks. Again, the girl easily escaped each one. When she wanted to really push Karolina, she told her to lie flat on her belly as if she had been tackled. Pennie mounted her back to put her in a rear naked choke hold. As one of the most inescapable submission holds, she contemplated how Karolina might escape.

Immediately, Karolina tried to find some leverage to roll them over, but the attempts weren't successful as Pennie had twenty-five pounds on her tiny daughter. She grabbed at Pennie's arms without any favorable outcome. Pennie maintained the hold securely without hurting the girl. As she shifted to regrip tighter, Karolina made a quick move that Pennie didn't expect.

In the next moment, Karolina pushed her closed hand backwards, nearer to Pennie's face and opened it to reveal a cricket. The disgusting bug jumped straight at her mouth. With a retching noise, Pennie rolled off and stood up as quickly as possible.

"Mom, it's just a cricket!" Karolina laughed from the ground, but Pennie couldn't hear over her own dry heaving.

"Come on, Mom. If you ain't cheatin', you ain't tryin'." She giggled at her exaggerated fake Southern accent. "That's what Chip said, and I know you're scared of crickets."

Finally getting the retching feelings under control, Pennie answered hoarsely, "That's a plague-infested, nasty, repulsive devil-spawn. I'll have you deported if you ever pull a stunt like that again."

The girls laughed at Pennie's pain. Chip had already formed a new strategy for their lesson.

"Karolina, I'm astonished. Your muscle memory isn't failing at all," Chip said as he reconsidered their mode of teaching. "Now, I'll tell you what attack to perform on Francelia, and we'll walk her through each defense. We'll start off slow and make her work for it as we progress."

Francelia enjoyed the physical practice, and eventually, Pennie became the attacker to add some weight and resistance to the drills. Before going much longer, Tony stepped out the back door and encouraged everyone to come inside.

The blast of cold air brought a wave of relief to the overheated foursome, but it was short lived. They all gathered around the television to see Cabral's latest message. Tony rewound live TV so they could watch from the beginning. With the close-up view of the terrorist, Pennie could easily see the crazy in his eyes before he spoke.

"This is a week of celebration for the Dominican Republic. The Merengue Festival starts tomorrow evening, and our streets will be filled with parades, music, and dancing. Inside the National Palace, twenty-four hours from now, I'll start my own festival. This establishment will be filled with pain, screaming, and death. I'm tired of the people saying they don't negotiate with terrorists. I'm not a terrorist. I'm an activist who wants what's best for his country, and female leadership is not what we need."

The camera panned out to show Daniela seated in a chair next to him. "If the elusive Francelia comes home between now and five p.m. on Sunday, I'll graciously let the women live in jail rather than be executed. That gives the Tiger over two days, but if she hasn't revealed herself by then, Daniela and all my hostages will be executed for the world to witness."

The commentators on the news program mostly filled the airtime with jibber jabber. They asked the same questions that were on everyone's minds. *Where was Francelia? Will the US intervene? Will Daniela be murdered on live television? How many hostages did Cabral really have?*

Oh, and one other question... *Why did Cabral keep referring to Francelia as a tiger?*

The darkened expression on Tony's face revealed his state of mind before he spoke. "Francelia, can you think of any reason he's calling you a tiger? You might be the only one who can shed some light on this, and we need all the insight we can get right now."

She slowly shook her head. "I can't think of any reason. Honestly."

"This is the second time he's issued a time limit, so that's a sign of him becoming desperate. I still don't think he'll do anything rash before he locates you," Tony consoled the girl who might be on the verge of a panic attack.

"Francelia, why don't you take a long shower? We'll eat a quick lunch after you've cleaned up and cooled down."

Karolina occupied the hall bathroom so Francelia could decompress in Pennie's shower. When the girls were both out of earshot, it was time to have an adult conversation.

"Okay, guys. These *tiger* references are totally freaking me out. Is there any conceivable way to figure out what he's talking about?"

"Not that I can think of," Tony responded. "When I spoke to my cousin earlier, I asked him about it too, and he had no input either. He might be quoting the 'catch a tiger by its toe' rhyme; it might not be anything."

"I don't like it either," Chip said. "But I really don't like this new deadline. I agree that Cabral is getting desperate, but I suspect he's going to do something stupid forty-eight hours from now. He's been sitting still for the past two days, and he's gotta make a move to maintain his control."

The conversation remained grim for the next half hour. Ambassador Hernandez called but promised to call back later when the girls would be available to talk. Without anything new to share, she only wanted to check on Francelia's well-being.

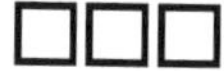

As much as she hated to leave, Pennie had to go to work. A late start to the day gave her some extra quality time with the girls this morning, but it cut into her investigating time. Mostly, she felt frustrated because she wasn't quite sure where to go with her part of the research. Judy was still concerned about the Acevedos. Pennie still needed to get a visual on Cynthia to confirm her presence in Bartlett, but she felt confident they weren't participating in anything malevolent.

During the past few days, she'd cleared Coach Richard Ewers along with his compadres, Ricky and Manny Guzman. Frank Fox was also cleared along with his old coworker, Diego Castellanos. Chip and Pietra found their way to Judy's list, but Pennie didn't need to, nor did she want to, dig into their relationship at all.

This left Toy Gunn along with the two Dominicans she brought back to the States. With her own eyes, Pennie witnessed a man in Toy's apartment wearing a *Thunder Swarm* shirt. Even though she had no way of knowing if this superhero wasp shirt had anything to do with terrorists, it still gave her the creeps. How could she find out more about Toy's dealings outside of work?

Also remaining on her list of potential terrorists were Thomas and Jamie Reyes. Thomas worked for an AC company. What were the chances of getting Thomas to repair her AC if she broke it on purpose? What possible scenario could she come up with to visit Jamie in the tool plant she worked for?

Without coming up with any suitable course of action for when she had another chance to investigate, Pennie pulled into the parking area at Avocado Farms. Most of the entrance area was congested with more rectangular bundles of hay. Adriana met her as she exited the truck to go over the goals for the day.

"I have two more truckloads of hay being delivered. Can you get it all relocated to the other side of the property? Next week, I want to use the bales to map out the future hayride, displays, and exhibits. Also, that reporter lady keeps coming around, but I asked her to leave us alone. You can kick her out if she shows up again today."

"Sure, is there anything else I need to do?"

Adriana shook her head, "No, Lupe has everything watered. Clearance plants are marked. I'm meeting with a construction company Monday morning to add a second parking area and road entrance on the opposite side of the property."

Pennie spent the next couple of sweaty hours loading and relocating hay. After the workout this morning, and the soreness from her couple of tumbles this week, she decided to take a break in the cashier shack. Perched on a stool, she leaned her head back against the wall, enjoying a little bit of relief offered by the box fan.

The whirring of the fan had just lured her into a trance when a male voice broke the spell.

"I believe you have exactly what I'm looking for."

She opened her eyes to see Thomas Reyes in the window of the shack. Before she could answer, he spoke again. "Where have I seen you before?"

She didn't reply, waiting for him to recognize her as the one snooping in his neighborhood yesterday. His eyes squinted, and he reached his hands into his pants pockets. Pennie slowly leaned forward to see how close she could get to the shotgun.

"I'm serious. What's your name? Where do I know you from?"

He eased his left hand out of the pocket about the time Pennie's fingers touched the cool steel of the shotgun barrel. It wasn't her gun. She'd never shot it. But she had to hope it was loaded and reliable because her life, and life of a defenseless Dominican, might depend on it.

Then he raised a vaping device to his mouth. Through a puff of smoke, he asked, "Didn't you work at the BARK animal shelter?"

The vape wasn't deadly, but she didn't know what his right hand might be reaching for. Her own hand remained on the shotgun. He looked so familiar. His Pacific Islander face and long beard with hints of grey. His keen brown eyes. Pennie affirmed his question with a quick nod, but she still hadn't found her voice.

"That's right. I've seen you at the shelter a few times."

She still couldn't place him. Her hand traced the barrel until it found the grip and the trigger guard. "Why were you at the shelter?" she asked, hoping to find out more before the situation turned violent. Slowly wrapping her fingers around the grip, she waited for his answer.

"My wife and I transport dogs, you know? When that shelter in Arkansas was damaged by the tornado a couple of years ago, we delivered about fifty dogs and cats to BARK. Then we picked up some from New Orleans after a hurricane last year. Just a week ago, we flew to the Caribbean to escort twenty dogs back to the States."

"Dogs?" Pennie couldn't believe her ears. She dropped her hand from the shotgun.

His right hand appeared holding nothing more than a wallet. "Yea. The shelter in Ohio isn't ready for these dogs yet, so we're keeping them at our house for another week. It's too early in the year for stores to sell hay, but I noticed yesterday that you got a load in. That's just what I need to spread out in my backyard runs and dog houses."

Pennie's frazzled brain could barely comprehend. One minute ago, she was convinced that she might have to defend herself with deadly force. Now, she knew Thomas and his wife were the opposite of terrorists. "How did you get started transporting animals?"

"I made a few mistakes in my youth. My wife and I both did. We were partners in crime before we made some changes. We got arrested, and it scared us straight. Since then, we started legitimate careers and had a couple of kids. They're grown up now, but my daughter signed us up to help animals fifteen years ago. Now, we do it because we love it. It keeps us grounded."

Pennie sold him some hay, helped him load it, and tried to get her agitated braincells back in line. The investigation, along with its direct bearing on her home, drove her bat crap crazy. Ever since she got home with Francelia, Pennie feared danger lurking around every corner. She saw potential terrorists everywhere she turned around.

Was this fear healthy? Did it keep her ready to defend her home? Or was it chipping away at her sanity?

Before her nerves had a chance to settle, Judy Thomas made another visit. Pennie recounted what she knew about Thomas and Jamie Reyes. Then she shared the details from her field trip to Toy's apartment, and how she saw a man wearing a *Thunder Swarm* shirt. Judy assured her that she was doing a great job. Then Judy mentioned she had a few promising leads without elaborating.

Pennie just wanted to go home. To spend a quiet weekend on lockdown to refresh her perspective. If the terrorists weren't located and arrested by Monday, she'd come up with a new angle to research Toy Gunn, the final suspect on her list.

The girls retired to the bunkroom after dinner. Pennie sat on her recliner in the living room with Chip and Tony, attempting to unwind her mental state. The news droned on with nothing new.

Just when Pennie thought they might have a quiet evening, Francelia ran into the room moaning, holding her phone in front of her. "Look, he sent a picture."

Hearing the distress in her friend's voice, Karolina followed her to the living room.

"Look!" she shrieked again.

Francelia's picture was a selfie in the bathroom mirror. She already wore her pajamas, and nothing appeared in the background except for a framed picture of a peony flower. The return image showed a bathroom selfie, but the bathroom was full of marble and heavy wood trim. Cabral took the selfie with Daniela seated on the side of a clawfoot tub behind him. In place of the festive Merengue dress she wore earlier, a long, black dress now hung shapelessly over her body.

Pennie's mind immediately decided Cabral had dressed Daniela for her funeral. Rather than voicing her morbid thoughts, she kept her mouth shut. Nothing else stood out about this picture. It was just a bathroom selfie in response to the one Francelia sent.

"Oh hell." Tony's whispered exclamation surprised Pennie. What did he see?

"He's going to torture her!" Francelia screamed.

Pennie still studied the picture until she found it. A small black and white box on the counter. She couldn't read the Spanish label or description on the box. The words weren't big enough to read in any language. But the warning symbol for a corrosive substance was universal. It was some kind of acid. Her heart fell in her chest at the thought of Daniela being afflicted with that kind of agony.

Once again, they surrounded Francelia with a group hug. Tony murmured reassurances about empty threats. Meanwhile, Chip offered his own assertions that Daniela was mentally strong and beyond intimidation.

A call from Ambassador Hernandez prompted the girl to control her breathing and get a grip.

"Hola, amorcito. ¿Como estas?"

"I'm scared, *Señora*," Francelia softly said. She recounted the details about the container of sulfuric acid in the latest photo. The ambassador offered similar soothing statements about Cabral being a coward. Only a few quiet tears fell as she accepted the encouragement. The call lasted less than five minutes since nothing could be solved.

Pennie took Francelia back to the bathroom to blow dry her hair and talk about her childhood. Francelia shared tidbits about playing card games with her parents. She smiled as she recalled her first musical recital where her father proudly watched from the front row. Everything remained peaceful until she turned ten.

Her dad had already been an activist, working tirelessly to empower women. When he was abducted, her mother went on a warpath to champion his cause. As proud as she was of her mother, and as much as she desired this change in her country, Francelia missed the untroubled days of her childhood. Pennie let the conversation end there, on the pleasant memories rather than anything beyond that.

They all moved to the breakfast table to play Uno and distract themselves from any pending deadline or potential torture. Karolina spoke more than usual, sharing all her experiences as an international student. She relished the opportunity to become a diplomat for future exchange students. The overachieving Brazilian created her own *TikTok* page to help new students assimilate.

Intrigued, and obviously needing her own diplomat, Francelia asked, "How can you help students adjust to life in the States when you're not American?"

"I forget I'm a foreigner sometimes. As soon as I knew what high school I'd be attending, I found some classmates on social media. Within twenty-four hours of landing in Memphis, I went to my first volleyball practice at school. I joined every extracurricular club. I made a variety of friends... athletes, musicians, intellectuals, teachers... I accepted the culture as my own from day one. Mom and Daddy Johnny supported me. They drove me to all my events. They allowed me to travel with them. We did cruises, camping, weekend trips to Gatlinburg and Hot Springs. They even let me ride with a friend's family to the beach one year."

Pennie saw the wheels turning in Francelia's mind. The freedom and opportunity she had never been afforded. The girl asked, "How did you learn to drive? When did you get a car?"

Karolina grinned. "Mom made me take lessons through a driving school. When I got my license, she became my passenger and let me drive around the city in an old minivan she bought from a neighbor. When I graduated high school, she bought me the Camaro as a gift."

"If you didn't have a car, how would you go to college?

How could I go to college?"

"Most universities have an international department that gives students a ride to and from the airport, and they coordinate transportation to the store a couple of times a week. Most international students who come here for college don't have a car or a host family. They completely depend on the school for the things they need. That's why I bring so many friends home, and I help anyone who needs anything. I know I'm blessed."

Then Pennie noticed something new in Francelia's eyes. Hope. This terrible situation might become the catalyst for a future she never dreamed was possible. A chime from Pennie's iPad disrupted their dinner talk.

"Dammit," Tony muttered as he got up from the dining room table.

"Do we need to hide?" Pennie asked to his back as he went to open the front door.

Pietra entered with a casserole dish in her hands. "I just thought I'd bring a treat since I know this has been a stressful day."

She placed the dish on the table and removed the top to reveal cinnamon rolls. "I made them from scratch."

"You know Pillsbury makes them in a can? They're ready in fifteen minutes that way," Chip said.

"I thought you might like a homemade dessert. I don't get many opportunities to bake for people, and I wanted to try this new recipe I found."

Everyone except for Karolina dug in and complimented the sweet treat before Chip escorted Pietra outside. Pennie knew what was happening. That competitive wench was trying to prove to Chip how domestic she could be even though she didn't have a domestic bone in her body.

Then thoughts of a honeybee flitted through Pennie's mind... Upon stinging its enemy, the honeybee would proudly end its life to bring someone that small amount of pain. Tonight, Pennie could relate to that level of pettiness.

Instead of dwelling on the pettiness, she said goodnight to Tony and the girls without waiting for Chip to come back inside. She was beyond stressed out from hiding a foreign refugee. The investigation was over her head, but she had to try. Then this ridiculous, fictitious competition over Chip when he had already chosen to be with Pietra. *Ugh*. This might be a good night to start drinking except that Pennie didn't keep alcohol in the house. A long lavender shower was her only reprieve before diving into bed for the night.

SATURDAY, JULY 23

Going to bed in a fit of jealousy guaranteed that Pennie would wake up to a sink full of dirty dishes. She never left dishes in the sink before, and she shouldn't allow a trivial grudge against Pietra to bring her down to begin with. Here it was, seven in the morning… way too early to be clenching her teeth while Pietra and Cole switched places with Tony and Chip. Since the vehicle swap situation was so messed up now, it seemed like the teams of two would only be driving Pietra's Mustang to and from Pennie's house each morning. Before she could finish wiping down the counters, her phone rang.

"Hey, Jenna! What's going on?"

"That floozy is what's going on! I can't believe I trusted him!"

The growling in her ear made Pennie pull the phone back for a second. "Hang on… Who? What? Huh?"

"Ooh, Cole was so smooth last week, telling me that Pietra wanted to drive his Tesla to see if she liked it before buying one, so they swapped vehicles for the day. But today… I'm driving down Highway 64 to take Dolly to the vet, and who do I see? Who, Pennie? Who do you think?"

She snuck back to her bedroom before answering, "Um, I'll go out on a limb and say you saw Cole?"

"Not only Cole! I saw Pietra too, and they were both in her car. I wanted to turn around and follow them, but I couldn't do a U-turn in time. I just now pulled into the parking lot at the vet's office. Do you think the doctor here might give me some valium?"

The anger in her best friend's voice was seriously concerning. "Did you try to call Cole? I'm sure there's a logical explanation."

"Are you listening to me? Cole told me his stupid bodyguard shifts changed to twenty-four hours on and twenty-four hours off until the assignment is completed. But instead of being on the way to work, he's cruising around with that harlot!"

"While I find it amusing that you're using the term for a fifteenth-century prostitute, I think you're overreacting before finding out the whole story. Cole would never do anything shady, Jenna. Just please—"

"Quit defending him! I'll find him later, and I'll castrate him with my bare hands! Look, I've gotta get Dolly checked in for her appointment now, so I'll call you later." Click.

"Cole, you should know that Jenna saw you riding in Pietra's car this morning. She's on the verge of homicide." Pennie watched Cole's eyes widen as he sucked in a breath.

He set down his freshly poured cup of coffee. "Do you think she'd believe that Pietra and I are doing the security detail together? I don't want to lie to her, but I can't reveal anything else."

Pietra sauntered over to fill her own mug, lightly touching Cole's forearm with her fingertips. "Cole, if she doesn't trust you, that's her problem. You shouldn't be dating someone who jumps to conclusions and flips out like that."

"Pietra Russo!" Pennie blurted out. "You back away from Cole right now and quit acting like the harlot that everyone already thinks you are."

"Harlot?! You need to get your imagination under control. Just because you weren't woman enough to hold onto Chip doesn't mean you have to be jealous of me. So quit your name calling and grow up."

Pennie's temper was getting the better of her. She wanted nothing more than to beat Pietra into a greasy spot on the kitchen floor, but that wouldn't be a good showing of women supporting women. Deeply inhaling through her flared nostrils, Pennie opted for a better approach. "Pietra, relationships are hard enough without you messing with them. I've been intentional about not interfering with you and Chip, and you need to offer them the same respect. I won't have it under my roof."

With that, Pennie retreated to her bedroom. At least the younger amigas weren't up to witness that trifling exchange. A hot shower helped get her blood pressure under control, but the heart burn was relentless these days.

She returned to the kitchen a half hour later to find everyone eating cereal at the breakfast table. Pennie took an antacid and put some bread in the toaster. It was disconcerting to her that no one was talking. Everyone was frazzled. The mental well-being of everyone in this room had paid a price to keep Francelia safe. Raw nerves made things terribly uncomfortable for the forced company.

Even though her nerves had settled just a little, Pennie still felt like a ticking time bomb. Weeks of pushing down her frustration and anxiety resulted in some kind of internal sickness that she'd never experienced before. Despite her own choices to keep a young girl safe from death threats, Pennie was becoming infected with the noxious situation. A lingering headache from clenched teeth had to be the number one symptom of her sickly state.

When the toast popped up, Pennie ate it dry, swallowing it down with some water. She didn't need any coffee to exasperate the heartburn. Something had to give, and it had to give soon.

Then her phone rang.

"Hey, Adriana."

"Hola, Pennie. Do you have a free minute? I need some help with a couple of decisions here at the nursery. It won't take long."

Getting out of the house might be just what she needed this morning.

The nursery was vacant at eight in the morning. Turning off the truck engine, she slowly exited her vehicle.

"*Hola*, Pennie!" Adriana waved from the cashier shack.

She walked over to speak to her boss but stopped dead in her tracks when she saw who accompanied Adriana.

"Hey there, Tiger!" He stood there with a cocky smirk on his face, matching his little brother's dimpled smirk beside him.

"Nick. JJ. What're you doing here?"

"Karolina didn't want to share your address so we could surprise you at home, so we found out where you worked. It was easy after she sent a picture wearing an Avocado Farms shirt." His creepy grin evoked Pennie's fight or flight response.

Pennie scanned the area for something she could use as

a weapon. She wasn't close enough to the koi pond to grab a loose stone, and the brother stood between her and the cashier station. Adriana wouldn't have known the threat they posed, and now Pennie needed to figure this out on her own. She couldn't let these potential terrorists get close to Karolina or Francelia. Could she outrun them and get to her truck to escape and call for help? Her slow step backwards only invited Nick to take a step forwards.

"Why are you playing hard to get with us? Why didn't you bring Karolina with you?"

He must think Karolina and Francelia were the same person. Pennie didn't know how to react, so she took another step backwards.

Nick lunged forward to grab her arm. "Don't run away from me..."

Poor Nick. He had no idea about the frustrated destroyer that lived inside Pennie this morning. Some of the events that followed would be forever lost to her rage-induced blackout. She didn't remember wailing on Nick, but she regained her senses as she straddled him on the ground. Still using his face as a punching bag, JJ tried to grab her in a bear hug from behind to stop the assault.

With more than a little fury to spare, Pennie slammed the back of her head towards his face, effectively crushing JJ's nose. He let go of the bear hug long enough for Pennie to turn around and knee him square in the groin. With a high-pitched screech, he fell hard on the ground.

"What's wrong with you?" Nick shouted from his own spot on the ground.

Pennie stood back and looked at the guys she had just beaten down. A renewed flood of consciousness revealed a lot of things. She didn't lack confidence when it came to self-defense, but she couldn't have single-handedly fought off two terrorists. Nick and JJ were both coherent. If they were here with any evil intentions, they'd both still be on their feet and fighting harder. The last minute went by with only the brothers defending themselves, not trying to harm or subdue Pennie. She had just unleashed her demons on two men who were only seeking friendship even though they were going about it in a creepy way.

She looked up to see Adriana standing a few feet away with her hands on either side of her face. With Pennie's slightly blurred vision, Adriana appeared to be the subject of *The Scream* as painted by Edvard Munch. She took a few deep breaths.

"Nick, I'm so sorry," she whispered, hoping it was loud enough for him to hear.

The brothers slowly got to their feet, maintaining a little distance from the lunatic they came here to meet.

"Seriously, I'm sorry. I don't know what came over me."

Nick shook his head. His face was covered in red whelps. His little brother still clenched his legs from the crotch shot while blood gushed from his nose.

"Why?"

She needed a cover story. What would warrant her display of violence? "I've been getting some anonymous threats lately. If you want to call the cops, I understand. I... I... I have no excuse for my behavior."

Pennie found herself up a creek with no paddle in sight. If she were arrested for assault, the felony on her record would ensure she'd never be able to host another exchange student or serve at her church again. Francelia's safety would be compromised. Adriana would fire her.

"The cops? I'm not admitting that a girl just kicked my ass. I thought we had a connection, and you were just playing hard to get. I didn't realize you were psycho. Look, we'll leave you alone. Come on, JJ."

They retreated to a parked car on the street without looking back.

Adriana found her voice. "Pennie, what was that about?"

"I'm dealing with some stuff, like a stalker, and it's not something I can talk about. The police are already involved, Adriana. I just acted out of fear, and I'm sorry you had to see that."

"No, *amiga*. I'm sorry. They looked like nice boys. I let them convince me that they met you on the cruise, and they wanted to see you again. This was supposed to be a nice surprise. I shouldn't have gone along with that. I should've told you why I wanted you to come here so you could decide for yourself."

"Thanks for understanding. I'm sure now that they didn't pose any threat, so you didn't do anything wrong. And they didn't lie about anything. The only one who messed up today was me. I'll work harder to keep the crazy under control."

Adriana offered a hug, consoling Pennie for a moment. "It's okay. I didn't realize you were dealing with these things. Try to have a peaceful day and let me know if you need anything."

Sitting back in the driver's seat, Pennie allowed the AC to blast her in the face for a few minutes. Guilt. Humiliation. Frustration. Shame. Confusion. The whirlwind of feelings suffocated her. The Metallica song that hyped her up earlier only served to intensify the negative feelings now. She flipped the station until she found some hallelujah music. Time to roll the windows down and put the truck in reverse... Backing away from the situation was all she could do now.

Another level of shock brought about some sudden tears before Pennie even took her foot off the brake. The hands that gripped her steering wheel were now skinned and red from the physical attack that she inflicted on the undeserving victims. Then she realized her yoga pants were covered in dirt and ripped at the knees. A glance in the mirror revealed the wild state of her hair. The tangible evidence of her behavior was worth shedding a few tears over. But not here.

A few minutes later, Pennie found herself at Freeman Park, next to the same baseball fields where they ate lunch earlier in the week. A team of teenagers practiced softball while the coaches pointed and yelled at players as they saw fit. Pennie rolled up the windows and turned the AC back on. Leaning her head back, she allowed herself a few minutes of crying. No heaving sobs. Just quiet tears rolling down her cheeks.

Watching the girls playing ball, Pennie took a trip down memory lane. Her father taught her the fundamentals of the game. He took her along with her three siblings to the ball fields to practice every day during the summers, then he took them for milkshakes after the intense practice sessions. This gave her mom time alone at home to clean or take a bubble bath. Honestly, Pennie had no idea what her mom did during those hours.

The sniffles brought her back to the present. Nick was a nice guy who enjoyed cruising and valued family. Instead of getting to know him, she beat the snot out of him. This certainly wasn't the best way to start a relationship. Within the next decade, Pennie wanted to be sitting at these same ballfields, watching her first-born child playing tee-ball. She wanted her future husband to teach their children how to play sports, while Pennie stayed home to do yardwork.

Instead of being lost in thought about future kids, Pennie needed to focus on the two children who currently lived under her roof. Two girls who needed security, love, encouragement, and guidance. The way Pennie acted today, she wasn't the best role model for anyone. This was the wake-up call she needed. It was time to operate with an even keel. Stop being so offendable. No more acting rashly.

Finally, she aimed her truck in the direction of home. The clock on her dash showed 8:58. That was a lot of crap to go through for not even nine in the morning.

"Mom, are you okay?" Karolina asked as Pennie entered through the garage.

"I'm fine, but I don't want to talk about it."

"Pennie, what happened?" Cole asked. He appeared concerned.

"Seriously, Pennie." Pietra sounded more condescending than concerned.

"I just want to take another shower. I'll explain later."

Another shower. More antacids. More aspirin. This absolutely wasn't a healthy cycle to be in. Leaving her hair wet, Pennie returned to the living room to face what she felt would be an execution.

Cole and Pietra sat in recliners, watching the news. Peach sprawled on the floor at Cole's feet.

"Where are the girls?" Pennie asked.

"They're giving themselves manicures so we can talk without them. You ready to explain?" Pietra asked.

She perched on the coffee table where she could face both officers. "I'm mortified with everything that's transpired this morning, guys. We may need to involve Tony and rethink this plan after I tell y'all about it."

Before she could share the first detail, her iPad sounded. The security system alerted her that someone pulled into the driveway. Pennie rushed to the window to see a dalmatian jumping out of an Infiniti. "Jenna's here. Y'all need to get out of sight."

Cole and Pietra ducked into the bunkroom where the amigas were busy choosing nail polish colors. Pennie allowed her best friend and Dolly in the front door to find that Jenna might have been crying this morning also.

"Jenna, what's wrong? Is Dolly okay?" Pennie watched as Peach and Dolly romped through the living room and ran laps of excitement.

"She's fine." That was all Jenna said as she entered the kitchen to pour some coffee. The cops must have made a fresh pot before being banished to the bunkroom. Pennie got a cup as well.

They sat at the breakfast table and stared out the windows for a minute before either of them spoke again. Some clouds appeared on the horizon. A storm was brewing, but it couldn't compare to the hurricane of lunacy inside Pennie's head. And any pending storm couldn't compare to the gale-force madness that gleamed in Jenna's eyes right now either.

"Have you been at the vet's office all this time? What's going on with Dolly?"

"She was due for a recheck after the rounds of heartworm treatment. I requested extensive bloodwork and X-rays to be sure she was healthy. Then their groomer gave her a bath while I waited. Dolly's good."

"But you don't look good, Jenna. What's wrong?"

"I should ask you the same thing. Your knuckles are bruised like you just used a brick wall as a punching bag. And I don't see you cry often, but I can tell you've wept already this morning. I guess it's nothing but toil and trouble for the both of us."

"Wept? Toil and trouble? Why are speaking to me in Shakespeare?"

Jenna drummed her manicured fingers on the table as she answered. "I'm trying to expand my vocabulary lately. I'm working with tons of different people to get this expo ready in February. Toy Gunn, the woman you met in my office, is making me feel uneducated, and I don't like it."

"So, you're using words like *toil* and *wept*?"

Defensively, Jenna snorted and looked away.

"Why've you been crying, Jenna? You go first. Then I'll tell you about my morning." Hopefully, Jenna's story would take precedence without them getting around to Pennie's morning. She had no idea how to explain one single minute of the day so far.

"I don't know if I can trust Cole. I love him, Pennie. I really do. This attachment... devotion... this affection... it's unreal. I don't even know how to process the emotions. The thought of Cole being unfaithful for even a second turns me into some kind of wacko."

Pennie reached out one of her mangled hands to place it on Jenna's. "Cole would never be unfaithful. You know that."

"I just spent two hours sitting in a veterinarian's waiting room lost in thought. I can't think of a single reason that Cole and Pietra should be driving together this morning. I'm trying to give him the benefit of the doubt. Any reasonable doubt at all, and I'm coming up empty. Why should I trust him?"

"Have you sent him a message? Given him a chance to explain?"

Jenna shook her head and pulled her hand back. Crossing her arms over her chest, she refocused on something outside the window. Pennie followed her gaze to see a squirrel outsmarting the squirrel-proof bird feeder.

"Look, I don't think Cole is a cheater. But I don't trust Pietra. She's like that squirrel right there. Always wanting something that isn't hers. She thinks she's clever. Cole might not even see that her end game is to ruin our relationship. It doesn't matter what we do to thwart her efforts, she keeps working harder to make sure we aren't happy. If she'd find a man of her own and put that same energy into her own relationship, she might find her own happiness. But since she's miserable, she's going to make sure all other women in her vicinity are suffering as well."

"That's harsh, Jenna. Not that I completely disagree, but I know that Pietra and Chip are dating right now. She didn't steal him from me, and she isn't trying to mess up things for you and Cole." Of course, Pennie had no idea why Pietra was acting so sultry around Cole this morning, but she wouldn't share any of that right now.

"You're so stupid sometimes."

With raised eyebrows, Pennie had to fight the urge to punch her best friend in the face. "Excuse me?"

"You think Pietra and Chip are dating, but I think Chip doesn't care about her. Pietra is trying to date him, but he isn't falling for it. And she'd kill for a chance to date a man as wonderful as Cole. I don't know why you can't see her for what she really is."

"Ummm… I'm sure they're dating. I don't think all her scruples are intact, but I can't imagine Cole would get involved in any games she might be playing. Surely, you can't believe that."

"I'm freaking out, Penn. I'm ready to commit to Cole in a way I can't even put into words. So, the idea that he isn't feeling the same level of commitment scares the hell out of me. He's doing something secretive this week, and it involves Pietra, the Jezebel in cop's clothing. What do I do with this information?"

"You give him a chance to explain. That's it, Jenna. Cole is trustworthy, and he only has eyes for you. Did he tell you that he had a security shift today?"

"Yea. That's why I haven't called him yet."

"Then tomorrow, after he's had a chance to get a little rest, go back to his house and talk to him. You'll know if he's being honest because you can trust your gut. Give him a chance to explain. He works with Pietra, so there may be a plausible explanation to them riding together this morning."

"I'll think about it. Now, tell me what happened to you."

"Well..." Pennie glanced at her battered hands with renewed embarrassment. "I went to the nursery earlier to talk to Adriana for a minute, and I tackled a guy who was trying to steal some stuff."

"You attacked someone trying to steal plants?!"

"It escalated quickly, Jenna. I couldn't explain if I tried. We didn't even call the cops."

"We gotta find you a man. For real. You need someone to give your energy to. I'm gonna take Dolly home and then get a mani/pedi. I'll let you know how it goes tomorrow."

"Thanks for talking her through that, Pennie. I'll have to explain that we're on the same security detail. Jenna won't like it, but she'll understand."

Beside Cole, Pietra postured with her hands on her hips like she was offended. "You're worried about your crazy girlfriend when we haven't even determined why Pennie looks like something the cat dragged in. Quit letting that woman cloud your judgement so you can focus on your job."

As if some curtain had been pulled back, Pennie got a clear view of what Pietra had become. She truly was miserable. She was trying to plant seeds of doubt in Cole's relationship. What was her deal with Chip? Did the relationship not satisfy her? Or was Chip not really committed to her? Regardless, Pietra had become a wretched woman with a deplorable attitude.

Pennie would have to double up her efforts to extend grace and find out what happened that caused Pietra to become so toxic. No more cattiness. No more being offended by Pietra's appalling behavior. She would address Pietra head-on. Cutting through her awful exterior to get to the root of her problem.

"Pietra," Pennie said her name just loud enough to get the woman's attention. The condescending eyes turned in Pennie's direction. "Why are you trying to sabotage his relationship?"

Pennie wasn't buying the hurt expression on Pietra's face, so she asked again, "Why, Pietra? Why does it bother you to see them happy together?"

"It doesn't bother me. I want to see my friends be happy."

"Then quit making problems for them. I know you just overheard our conversation. You know how Jenna feels about him. If she's crazy, it's because she's crazy in love. So just stop, Pietra. We can talk later in private if you need a friend."

The female detective stomped to the recliner and plopped down. "I just need to know what happened to you today. Do we need to get Tony on the phone?"

"Oh, probably so. Have a seat, Cole. This one's a doozy."

She didn't leave out a single detail of the dreadful morning. Clobbering the Tulane fans wasn't gratifying. Crying in the park wasn't her proudest moment either. Mistaking Nick and JJ for terrorists might be the most disturbing jump to conclusions she'd ever made despite the background Judy shared on their family. Pennie mentioned her explanation about an anonymous stalker so that Adriana wouldn't be alerted to anything else going on.

Tony wasn't thrilled to get a phone call after only two hours of sleep, but he expressed more understanding than Pennie expected. Could his sleepy state have helped her cause?

The events of the morning only revealed a few things. First, they knew that Nick and JJ weren't the terrorists on US soil right now. Second, nothing would change with their plans to lay low. Third, Pennie only had Toy Gunn left to investigate when she got time to do so.

Then Karolina stormed into the room.

"Mom, JJ just sent me a text and told me you're crazy! What did you do?"

The fourth revelation that she didn't consider: Karolina would be terribly embarrassed by Pennie's actions.

"Oh, honey. Did you tell them to come here?"

"No! What are you talking about?"

"Karolina, they surprised me at work this morning, and I felt threatened. I have felt a little crazy these days. I know I didn't handle it well in hindsight."

"Mom, what did you do?"

JJ must not have gone into detail about their violent encounter. How much should Pennie share now? "I might have broken his nose."

The rumbling sound Karolina made was somewhere between a growling puma and a roaring grizzly bear. Her AmberLou colored hair whipped around right before she trudged back to the bunkroom.

"That went well." Pietra had to punctuate the encounter with her own uncouth remark.

Rather than respond or stick around for any additional criticism, Pennie grabbed her phone with earbuds and headed outside. Her yard had been neglected, so she dedicated several hours to mowing, edging, and cleaning up, grateful that the cloudy skies offered a break from the relentless July sun. By the time she finished, her hands hurt like the dickens, but the prior aggression and hostility had been replaced with exhaustion. A light rain had just started falling when she returned the lawn equipment to the garage.

A nap followed Pennie's third shower of the day.

Peach nudged Pennie to wake her. Peach experienced the same hunger pains as Pennie. Since she had skipped lunch, and a glance at her phone revealed that dinner time was approaching, Pennie's stomach rumbled louder than the thunder outside. Back in May, Bartlett was ravaged by straight-line winds and nasty storms that wreaked havoc on her neighborhood for several weeks. Since then, she hadn't been able to sleep through any kind of weather incident.

Easing into the kitchen, she found the amigas making Karolina's favorite... chickpea stroganoff. A closer look revealed that Francelia made her own pot of stroganoff with steak. It was still an unusual recipe using potato sticks as a topping and white rice on the side. Not at all like the Velveeta version of the meal that Pennie made on days she didn't feel like cooking.

Any conversation was still lacking. Cole and Pietra watched the news in silence. Pennie stepped on the back porch to listen to the rain drops drumming against the roof. The cool breeze and soothing noise were nothing short than a gift from God. She felt the tension leaving her soul as she inhaled the scent of the summer shower and freshly cut grass. It was time to get her motley crew of a family back on the same page and cope with their situation in a healthier fashion.

"Pennie, come on," Cole hollered at the door, insisting that she come inside for something urgent.

They all watched the television screen as Adolfo Cabral gave his latest message. In this image, an open window behind him revealed colorfully dressed people marching down the streets.

"You can see the parades have started for our Merengue Festival, and the timing is perfect. We can celebrate our country's heritage while ushering in a new era of leadership. Twenty-four hours from now, it looks like the incumbent president, Daniela Vasquez, will be executed for her crimes against mankind. When her daughter is found, her execution will be slow and painful as well."

Cabral adjusted the camera so that the window was no longer in view. He sat on an uncomfortable-looking fancy couch next to Daniela, who now wore a different red dress. Her festive attire didn't match her despondent expression. "Maybe I can convince Vasquez to disclose the location of her daughter so this can end peacefully. Even if she doesn't, my men are actively hunting tigers as we speak. Remember, I have many prisoners I could exchange for one insignificant girl if anyone wants to make an exchange. For now, though, a night of vigorous persuasion awaits."

His evil leer froze on the screen for an extra beat before the anchor appeared. They continued asking the same questions as the night before... questions about Francelia's location, about the US military's plans, about the tiger reference... No one had any answers. Various news correspondents tossed around a few suppositions, but everyone watching the news from Pennie's living room in Bartlett, Tennessee, knew they were wrong.

The suggestion that Francelia was in a hidden saferoom in their National Palace wasn't based in any fact. One newsman tossed out the idea that the Dominican Republic wanted Cabral to be their new leader. Francelia scoffed aloud at that statement. No one had any input on the tiger reference. A few random ideas were tossed around about who "Maria" might be, even though Cabral didn't mention her alias this time.

Pennie wondered if the message spoken in Spanish came across worse than the English translation she read across the screen.

"Francelia, have you had any *ReelLife* notifications today?" Pennie asked as they all still stared at the television.

"Just one." She retrieved her phone from the kitchen and showed Pennie the photo exchange from this morning. Francelia sent a shot of herself sitting on the back porch, wearing pajamas, with only bricks behind her. The return photo featured Adolfo and Daniela sitting on the balcony of the palace. Daniela still wore some kind of nightgown, while Adolfo wore his self-assigned military uniform with the red band around his arm in every picture.

"Please know that I'm sorry and appalled for my tantrum this morning and for abandoning everyone today. It was selfish of me, Francelia. I'm refocused on what's going on here now."

"It's okay, Momma Pennie. This has been hard on us all."

"Why don't we eat? That'll make us all feel a little better," Karolina added as she led the way to the kitchen.

Dinner passed without much conversation. A *ReelLife* notification prompted Francelia to share a photo of her dinner plate. The response was a photo of Cabral's dessert. It looked like some kind of round fried pie with a bite taken out of it.

Karolina asked the obvious question. "What do you call these, Francie?"

"*Pastelitos*. They're like empanadas. You can make them with any kind of filling, usually meat, but that looks like peach. My mother's favorite dessert."

"In Brazil, we have *pastels*. They serve them at the farmer's markets, but I can't eat them. I do drink the *caldo de cana*."

Continuing their own private conversation, excluding the three older adults at the table, Francelia asked, "Is that like our *guarapo de caña*?"

"Yes, it's juice from sugar cane."

"Hang on," Pennie interrupted. "Y'all drink straight-up sugar juice? No fruit or anything added?"

Both rolled their eyes in response. "You have to try it to understand."

Rather than inquire about their drinking habits any

further, Pennie gathered dishes and proceeded to clean the kitchen. As she scrubbed the first pan, her phone indicated Vale Hernandez was calling. Pennie summoned Francelia to come answer it.

The young Dominican took the phone back to the table and spoke to her ambassador for only a few minutes. Pennie didn't participate in their conversation, but the officers stayed close and chimed in when necessary. Nothing new had been discovered. The second deadline issued by Cabral left them twenty-four hours to see what would happen next. In Santo Domingo, the time was one hour ahead of Bartlett, Tennessee, meaning tomorrow at six Dominican time, five Tennessee time, something majorly bad might happen. And all the world could do was watch.

When the girls got off the phone, they mentioned their plans to watch a movie in Karolina's bedroom. Pennie followed them to talk privately.

Once in Karolina's room, she asked, "How are you doing right now, Francelia?"

"I'm frightened. I feel heavy. Like the day of… um…" She paused, searching for the right word. "*¿Cómo se dice condenar*?"

"Doom," Karolina translated. "She feels like tomorrow is a day of doom. I feel it too."

"Me too," Pennie admitted. "I don't think Cabral will extend the deadline again. As of right now, it doesn't look like your mom has been tortured other than the mental anguish. And at least she has a slight amount of peace knowing you're safe."

"I won't sleep tonight, but I'm staying in here with Karolina. We'll just watch movies and try to stay calm."

"Do y'all want to come to my room? We can all fit in the bed, but I don't have a TV in there. We'd have to watch stuff on my iPad."

"No, Mom, we're okay. This movie is in Spanish, so you wouldn't understand anyway."

"Then let me pray with you." Pennie spent the next five minutes calling the angels down… Building up hedges of protection… Demanding peace for bothered souls… Insisting the evil should bow in the presence of their Lord… Petitioning the heavens to open and grounds to shake…

Within twenty-four hours, the forces of good and evil would collide. The trajectory of Francelia's life would change depending on the outcome. Pennie couldn't imagine the turmoil going through her mind right now. Then Pennie wondered if she could officially adopt a twenty-year-old if Daniela didn't survive tomorrow. She quickly reined in that thought to stand by her faith. Daniela would be delivered from the clutches of Adolfo Cabral. She had to believe that.

The thoughts and tears were interrupted when Pietra came through to make sure the windows were secure. As she checked the lock, she turned her head to softly say, "We're keeping an eye on the news all night. We'll come get you if anything develops."

Pennie gave the girls kisses, and Peach jumped in the bed to offer her own affection. Karolina responded with, "*Saia daqui!*"

The only command Peach understood in Portuguese was "Get out of here." Karolina loved the dog but not the hair. She especially didn't like Peach's hair in her bed.

Pennie smiled and took Peach outside to use the bathroom one last time. The rain had moved out, so she only had to towel off her dog's feet before they went back into the house. She put on a fresh pot of coffee for the officers and retreated to her own bedroom.

Thanks to the early time and her earlier nap, Pennie wasn't the least bit tired. Her hands were sore and stiff from the skirmish earlier. The back of her head throbbed from the impact with JJ's face. Her ribs were bruised from her scramble over the fence the other day. She needed her own peace right now. Sitting up in her bed with Peach tucked close by, she opened her Bible and read the first passage that caught her eye.

First Peter. Book One. Verse Six. "In all this you greatly rejoice, though for a little while you may have had to suffer grief in all kinds of trials."

Pennie scratched Peach behind the ear and contemplated her level of non-rejoicing lately. Taking a few minutes in the quiet, she counted her blessings. The suffering would only last a little while. Regardless of how everything with Daniela Vasquez went down, Francelia was still safe, and Pennie still had a stable home, money in the bank, an amazing family... Why was she so fixated on wanting a husband and children?

A light rapping on her door preceded Pietra entering her room. "I'm just checking the windows." The officer went to the bathroom to ensure that window was locked before verifying the window in her room was secure. Rather than leave after performing her duty, Pietra sat in one of the two chairs that occupied the space in front of the window. It struck Pennie as odd that she'd lived in this house for two years now, and this might be the first time anyone has ever sat in one of those decorative chairs.

Rather than say anything, Pietra huffed and stared at the floor. She wanted to talk. Pennie did offer to talk later if she wanted to, so this would be a deep conversation that she might not be ready for. If anything, she wanted Pietra to go away forever. Instead of acknowledging Pietra's prolonged presence in the room, Pennie glanced back down at her Bible where a later verse caught her eye.

The second half of verse twenty-two. "...Love one another deeply, from the heart." Swallowing her pride, Pennie decided to tackle the conversation head on.

"What's going on with you, Pietra?"

"I wish I knew."

"If I had to guess, you're a little jealous of seeing people around you so truly in love."

"Why would you guess that?" Pietra asked, even though her expression confirmed it.

"Oh, I don't know. Maybe because I feel the same way." Pennie abandoned her spot on the bed and sat in the second chair next to her frenemy. "I'm ready to start my next chapter. To be a wife again. To be a mom. To plan a family vacation. I feel like these days are just filler until those dreams come true. That's why I jump at the chance to help with these missions. It's like I'm fading away. But that's my burden and not yours. You have Chip, so why are you longing for love?"

Pietra pursed her lips and looked around the room. She huffed again. "I've never really wanted anything serious with a man until I met Chip. He's keeping our pace slow, and I don't know how to interpret that."

"It sounds like he wants to build a strong foundation for your relationship. He wants y'all to get to know each other." Pennie inquired.

"You think so?" Pietra's expression brightened considerably. "This is the first time I've pursued a long-term relationship, so that might be reasonable."

"Do you think maybe the way you've been acting flirty with Cole is just a ploy to keep your options open in case things fizzle with Chip?"

Pietra nodded. "I've always kept my options open."

"Don't you think Chip deserves better than that? You wouldn't want anyone flirting with Chip or badmouthing you to him. Yet, that's what you're doing with Cole. If you seriously want a relationship to work, quit looking for other options. Quit comparing relationships. Give Chip your full attention."

"Thanks, Pennie. I think the strain of this operation and worrying about things unnecessarily has caused me to lose sight of what I need to do. I still don't understand why you're helping me when I can tell you're hanging onto some feelings for Chip."

"Chip's a great guy, but our timing was off. He isn't ready for marriage and family like I am. So, if he wants to take it slow, you should be patient with him. I bet he's one of the few men on earth worth the wait."

Appearing quite a bit happier, Pietra agreed and left the room. Pennie pulled the curtain back enough to see that it hadn't gotten completely dark yet. She still wasn't sleepy. Despite having three showers today, she opted for a bubble bath to help her relax.

SUNDAY, JULY 24

Incoherent dreams filled Pennie's subconscious after she finally succumbed to sleep. Fighting her way out of a mob, she heard the rat-a-tat of gunfire and screams in the distance. Another bout of struggling woke her enough to realize it was only her blanket that had her trapped. Was she still asleep? Was she awake? She glanced at the clock. A few minutes past midnight. She sat up to ensure she was awake. Peach had sprawled out on the floor to escape Pennie's restless thrashing.

Another rat-a-tat and screams in the distance. Then a light tapping on her bedroom door. Waking up fully, she jumped up to find Cole on the other side of the door. "Come on, there's some action in Santo Domingo."

Just as Pennie had a seat on the couch, Pietra entered the living room from the opposite side of the house with the two amigas in tow. Francelia and Karolina joined her on the couch, allowing Pietra to sit at the opposite end to sandwich the girls in place. Cole turned up the volume so that more distant gunfire and bursts of light punctuated the darkness around the National Palace. Whatever was taking place had no real narration, but an anchor did his best to make sense of the scene.

"...The streets and buildings all went pitch black about fifteen minutes ago. The parades and street performers seemed to disappear, abandoning the festivities for the evening. We still haven't found out the source of the shooting or what caused the power outage. The cameras on our drones aren't equipped for filming in total darkness, but we're keeping an eye on the scene..."

The five people in Pennie's living room watched in shock. They had no idea what was taking place. Francelia trembled enough for Pennie to notice. She wrapped her arm around the frightened girl. No words were spoken. The lady on the screen recounted the events of the past week, including the impending deadline for later that day.

The reporter had nothing new to add, so she started over with how the day went near the National Palace. The camera switched to earlier footage of parades and other jubilant activities in the streets of Santo Domingo. Blissfully unaffected by the events within the palace, the citizens enjoyed the celebration of the Merengue Festival across the Dominican Republic. Brightly dressed dancers and street performers put on a show on the roads right in front of the palace.

As Pennie tried to process the scene, she felt Francelia sobbing. "What're the tears for?" she quietly asked the girl.

"My mom could be dead by now. I have no home. No family." The sniffly whimpering turned into bawling once the words were spoken.

"You don't know that, sweetie. Let's stay hopeful."

Karolina scooched closer to hold Francelia tightly between her and Pennie. Peach moved nearer as well, laying her head on Francelia's lap to console her as only a sweet dog could.

Then nothing new for a half hour... A quick phone call from Ambassador Hernandez ensured they were watching the events unfold on television, but even she didn't have a clue what was going on. Pennie's patience wore thin listening to the nasally reporter talk about things that don't matter just to fill the silence. No one else in the living room had anything to say.

Just a waiting game. A terribly painful waiting game for one grieving Dominican.

Pennie's mind had entered a trance by the time the television made a noise to indicate breaking news might be shared. The reporter's face was instantly replaced by a scene from a press conference that was just getting started. A podium featuring the seal of the President of the United States was center screen with an American flag displayed in the background. President Jerome Carson stepped into view, gripping the podium with both hands.

When Pennie voted last year, she didn't cast a ballot in favor of the president who recently stepped down, but she was very pleased with the vice president who stepped up to run the country. In the few months Carson has been acting as Commander-in-Chief, his economic reform and foreign relations had gained traction, making him a true bi-partisan leader for the nation.

Now, he stood in the glare of a spotlight with a stern expression. His dark face and short gray hair reminded Pennie of Danny Glover from his role in *Shooter*. A few distinguished lines across his forehead gave him an air of wisdom and experience. As the camera panned closer to his face, his perceptive eyes took stock of everyone in the room as well as everyone watching through the camera. Finally, he leaned closer to the microphone to make his announcement.

Everyone in the room held their breath.

"Good evening, fellow Americans and viewers all over the world. Tonight, I can report that the United States has conducted an operation to take down the *Mata Cacatas*, also known as the *Wasps*. During this operation, we have killed Adolfo Cabral, who has led this terrorist group into taking over the Dominican National Palace by force and is responsible for numerous murders and abductions."

A collective gasp in the living room in Bartlett, Tennessee was the only response. Taking down Cabral was only the first step. They needed to know about Daniela's well-being.

The president continued, "With the cooperation of the Dominican police and military, US Special Forces have worked tirelessly over the past few days to bring about an end to this terrorist takeover. We stand united with our Caribbean neighbors, and tonight, a small group of courageous Americans carried out this targeted mission to restore the rightful power of the Dominican Republic to President Daniela Vasquez who was unharmed during this operation."

At those words, a noise escaped Francelia's lips that conveyed every emotion from ecstasy to relief, exhilaration to deliverance... Tears of joy flooded every eye in the room.

"The only casualties from this operation were members of the *Mata Cacatas*. No Americans, civilians, or Dominican officers were harmed or killed during the brief skirmish that took place. This is only the first step in dismantling the terrorist network, but we strongly believe the network was still in early stages of forming. We will stand strong with our friends and allies to ensure the *Mata Cacatas* are completely defeated, and the democracy of the Dominican Republic will stand strong.

"When the ambassador from multiple Caribbean nations implored help from America, we chose not to stand idly by while our friends and allies were killed. We understand the cost of war, but the cost of allowing terrorists to trump democracy is a price we were unwilling to pay. Tonight, I can tell you that justice has been done.

"I want to personally thank the military leaders, counterterrorism personnel, intelligence professionals, and the brave men and women of our Armed Forces. Tonight, we see the result of their tireless pursuit of justice."

When Carson had reached the end of his speech, he took a step back from the microphone, then he leaned back in to add another statement.

"Our work isn't complete yet. Cabral's younger brother Julio wasn't found in the National Palace, and his whereabouts are unknown. Also, the president's daughter Francelia wasn't accounted for. As we seek the safety of Francelia, we are seeking the arrest of Julio Cabral. US Special Forces will not rest until Julio is in custody, and Francelia is reunited with her mother. The Dominican police are currently searching for the prisoners that have been abducted by the Cabral brothers to account for all missing Dominican nationals.

"In the meantime, the world can rest assured knowing that good has prevailed over evil. We know that the history of our country has always been to stand up for our values and endeavor to make the world a safer place. Please continue to pray for the people of the Dominican Republic as they recover from the incidents of the past week.

"Thank you. May God bless you and continue to bless the United States of America."

The president didn't stick around to answer any questions from the members of the press.

"My mom's alive. How did this all happen?" Francelia'

smiling face didn't need any explanation of how. She was just thrilled that her mother was unharmed.

Rejoice. That's the only word that went through Pennie's brain.

Pietra sat up taller on the couch as she asked, "Does that mean it's over? That's it?"

"No, it's not over," Cole answered. "Julio Cabral is still out there, and he might be in our country right now with a few other Wasps. We can't let them find Francelia."

Choosing to be contentious, Pietra touted, "Carson didn't acknowledge that any terrorists are on our soil, so I'd bet that's just a rumor the Wasps started to scare us. It's not up to you anyway, Cole. It's over if Tony says it's over."

"Pietra, I'm not arguing with you. Of course, we get directions from Tony, but it's not over even if our involvement is. And personally, I'm going to stay committed to keeping Francelia safe as long as it takes to put Julio Cabral behind bars."

"Even if it causes problems with your girlfriend?" Pietra questioned him with an unnecessary attitude. Pennie couldn't believe this exchange was taking place after such major news.

"Jenna will understand. She cares about people. In fact, she'd let Francelia hide at her house open ended if that's what it took."

Finally, Pennie had to interrupt, "Guys, Francelia is safe with me until her mother says she can come home. I don't work for Tony, and I don't work for the government. She will simply be Maria from Honduras until the coast is clear."

The bickering stopped. Cole moved to the kitchen to make more coffee. Pennie wondered why Tony hadn't called, but she didn't have to wonder for long. The iPad on the coffee table notified everyone of a visitor on the front porch.

Upon entering the house, Tony wasted no time embracing Francelia, whispering encouraging words as she shed fresh tears on his white t-shirt. They all gathered in the living room where Tony gave his official orders as police chief. The security rotation would continue as it had been until the threat of Julio Cabral had been eliminated.

As he spoke, Pennie's phone rang. She answered it on speaker so Ambassador Hernandez could address everyone.

"Francelia, *amorcito*, your mother is okay. President Carson called me personally a few minutes ago. Your mother was given the opportunity to come back to the USA for safety, but she wanted to start working immediately to get our country back in order. I don't like that she stayed behind, but this woman, she's hardheaded."

"I know, *Señora*. I'm just happy that she's safe. When can I talk to her?"

"Until we know you're safe, we aren't giving anyone access to you. I don't want anyone tracing phone calls or anything. Even President Carson doesn't know where you are since Julio Cabral is still on the loose."

"I understand. I've never been away from my mother this long, and I miss her. But we'll wait until it's safe."

The call ended. Tony went home to get a couple of hours of sleep before returning for his shift. Despite the massive relief everyone felt, Francelia didn't want to go to bed by herself. A few minutes later, Pennie found herself in her king-sized bed with Francelia, Karolina, and Peach. Pennie didn't quite understand the prayer Francelia whispered in Spanish, but she knew rejoicing was the theme.

For five whole hours, the ladies rested peacefully. The best sleep they'd had in over a week. Just knowing the Wasps were unraveling brought a wave of relief through Pennie's home. She stared at the twirling ceiling fan, afraid to move so as not to wake the amigas who still enjoyed their slumber. The end was in sight. Eventually, Julio would be captured, and Francelia would return home. Pennie's life would go back to normal.

As of this morning, the birds outside chirped like normal. The sun shined through the windows as usual. Her comforter and sheets still smelled like Gain fabric softener just as they had in the past. Peach's hair ensured she needed to wash the bedding again as she did every few days. The AC unit was already running at seven in the morning to combat the heat of the Midsouth as it did every July.

But for everything else in her life, she didn't quite know what normal was anymore. She'd have to figure it out. Her future would include no more missions. No more danger. No more investigations. No more cold cases. No more extractions. She'd tend to her garden, get back to Krav class, and pray that God would send a man worthy of being her future husband and father for her future kids.

Being lost in this train of thought wasn't a good start to the day, so it was almost welcomed when someone lightly rapped on her bedroom door.

Without waiting for a reply, Tony poked his head in. "You awake?"

The girls stirred beside her. "Yea, give me fifteen minutes, and I'll come in there to cook some breakfast."

Something that wasn't normal… Pennie's knuckles were bruised and swollen from the beatdown yesterday morning. Her head still ached but not as bad. She slowly extended and curled her fingers several times to loosen up the stiffness. After sending a text to her family's group chat to say she wouldn't be at church that morning, Pennie got up to face the day.

Pietra and Cole had already gone to their respective homes, leaving only Tony sitting on a barstool to chat with Pennie while she chopped potatoes for a breakfast casserole. Tony made the decision to go back to one officer per day to keep watch over the women.

"Before the girls get up, can you please explain again how everything went down yesterday?" Tony asked. "I was slightly sleep-deprived when you called."

She did notice a few signs of fatigue in Tony. He no longer had that twinkle in his eye as she was accustomed to seeing. This operation took a toll on all of them.

"Well, Nick and JJ surprised me yesterday, and it felt like an ambush. I never told them where to find us, and I never so much as gave them my phone number. Even without our current situation, that behavior's a bit stalkish. Looking back, I'm mortified, but in the moment, I only felt the need to protect myself and my girls."

Pennie explained everything in more detail while she finished cooking. The adults were pleased to see the girls come through the kitchen wearing genuine smiles. The turmoil was moving out, making room for hope. During breakfast, everyone kept one eye on the television to see if any new stories might come on. Any sign that Francelia could go back home and relieve the women from the lockdown they'd endured... And further relieving the four officers of the security detail that had commandeered their lives.

By mid-morning, everyone had showered and settled in the living room. One photo exchange on the *ReelLife* app showed a cheery Daniela in a darkened room. No one knew if the president was still in her National Palace or if she had been transferred to some safer location. The photo she sent Francelia didn't give anything away.

Finally, an update from a national news station. The heavily made-up woman at the broadcast desk shared some insight from the events of the past nine hours. All eyes and ears were on the television.

"The rescue mission that took place overnight is still shrouded in unknowns, but we have a few pieces of the puzzle to share with you this morning. The US Special Forces sent in a small contingency of manpower to help our Dominican neighbors regain control of the National Palace. Under the cover of darkness, the members of the US military along with the Dominican military infiltrated the palace. People close to the scene say the armed forces surrounded the palace under the guise of a parade celebrating the Merengue Festival. At a precise time, they shed their disguises and quickly overtook the guards who were protecting Adolfo Cabral."

Wasn't that ironic? Pennie knew Cabral was so vain and confident in his support, he wanted the celebrations around him as some kind of victory jubilee. She loved that it helped bring about his demise.

"Sources in the Caribbean also tell us that the remaining members of the *Mata Cacatas* within the palace have peacefully surrendered. Across the island nation, demonstrators for this machismo group have abandoned their posts this morning. It seems this quick rise to power has fizzled out almost immediately with the death of their leader.

This could be the beginning of a new era for the people of the Dominican Republic."

Almost immediately, the station switched to a reporter somewhere else. "Our drones were destroyed in the skirmish last night, but we're actively working to deploy more cameras to Santo Domingo and get a correspondent closer to the scene. The world actively awaits for any update on President Daniela Vasquez. Our own president said she was unharmed, but I think I speak for everyone when I say we want to see for ourselves."

The reporter cocked his head and found an adjacent subject to speak about when he opened his mouth again. "When Daniela Vasquez was elected president last year, her running mate Victor Cano stood strong throughout the early months of her presidency. When the initial death threats started, Cano went into hiding, much like Vasquez. The public doesn't know where he is much less whether he has survived this recent uproar. Some sources say he was a supporter of the *Mata Cacatas* all along. When he finally emerges from his hiding place, we'll see which side he stands on."

"Francelia, how close were you to Victor Cano?" Pennie inquired since she didn't know much about this Dominican vice president.

"I called him Uncle Vic. He was my dad's best friend. He's one of the good guys. I can't believe anyone would spread lies about him. Throughout the election, people spread rumors about my mom having an affair with him. It's all lies. He has a wife and two young sons. They all went into hiding when we went into lockdown at the palace. I don't even know where he is."

With that bit of information, Pennie hated to ask her next question. "You're sure there's no chance that he's one of the Wasps? That he's walking around like a wolf in sheep's clothing?"

"No! Why would you say that?"

"If your mom dies, Cano has the most to gain. I'm just making sure, sweetie. If you trust him, so do I."

The rest of the day was spent with other uninformative news reports. Francelia and Karolina did a little sunbathing to relax. Adriana surprised her with a visit after lunch to make sure Pennie saw the overnight excitement in Adriana's home country. The ten-minute visit happened with Tony hiding in the bedroom.

The next surprise visitor came in the form of her big sister. Alice stormed into the house with a demeanor halfway between concerned and controlling as only a big sister can do.

"You've been distant since you came back from the cruise, Pennie. You barely chime in on the family group chat. Last Sunday, you went shopping with Pietra instead of eating lunch with your family. Mom's in a tizzy because she thinks you're on drugs or something."

"Come on, Alice. I've just been tired. This heat is getting to me, and it's always a little sad to come back to reality after a vacation."

"Don't give me that crap. Now that I'm here, I see that we do need to be concerned about you. Penn, you look terrible. I've never seen you with these bags under your eyes, and you have bruises all over your arms." Alice exclaimed all this as she reached for Pennie's hands. "What did you do?"

"Look, I didn't want anyone to worry, okay?" Pennie replied as she tried to come up with a good explanation.

"As your sister, it's my job to worry! What happened to your hands?"

Pennie fabricated something on the fly to go along with the lie she told Adriana… "It's a stalker situation. You'll be glad to know that I beat him up, and he won't be messing with me anymore. Karolina and Fr… Her friend Maria are still staying here with me, so that's taken a lot of my energy also." Whew, that was close. She almost used Francelia's real name.

"Where did this stalker come from?"

"From the cruise ship. I only talked to him a couple of times, and he figured out where I worked when he saw one of Karolina's social media posts. When he showed up at my work yesterday, I freaked out and attacked him. He's gone now, but I couldn't come to church this morning with my hands like this. I'll be back at church next week, and I'll be good as new. I promise, Alice."

"We gotta find you a man to fight off any stalkers. Where did Kennedy find that hunk she married?"

"My neighbor Kennedy? He's a fireman, and they met when he brought her an orphaned rabbit after a house fire."

"So, we need to set a house on fire? Do you think a hot fireman would come rescue you if we lit it up right now?"

Was Alice crazy? Setting fire to Pennie's house to see if a hunk would come to her rescue? Was Pennie a little crazy too since the idea didn't seem half bad given the state of her love life lately?

"Stop it, Alice. I'm not setting anything ablaze, and I'll find a man in good time."

She finally shooed Alice out of her home before they formulated an arson-based dating game. When Tony re-entered the living room, they discussed several theories of who the rumored terrorists might be.

"I don't really want to believe Victor Cano is a Wasp in disguise. Adolfo Cabral could've sent a couple of his guys here undercover to intercept Francelia."

Tony inclined his head. "I'd like to agree with you. Since this all started, we haven't seen Julio Cabral or Victor Cano. It could be these two men are here together, and Cano might be using his relationship with Francelia to get close to her."

"I'm sorry, Tony. I'd rather see the good in people. I only asked Francelia about him to get her input. She says he's a good guy, so I'm going to trust her."

"She's only a kid, Pennie. She doesn't have the instincts to make that call."

"She's been in the political landscape her whole life. She's much more mature than other girls her age."

"I just don't trust politicians in general. It doesn't matter right now anyway. Daniela will decide when she wants her daughter to come home, and it'll all be out of our hands."

After dinner, the repetitive news stories finally had a break. Vice President Victor Cano emerged from his hiding place in the resort town of Puerto Plata on the north side of the island. He made a brief remark that his family was heading home to Santo Domingo to help Daniela Vasquez come back from this recent chaos. Francelia seemed genuinely pleased with this report, so everyone shared in her delight. By the time the seven o'clock news came on, President Vasquez made her own address to the nation.

With her own press conference, behind a wooden podium and in front of a Dominican flag, she looked directly into the camera. Even with a black eye, she sounded strong and confident. Francelia moved to sit on the front edge of the coffee table, closer to the television. Pennie scooted over so she could read the English subtitles.

"I'm here to express complete humility and gratefulness... for the Dominican citizens who supported me... for the US soldiers who aided in my release... and for my God who protects me. My faith has kept me strong through this ordeal, along with knowing my daughter is safe. Francelia will stay out of the public eye for the time being while I work to promote stability and unity throughout our nation. When Vice President Cano arrives in the capital city, we'll have our work cut out for us. Let us not look back at the past few months as a black eye on our country but view this as a growing point."

Daniela smirked and indicated her own black eye before continuing. Pennie absolutely admired this woman's sense of self-awareness and bravery. "Good has triumphed over evil. The people's voices were heard, God's plan was not thwarted, and I will remain president to serve the fine people of the Dominican Republic. Thank you and God bless."

"Did you see it?" Francelia asked softly.

"See what?" Tony answered.

Francelia grabbed the remote control to rewind the short speech. "There." She pointed to Daniela's hand. The long-sleeved blouse covered her entire arm, but they saw scarring on the back of her hand. The expression of disbelief descended over Francelia's face. "That's acid burns. He really did torture her."

Tony moved next to Francelia on the coffee table and pulled her into a sideways hug. "Your mother endured insults, physical abuse, and threats of execution. But she remained strong and steadfast despite all that. The men behind her torture are dead, and she's going to be the best president your country's ever seen. Don't look defeated now that you have everything to look forward to."

"He's right, Francelia." Pennie moved to the other side of her. "You have the strongest role model a girl could ever ask for."

Pennie's ringing phone cut the encouraging moment short.

"Hey, Jenna, let me go to my bedroom so I don't interrupt the girls' movie on TV—" Pennie dashed towards her bedroom and shut the door. "Okay, what's up?"

"I just had dinner with Cole. I've missed him so much."

"That's great; did y'all talk about everything that's bothering you?"

Jenna huffed through the phone. "I guess. He said that Pietra is working the same assignment with him, and he couldn't share any more information than that. His shifts changed, so we planned another date for tomorrow when I get off work. I just have to trust him."

"They do work together, so at least it's a legitimate explanation. You can trust him."

"I still think it's suspicious though. I'm going to order one of those transmitter things you put in kids' backpacks to keep up with their locations so I can see where he's really going. If I can find one in town in the morning, I'll try to hide it in his car after our date tomorrow night."

"Jenna Marie Martin! Don't do that. Don't violate his trust. You'll find out that he's being honest, and he'll break up with you for being crazy. You'd be throwing your relationship away."

"I am crazy, Pennie! I'm one step away from hiding in his trunk to see where he goes when he isn't with me. I can't handle the idea that he's potentially cheating on me, especially with that skank Pietra."

"You and I both know he's got better taste than that. He chose you. He's not a cheater, and you're not crazy."

"Something else has me thinking I'm crazy. My best friend lied to me. If I can't trust her, who can I trust?"

Pennie sat on the foot of her bed in confusion. "What? I'm your best friend; what're you talking about?"

"You looked me in the eye yesterday and told me you attacked a shoplifter. Your sister called me today because she's worried about you. You told her you attacked a stalker. Normally, I can see right through you, but I'm willing to bet you're lying to both of us. I don't know who you got into a fight with, but you aren't being honest with anyone about it."

Oh crap! The tangled web of lies had caught up to Pennie, and she wasn't out of the woods yet. "I couldn't tell her the truth, Jenna. Alice already thinks I'm half-cocked all the time. If I told her I attacked a shoplifter, she would've had me committed. Even worse, she would've told my mom on me."

"So, you're sticking with the story that you attacked someone who tried to steal some marigolds?"

"Yes." It sounded hollow to her own ears. She wasn't fooling Jenna.

"After this weird phase of the moon or whatever passes, I hope you'll be honest with me. And so will Cole. Until then, I'm going to try some online retail therapy. Call me when you're ready to be sincere."

Pennie stared at the disconnected phone in her hand. When this all started, she only wanted to protect an innocent

Dominican girl. She didn't want to be dishonest with her friends and family. She didn't want the drama that had permeated every area of her life. Now, she had pulled Cole, Pietra, and Chip into the mess. She had all but abandoned her job to investigate on her own. Now that she'd thought about it, she had abandoned her whole life. And it'd remain this way until Francelia could safely return home.

With a heavy heart, Pennie sat in her quiet bedroom. She knew it'd all be worth it when Francelia and her mother were reunited. Now wasn't the time to regret anything. She wasn't sure how much detail she could ever share with Jenna, but their friendship would survive this. Even if Jenna's coworker might be the key to locating the terrorist on US soil right now.

The phone rang again, but it wasn't Jenna calling back. "Hello, Ambassador Hernandez. How are you?" Pennie hurried back to the living room and put the call on speaker to include everyone.

Once greetings were made, the Dominican ambassador got down to business. "It's been an eventful twenty-four hours. Mostly, the events have been favorable, but I've received some disturbing news tonight."

"What's going on, *Señora*?" Francelia pleaded. No one wanted to hear disturbing news at this point.

"Victoria Peele has reached out to me. Remember, she works for the US Department of State. More rumors of terrorists on US soil have reached her department. Ms. Peele thinks I know where Francelia is, so she warned me to keep her hidden longer."

Tony added his tidbit. "That doesn't change anything for us, Ambassador. We already knew the potential for Wasps to be in our country, and safety wasn't magically restored with the death of Adolfo Cabral. We're keeping Francelia safe until you say she can return home."

"Thank you, Chief Lawrence, and our country truly appreciates all you are doing. I just hate that there are still members of this hateful group searching for Francelia. The intel indicates it's between two to four men. I hoped intel would indicate these men went back home, but they may be operating rogue to start their own movement."

"We're still keeping around-the-clock security here, and Francelia isn't leaving the house."

"But I notice that you're the only officer there tonight. Why did you stop assigning pairs?"

The chief grimaced. He obviously didn't like being called out. "Ma'am, that was completely my decision. I felt like the threat was significantly diminished after the overnight events, and my team is exhausted. We're retaining a four-man rotation, and that's all the manpower my department can spare. Not only that, but we also don't want any additional people knowing who we have here."

The voice on the other side of the phone still sounded disapproving, much like Pennie's fourth grade teacher. Ms. McChristian found a way to make that red A+ on the top of a paper seem disappointing. Ever since that time Pennie asked what time lunch break was, Ms. McChristian became fixated on making her feel belittled and insignificant. Not in an unprofessional way, but psychological. The annoyed glances... the unfair comparisons... the resentful tone...

The same tone Ambassador Hernandez used right now. "Chief, I perceive that the only threat against Francelia is the same one you defended against yesterday. Today, that threat, if anything, has escalated based on a sense of desperation. Again, we're eternally grateful for everything you've done, but I'd like to respectfully disagree with your decision."

Rather than respond to the ambassador, Tony turned to Francelia. "Would you feel safer if two officers were here each day?"

"Yes, sir."

"Then starting tomorrow, I'll reinstate the rotation of pairs of officers."

Pennie saw the exhaustion on his face, but she had no basis for input. These decisions were out of her hands. She offered to keep watch if Tony wanted to take a nap, but he refused the offer and encouraged everyone else to go to bed early.

Pennie stared at her ceiling fan again, but this time, the room was dark. Only the errant light from her window reflected off the edges of the blades as they spun endlessly. Her own life felt like it was spinning with no real goal or destination. When she committed to extracting Francelia from the Dominican Republic, her investment was intended to be half of a cruise and a trip to the Miami airport.

When she committed to keeping Francelia with her past Miami, she knew the timeline would be open ended. Ten days ago, her investment should've been nothing more than having an extra international under her roof, except she'd be using a fake name. There'd be no burden other than keeping her identity secret.

Seven days ago, the commitment shifted greatly. Constant police presence in her home. A complete pause in her personal life. A commitment to seek out the terrorists on her own. A mental taxing she never expected. For the safety of Francelia, she'd do it until she didn't have to. But the idea that it was over last night was so refreshing. Now, it was back to being an open-ended timeline. Infinite lockdown until the rogue Wasps were identified and arrested.

Sleep eluded her. Was she on the verge of depression? She had only found a new routine working for the nursery when she had to take off for this mission. The satisfying job, along with her workout regimen, brought her a sense of peace she hadn't felt since before Johnny died. Could she find it again? Was it forever out of her grasp now?

She rolled over to cuddle her sweet dog. Next month, she'd turn twenty-nine. Plenty of time to get her life back on track. Just a little mental fortitude... Pennie focused on perseverance and prayed herself to sleep.

MONDAY, JULY 25

Chip and Cole arrived, but the officer exchange wasn't nondescript like it had been on previous mornings. Pennie had just started a fresh pot of coffee and said goodbye to Tony while the girls got ready for the day. A split second after Tony pulled away, the excitement started in her driveway.

Pennie hadn't even closed the garage when an incensed Jenna squealed into the driveway.

As soon as Jenna stormed into the house, Cole asked, "Pennie, can we use your room to talk privately?"

When Pennie nodded, Cole and Jenna shut themselves behind her bedroom door. She knew Cole would keep Francelia's identity secret and give Jenna just enough information to allow them to finish this mission without compromising anything.

Giving them space, Pennie poured two mugs of coffee and invited Chip to sit at the dining room table. "I'm sorry Jenna's causing an issue this morning."

"It's not your fault. Cole already knew she was upset since he had to cancel their plans for tonight. She was coming by to apologize to him this morning, but she ended up following him to my house and then to here. I'd like to think two seasoned officers would've noticed a tail, but a scorned woman knows how to be stealthy."

"Jenna ain't happy with me right now either. She caught me in a lie about what happened Friday. I told her I took down a shoplifter, but I told my sister I defended myself against a stalker. I didn't realize they'd compare notes."

Chip glanced down at Pennie's hands as they clutched the coffee mug. He reached over and gently took her left hand in his own. "It looks like you've suffered a boxer's fracture."

Pennie knew the side of her hand was swollen, and something might be broken, but she tried to ignore it rather than visit a doctor. "I probably should've been icing it down or immobilizing it somehow, but it's not a big deal."

"You need to let it heal correctly." Chip's comment sounded full of sincerity. The way his fingertips lightly traced each bone in her hand gave her the chills. In fact, her bones turned to Jell-O. Nothing hurt anymore. A simple caress from Chip took all her pain away.

Suddenly, Jenna bustled into the dining room, interrupting the momentary break from reality. "You knew where Cole was the whole time and never told me?!"

"Jenna, leave her alone," Cole said to her back. "We're all required to maintain confidentiality."

Jenna spun around to face her boyfriend. "But you can't tell me why you're protecting her?" Then another spin. "Why is everyone protecting you? Penn, why're you acting like you can trust me? "

"It's not me, Jenna. Please understand."

"If it's not you, then who is it?" Jenna waited with her hands angrily on her hips.

"That's not what I meant. It's not up to me to share the details."

The headshake indicated that Jenna was done being lied to. "I've had it up to here with everyone's deceit and treachery!" Her hand moved from her hip to above her head while her green eyes flashed with anger. She was speaking in

Shakespeare again. That's when the girls entered the dining room to see what was going on.

Between the looming danger for Francelia, the inexplicable feelings for Chip, and the increasing rage from Jenna, Pennie needed an escape hatch. She was never so happy for her phone to ring.

Grabbing her phone, Pennie ran to her backyard to escape the insanity inside her house.

"Pennie, did I catch you at a bad time?"

"No, Adriana. What's up?" Pennie tried to keep her tone even despite her elevated heart rate.

"Are you still coming to work this morning?"

"Of course. I'll be there shortly," she answered, craving the tranquility of the nursery.

"I brought Cynthia with me. She wants to see you before she goes back to college. Then I just need your help with a few decisions, and you can take the rest of the day off."

She glanced through the windows into the house. She could read the body language well enough to know a heated discussion filled her once-peaceful home.

"Cynthia also wants to say hello to Karolina. You should bring her and Maria too."

After seeing the pandemonium inside her house, Pennie felt like she was at her breaking point. "I'm heading your way now."

Without saying a word to anyone, Pennie grabbed her

truck keys and exited through the still-open garage. Cole's Tesla was parked in the garage with Jenna's new Infiniti SUV blocking it in. Fortunately, her truck was in the clear. It didn't appear that anyone noticed her leaving, so she put it in reverse without hesitation.

Cruising down a few backroads with the windows down gave her a feeling of freedom from the insanity in her home. Unlike two mornings ago, Pennie tuned into some Jesus music instead of hard rock. She needed something to quell her soul. A reminder that all this would work out for the good. During the drive to the nursery, her heart rate returned to normal.

It would be over an hour before the nursery opened, so Pennie didn't expect to see the extra vehicles in the parking lot. Then she remembered some contractors were meeting Adriana to plan the new parking rea. Adriana's Avocado Farms work truck was pulled close to the cashier shack. About fifty yards past her stood the old building that was now slated for demolition. Pennie stepped out of her truck and inhaled deeply. The aroma of plants, flowers, and fresh earth gratified her spirit for a moment.

Walking towards the cashier shack, she noticed the bales of hay had been arranged into some kind of map on the adjacent property. Over the weekend, the Acevedos had brought in small mountains of mulch, garden soil, and sand near the old building.

An army of concrete statuary stood proudly—gnomes, angles, rabbits, and frogs—Pennie loved to see the expansion onto the newly purchased land, and she could easily picture all the future fun once this chaos ended. Her job was to help them grow, and it filled her heart to see the progress. When she was close enough to the cashier shed to greet Adriana, she knew something was wrong.

Adriana and Cynthia's frightened faces peered at Pennie through the open window of the shed, their ever-present smiles missing.

"Adriana, what's..."

The question trailed as four men stepped out from behind the twelve-by-twelve shed. Two men on each side. Pennie's best guess was that all the thugs were Hispanic, and given her circumstances, they were Dominican. Their ballcaps obscured most of their faces. She wasn't focused on them anyway. The *Thunder Swarm* logo on each hat caught Pennie's eye. Wasps. This wasn't good.

The rows of trees and shrubs blocked any view from the highway, so a passerby had no chance to see a disturbance and call for help. Three women against four men were terrible odds to fight their way out. The skinniest thug aimed a gun at the Acevedos, and Pennie felt safe assuming all of them carried weapons.

As usual for times of panic, Pennie's brain found a tangent that was in no way helpful for their situation. She compared these four thugs to characters in a Dr. Suess book and gave them ridiculous nicknames in her imagination. The tall one became *Giraffe*. She'd seen him once before at the Miami airport. The short, scrawny one became *Skinny Bones*. The pudgy one became *Chunk*. The one who struck fear in her heart—the obvious leader of the group—needed no nickname. He was none other than Julio Cabral.

"You know where Francelia is?" asked Giraffe.

Pennie shook her head since she couldn't find her voice.

"I'm so sorry, Pennie. They threatened to kill Cynthia if I didn't tell them."

"Shut up, bitch!" Cabral yelled as he sucker-punched Adriana through the open window. "Get out here, now!" he ordered in Cynthia's direction as her mom crumpled to the floor.

Cynthia didn't immediately follow orders, drawing the attention of Cabral.

"What are you doing?!" he yelled as he reached through the window to wrestle with Cynthia over something Pennie couldn't see. She knew exactly what it was when the shotgun blew a hole in the side of the shack. Cabral snatched it away from Cynthia's grip and threw it into the koi pond. "Now get out here!"

This time, she obediently exited the shed and came around to stand with Pennie. The women had only met a few times, but they held hands knowing they only had each other to depend on.

Cabral stepped towards them, speaking with a thick accent and a calmness that belied the situation. "Where is Francelia? We've been searching here for a week, and you're my last lead."

A car door slammed behind them, saving Pennie from having to answer immediately. She glanced over her shoulder to see Lupe skipping towards them, unaware of the danger. By the time she noticed something was wrong, Skinny Bones ran after her, grabbing her arm and dragging her into their little meeting.

He shoved her into Pennie, and she grabbed Lupe's hand to steady her. Pennie's already painful hands throbbed from the girls on each side squeezing, but she decided to remain strong.

Chunk inclined his head to Cabral and said, "*No se, Jefe.*"

Pennie knew that meant, "I don't know, Boss," but she hoped they'd continue speaking in English, so she wasn't forced to translate anything. She glanced at Lupe and Cynthia on either side of her. Both girls still sported the AmberLou hairstyle, and they had a similar build. The thugs must be trying to figure out if one of them truly was Francelia.

"Where is she?" Cabral hissed at her.

"*No se, Jefe.*" Pennie shouldn't be taunting him, but she needed to delay him long enough for someone—anyone—to show up and call the cops.

The slap across her face didn't surprise her, and she barely flinched as his hand cracked hard against her cheek. If Daniela could endure some acid burns to spare Francelia, Pennie could endure a little suffering herself. The ringing in her left ear would subside soon enough. Pennie regained eye contact without giving anything away.

"You think you're so smart, *mujer*. We can go search your house right now. I bet she's there."

Trying to maintain her poker face, Pennie again declined to answer. The thugs would have to get her address if they wanted to get to her house. She wasn't offering the address, and her driver's license was in the wallet in her truck's console. If she just delayed them, created a goose chase to keep them busy, some kind of help would show up. The landscape crew should arrive shortly.

Another car door shutting behind her caused everyone to jerk their heads around. It wasn't the best day for Cole to wear his Bartlett Police t-shirt as he stepped out of Jenna's

Infiniti. Before he got all around the stacks of flowers to check out the scene, Cabral had already pulled his gun and sent several bullets flying in Cole's direction.

Pennie screamed when Cole fell to the ground, clutching his chest. Time stood still. Her mouth stood agape. The two girls buried their faces in Pennie's chest. Their bodies convulsed from the abrupt sobbing. "Shh, amigas. Stay strong," she whispered into the tops of their heads and stroked their hair to console them.

"Enough of this! Tell me where to find Francelia before anyone else shows up!" The frustration in Cabral's voice scared Pennie. She didn't want him shooting anyone else, and he wasn't going to make any levelheaded decisions while spittle flew from his angry mouth.

Again, car doors shutting caused everyone to look towards the parking lot. Pennie's greatest fear was happening in front of her. Karolina and Francelia ran towards her from the backseat of the Infiniti. She heard Chip yell at them to stop before he ducked behind a pallet of landscape stones. But they didn't stop. They ran up and joined Pennie with Cynthia and Lupe. After a group hug, they spread out in a line, holding hands in solidarity.

The four thugs eyed the four girls in bewilderment. Karolina and Francelia were practically twins. Add in the identical hairstyle, similar build, and same age... With the shuffle of the girls from the group hug, the thugs didn't know who was who.

Pennie had to take charge to prevent Cabral from hurting anyone else while Chip came up with a plan. "These are my exchange students—Maria and Karolina. They don't know where Francelia is, but if you let them all go right now, I'll take you to her."

The sneer on Cabral's face indicated he didn't like that plan. "No. One of these girls is Francelia."

"That one has a tiger on her shirt," Chunk offered that tidbit to help his boss.

Pennie glanced down to see Karolina wearing a 901 Tigers t-shirt. Where did they find out that anyone in her home was a Tiger fan? They used that reference more than once, but how did they know?

From Pennie's peripheral, she noticed that Cole had rolled from his initial spot on the ground to find a shady spot under a row of hydrangeas. The thugs were so fixated on the quadruplets, they must not have noticed his movement. Not that it would help them any, she simply found a moment of relief knowing he didn't just die right in front of them. He'd need emergency medical services quickly, but Pennie had to make sure no one else got hurt in the meantime.

"I'm telling you to let them go. I'll take you to Francelia, and you can kill me when you're done. Please just let these exchange students go. They came here for a better life."

"Maybe we should just shoot them all now."

Pennie didn't appreciate Giraffe's suggestion.

"No. We need her alive. When she dies, the world will be watching, and I'll take over where my brother left off. The *Mata Cacatas* will take over La Dominica, and then Haiti too. We'll rule the entire island. Bitches like you will be begging for mercy." With that, Cabral spat at Pennie's feet.

"Then maybe we can shoot them all in the knee?" Skinny Bones suggested, and Pennie didn't appreciate his input either.

Cabral replaced the sneer with a leer… "I like that idea," he said as he took aim at Pennie's knee.

The next few minutes would be critical, but Pennie couldn't fathom how things might play out.

Gunshots rang out, but Pennie and the four amigas were still standing. Everyone ducked and looked around, seeking the source of the gunfire. Then more shots. In the moment of confusion, Pennie yelled at the girls to run for cover.

As she fled towards the old building, she saw four heads covered in AmberLou-colored hair fleeing in other directions. When she arrived at the door to the building, she glanced back to find Giraffe hot on her heels. She ducked inside and turned the deadbolt into place even though the rickety lock wouldn't slow anyone down. Trying to outrun him any further would be futile. It was time for Pennie to take her stand.

The furniture had already been cleared from the space, so the only weapon Pennie found was an old wooden broom. She grabbed it like a baseball bat just as Giraffe kicked in the door. *Whack!* She struck him straight in the face. He faltered, but only for a second.

Oh crap!

He glared at her and reached for his gun. What could Pennie do now?

Grasping the broom handle, she rammed the other end of it into the ceiling tile above her. Pennie scampered back as the nest of furious racoons fell onto the unexpecting Dominican. His squeals sounded behind her as she ran through the back door. As a parting gift, she used the broom handle to knock down the wasps' nests that hung on the eaves above the door.

The pissed-off Wasp exited the house into a swarm of

angry wasps, but it didn't slow him down enough. He pounced on Pennie before she could get through the maze of concrete statuary. She fell face down on the ground with a thud, and Giraffe wasted no time dropping onto her back. He forced her to roll over underneath him so he could wrap his hands around her neck. She should've known how to get out of this position, but the oxygen was knocked out of her lungs when she fell. She struggled to inhale, to prolong her survival... Where was her guardian angel when she needed it?!

Before she could process what happened, a concrete angel statue crashed on top of his head. He collapsed to the ground next to Pennie. She looked up to find Jenna reaching a hand down to help Pennie up.

"Come on. We gotta help the girls," Jenna commanded.

They ran to the mounds of garden soil and sand where they heard a girl's scream. They rounded the piles in time to see Skinny Bones tackle Karolina. He immediately put her in a rear naked choke hold. Pennie hurried, but she couldn't get to Karolina quickly enough to stop the deadly move.

In a split second, Karolina grabbed a handful of sand and threw it back into the face of her captor. He jumped off, rubbing at his eyes. With some kind of scissor sweep, Karolina brought him back down to the ground to pin him in an arm bar.

"I'll stay with her; go find the other girls," Jenna insisted as she relieved the writhing Skinny Bones of his gun.

Pennie stopped and scanned the area for the next source of action. A flurry of two-toned hair dashed behind a row of flowers with Chunk following her. Pennie booked it in that direction, but she never saw anyone emerge from the other side of the row. When she finally got to the row, she peeked around to find Lupe and Cynthia wailing on Chunk. Lupe had already taken his gun, and his head bled profusely from a gash on his forehead. The girls had set up an ambush. While Chunk chased one girl, the other waited to strike him with a landscape stone from the koi pond. The bloody stone laid next to his head.

To her surprise, an officer showed up to take over the scene. Pennie never even heard the sirens, but she tried to tell them that Francelia was still in danger. Frantically searching the area, she couldn't find the one girl who truly needed protection. Officers were still trying to make sense of the scene. One officer found Cole under the bushes and called for the paramedics on his radio.

But Pennie knew the scene wasn't secure. Where was Francelia? Cabral? Chip? She ignored the officer who asked if she needed medical attention so she could run towards the pallets of landscape stones where she last saw Chip. Slowly, she meandered through the stacks. Along the way, Pennie selected a baseball-sized stone she could use as a weapon in case she needed it.

When she rounded one pallet, the spectacle was heartbreaking. Cabral held Francelia captive in front of him—his arm around her neck and a gun to her head. She didn't expect to see movement in the trees beyond where Cabral stood. Without identifying who the unexpected visitor might be, her line of sight found Chip nearby, partially concealed by a pallet of stones. His gun was aimed at Cabral.

Pennie stopped. In shock, she tried to hear the back and forth between Chip and Cabral.

Let her go.

Never, she's my ticket out of here.

No one has to die.

As soon as the news cameras are here, I'm killing her with on live TV.

Kill him. Don't worry about me.

Pennie didn't expect that shout from Francelia. She refreshed her focus to grasp the whole scene. Francelia acted fearlessly to bring this to an end. And Pennie just stood there with a rock. She couldn't see any way to help. With a decision he'd later regret, Cabral swiftly averted his aim and shot at Chip.

With only a split second to react, Pennie gauged her distance from Cabral—approximately the distance from home plate to second base. His gun was still aimed away from Francelia. Without even a hop and a skip, Pennie let the rock fly, but it wasn't quite like the scene in the Bible. She wasn't David, and that wasn't Goliath. Instead of knocking him out with a blow to the head, she struck him in the shoulder. He acted surprised enough to let go of Francelia and turn his livid gaze on Pennie.

One step was all he took. A gunshot from another direction dropped him. Pennie and Francelia whipped their heads to the tree line to find Toy Gunn standing proudly with her very real smoking gun. Pennie didn't even question what Toy was doing here; she just rushed to Francelia's side.

"I'm okay," Francelia exclaimed as she got back to her feet.

Joy flooded Pennie's heart. All the girls were unharmed. The Wasps had been taken down.

"Can I get some help?"

How did she forget about Chip? Pennie ran over to where Chip sat on the ground. His hands applied pressure to an area where his thigh was bleeding.

"We need a paramedic over here," Pennie screamed unnecessarily. The gunshots already garnered the attention of officers who arrived on the scene. They quickly pushed Pennie out of the way and started first aid to treat Chip's injury. The whirlwind of activity and adrenaline made her lightheaded, so she had a seat on the ground until someone gave her further instructions.

All sense of time was lost. No clock. No watch. No phone. The rumbling of Pennie's belly let her know lunchtime had passed. How did she always get stuck in a room, starving to death, while waiting to be questioned?

Being alone didn't help. Until the police sorted it all out, they didn't really know who should be arrested and who should be released. Pennie folded her arms on the table and rested her head. At least all the girls were safe.

The door opened to the small interrogation room. "We can hear your stomach growling from the next room. Here." Tony threw a granola bar towards Pennie.

"Thank you. It's bad enough that I missed breakfast. Missing lunch is about to kill me." She hastily dug into the bar.

"Lunch? It's only ten fifteen."

She looked up to find that same disapproving glare that Ms. McChristian had over eighteen years ago. Just like that, Pennie was back in the fourth grade trying to make it to lunch break. She didn't bother responding.

"The nursery didn't have any security cameras, but a nosy reporter hid a few cameras around the property. Not only that, but Judy Thomas called the cops to let us know she spotted the Wasps, and she followed them to the nursery. She filmed a little bit from her hiding place. Using that film, plus the hidden cameras, we're trying to piece the whole scene together now. My boss, the actual chief of police for Bartlett, gives me a lot of leeway for special operations, but he's going to head up this investigation. We'll be seeing other alphabet agencies and foreign officials show up since a Dominican terrorist group is involved."

"I understand. I'll cooperate every step of the way. Is there any update on Chip or Cole?"

The chief sat heavily in the chair across from Pennie. "Chip's wound isn't life threatening. They're stitching him up now. Cole went in for surgery almost immediately. I haven't gotten an update yet, but I'm heading to the hospital next. Someone will be in here shortly. Until then, write down everything that happened today." He pushed a notebook with a pen across the table.

Her already-injured hand was majorly cramping by the time she filled up a dozen pages. Since she had no way to gauge the time, Pennie didn't have a clue when the big dog chief came into the room. And she really didn't care about the time anymore when she noticed Francelia and Karolina entered with him.

"So, you're the one who brought all this trouble to Bartlett?"

Again, a disapproving glare from the stout chief. Even if he wasn't a foreboding who took up the entire doorway, she knew what the stars on his collar represented.

Pennie shrank back into her seat. "I'm sorry, sir."

"Don't be sorry. We've never officially met. I'm Chief Eubanks."

After standing up to shake his outstretched hand, Pennie winced only slightly from his firm grip. "Sometimes I bring cookies up here. I'm not always in the interrogation room, so I hate this is where you're meeting me for the first time." She turned her attention to the girls who wrapped her in a group hug.

"I've peeked at your history. You've even spent a night in jail here. But I know you didn't do anything wrong today. Do you need any medical attention?"

"No, sir."

"Did you provide an account of events to the best of your ability?" he asked, tapping the notebook with his thick forefinger.

"Yes, sir."

"We'll have questions as the investigation progresses. For now, I'm given to understand that Francelia Vasquez is staying in your custody. She's an adult, so I don't have to verify that with anyone else, but you need to make sure she's available for questioning as well."

"Yes, sir."

"I really thought you'd be more chatty, Ms. Nichols. But I suppose it's been a stressful couple of weeks for you. Go home and get some rest. I'll read over your notes and contact you when we need to meet again."

That afternoon, Pennie's brother, Officer James Walker, voluntarily came over to provide security. Everyone cleaned up and ordered pizza for nourishment as only a melty, greasy pseudo-Italian feast can provide.

She called Jenna to get an update on Cole. He remained in critical but stable condition. The doctors performed an exploratory surgery to be sure they assessed everything damaged by the bullet while repairing his collapsed lung. His lost blood was replaced, and Jenna chose to stay by his side until he could be released. For her peace of mind, Pennie drove to her house to retrieve Dolly the Dalmatian.

A call from Ambassador Hernandez ensured that everyone was safe and sound after facing the terrorists that day. Even though she missed a *ReelLife* exchange earlier, Francelia sent a smiling picture to her mother after pizza had been inhaled.

With James keeping watch from the living room and the security system fully armed, everyone collapsed into bed without any worries left to prevent a good night's sleep.

TUESDAY JULY 26

The dogs frolicked in the sunshine. Pennie and her brother sipped coffee on the back porch. The girls soaked up some of the morning rays. This was the first morning Pennie felt truly relieved of all anxiety in a while. The nursery would remain closed until the investigation was complete, so she had no need to report to work.

"How are we explaining this to Mom?" James asked.

"I don't even know what you know."

"Dominican terrorists showed up in Bartlett yesterday, and a political refugee is living with you. That sums up my knowledge on the subject." James rolled his eyes and took another sip.

She grinned at her little brother. Younger, not littler. James towered over her by the time he turned thirteen. "It was all a spur of the moment thing. Francelia wasn't supposed to be here, but you know me. I saw an opportunity to help, so I did. It never occurred to me that trouble would come to town or that anyone would be in danger."

"You could blame it all on Karolina. Say that she knew who Francelia was, and she wanted to help. Mom met Francelia —AKA Maria—at church a week ago. She'd be okay knowing y'all were helping."

"I guess we could come up with something plausible like that. Mom doesn't need any reason to worry about me when she already worries about you. Her baby boy, the police officer."

"You don't even need me here. I saw Karolina on the video. She might've blinded that guy with sand, she escaped from a rear naked choke hold, and she broke his arm with a Jiu Jitsu submission move."

Pennie leaned her head back and laughed. "I've never been so proud of her."

Her iPad notified them that someone was at the front door. James stayed out back with the girls, while Pennie let Chip inside. She poured him a cup of coffee and invited him to have a seat.

"How's the leg?"

"It'll be fine. The bullet went through my muscle, so they stitched me up. I'll be on light duty until the doctor clears me."

She glanced down at his leg. The bandage was higher than the hem of his shorts, so she couldn't assess anything for herself. "Is this the first time you've been shot?"

"Yea. It hurt more than I expected." He added a light chuckle, and the twinkle in his eye was so adorable. Then he turned towards Pennie. "How's your face? It looks terrible."

Instinctively, her hand moved to cover the left side of her face. She had a heck of a bruise developing. She knew that without Chip making her self-conscious about it.

"Are you really trying to hide your battered face with your broken hand?"

Pennie cut an evil glance his way. "The last time someone hit me in the face, I managed to cover the bruise with makeup before anyone saw me again."

"Ah, touché. I just wanted to check on you. After all this, you might need a real vacation."

"I'm good. There's a lot of reasons to rejoice right now.

The girls are unharmed. Daniela is safe. Adriana has a black eye, but she's no worse for the wear. Cole and you both got shot, but you'll both be okay. And now that all this is ending, I just need to get back to work and find my boring routine again."

Her phone rang. Chief Eubanks was calling her down to the station. Let the questioning begin.

"I guess I need to head to the station. Thanks for checking on me." Pennie walked Chip to the door.

She wasn't sure what she expected, but the warm hug exceeded anything she could've hoped for. He kissed the top of her head and whispered, "Take care, Skipper."

SATURDAY, JULY 30

A few days had passed. Multiple rounds of questioning, filling in blanks, and backtracking made sure the story was complete. The FBI Counter-Terrorism team visited Bartlett to get their own information firsthand. The *Mata Cacatas* were officially squashed like a nuisance wasp. Pockets of machismo groups would always exist, but the relevant threat to Daniela Vasquez and her daughter went away with the death of the Cabral brothers.

Multiple locations had been uncovered where prisoners were kept in the Dominican Republic. Mostly, the guards were found and freed from the attack on the National Palace ten days ago. Over the years, the Cabral brothers had detained a dozen *girlfriends*—plus their illegitimate children—along with other random hostages. Scores of captives were treated and released back to their families.

As new facts were uncovered, they found out that the *Mata Cacatas* had more technological sophistication than anyone expected. They managed to hack the *ReelLife* account created by Francelia. They weren't quite sophisticated enough to differentiate between Francelia and Karolina. Using the pictures from the app, they put together clues to find Francelia's location.

First, the Tigers shirt. It wasn't initially apparent to the Dominicans that the featured Tiger belonged to the University of Memphis, so that clue didn't lead anywhere to begin with. The Avocado Farms shirt provided the second hint. Without any real logo on the shirt, Julio and his thugs searched actual avocado farms in Florida. When a photo of Karolina was posted with a different Tigers shirt, they figured out Memphis was the place to be.

Julio Cabral arrived in Memphis the night before and found Avocado Farms on the internet. They simply showed up the next day and waited for someone to show up. Multiple girls who could be Francelia confused them enough to delay any hasty decisions.

Tony was notified of the emergency call from Judy Thomas that morning, prompting him to give a different call to action to Cole and Chip. The alert warned that Cabral was spotted in Bartlett that morning, and Chief directed his officers to bring Pennie and the girls to the station while a manhunt ensued. Cole and Chip had no way of knowing the Wasps would be waiting at the nursery. Cole suffered the worst injury, but he also saved their lives. When he overheard the threats to shoot them in their knees, he aimed gunfire into the air to create an opportunity for the women to scatter and avoid the torture until help arrived.

Chip had already called for backup and paramedics, so he stayed out of sight and added to the gunfire to cause even more confusion. The amigas and Jenna tagged along because no one needed to stay at the house alone, and they would all report to the police station together. The unfortunate series of events that followed at least brought an end to the chaos.

The one piece that didn't seem like it fit the puzzle was Toy Gunn. Pennie would later find out that earlier that morning, Jenna called Toy to let her know she wasn't coming to work. Toy had never heard Jenna sound emotionally unstable, so she wanted to check on her personally. Tracking Jenna down using a shared app, Toy quickly realized the danger everyone was in at the nursery. She recognized Cabral from a distance and used the cover of the trees to get closer.

The element of surprise gave Toy the opportunity to save the day. Who would've guessed Toy was an avid hunter and marksman?

Pennie had no way of knowing at the time, but the man inside Toy's apartment was her housekeeper. Just a guy there to clean who happened to be a fan of the *Thunder Swarm* movie.

As things would play out, Judy used the footage from her cameras to create the story of her career. She stayed hidden while the action ensued because she knew a news camera would motivate Julio Cabral to make a deadly statement with the world watching. Following strict instructions from the law enforcement agencies, she only touted the involvement of two heroic officers who were injured and gave credit to Adriana Acevedos for bravely protecting the girls. Avocado Farms blew up on social media, and they would certainly receive an influx of business after they could reopen.

With the cooperation of all agencies and departments, the names of the American officers and civilians involved in the extraction would remain confidential. Chip and Cole were only locally recognized as being the first on the scene with no additional involvement. Pennie didn't want any reporters hounding her or Karolina, and the officers didn't want any extra notoriety to prevent them from being considered for future undercover operations. As an occupational hazard, Daniela Vasquez would always be in the spotlight, one Francelia couldn't seem to escape.

For these few days, despite the constant interviews, Francelia enjoyed the reprieve from the political limelight. She wore disguises to remain incognito as Karolina took her new sister out for a few new experiences. As her first order of business, Karolina booked appointments for them to have their hair colored back to their natural shades of dark brown. They enjoyed coffee houses, shopping, movies, dinner, rock climbing... Uncle James tagged along every time they left the house except for the shopping trip. Pietra came by to take her favorite amigas to buy new clothes.

Upon Cole's release from the hospital this morning, he opted to stay with Jenna until he got his strength back. Pennie returned Dolly to her best friend and picked up Chick-fil-A for her family's lunch that Saturday, five days after the craziness went down. By the time they finished eating, Chief Eubanks called them back to the station.

In the conference room that started it all, Pennie sat with her brother and two daughters. Only Chief Lawrence joined them, and he engaged in a little small talk with the girls. The repetitive interviews were getting old, so Pennie wasn't pleased with getting called out here again... until the next person arrived.

Ambassador Valentina Hernandez entered the room. Technically, her smile entered the room before she did. Francelia ran into the open arms, grateful for someone from her own country to be there with her.

"*Amorcito*, how are you?" Vale whispered.

In lieu of answering aloud, Francelia nodded against Vale's shoulder.

"Are your new friends taking care of you?"

Another nod.

"I have a surprise for you."

Francelia stepped back to see the surprise. Vale motioned behind her. Daniela Vasquez was crying before she made it all the way through the doorway.

The reunion of mother and daughter brought tears to Karolina's eyes, like how she cried at the happy ending to a Hallmark movie. Pennie might've shed a tear or two, like the happy feeling she'd experience if the Tigers ever won the college basketball championship.

Everyone planned to come back to Pennie's house for dinner. A personal security guard stayed close to Vale. Chiefs Lawrence and Eubanks joined James Walker to provide extra security for all the women. Everyone spent the evening laughing, crying, and everything in between.

As bedtime approached, no one wanted to go back to their hotel. So, the women hashed out sleeping arrangements. Vale and Daniela had their bags in the car since they came straight to the police station without checking into the hotel first. Even though the sense of danger had passed, Vale's bodyguard and Tony volunteered to keep watch that night, taking turns napping on the recliner.

SUNDAY, JULY 31

James Walker reported to his sister's house in time to eat French toast with the women. Tony went home with the sentiment that he never wanted to see Pennie again, but he meant it in a nice way. The general conversation around the table that morning was hopeful and positive. When Daniela talked about taking Francelia home, the tone changed.

The twenty-year-old daughter found her own voice. She grew tired of the political world. Being a puppet on a string… Smiling and nodding… No more. Francelia wanted to start college and begin her own life effective immediately.

"But Francie, our home… My job… I can't be president of a nation while I'm worried about my little girl away at college."

"No, Madre. I'm ready for school and a career. Politics has taken everything away from me."

Daniela's face softened. "We've come so far for women in La Dominica. We can't stop the progress now."

Refusing to make eye contact, Francelia shook her head. "Everyone in La Dominica is celebrating Father's Day today, but not me. Politics took Padre from me. Politics took safety away from me. From us." Her lip quivered from the pain she'd been holding in for years. She tried to hold back the tears.

The mother and daughter went outside to have some one-on-one time. They clearly had a lot to discuss. Pennie didn't envy the position Daniela found herself in today. The intention was for all the Dominicans to fly home the next morning, but Francelia wasn't having it.

Between Karolina and Pennie, they kept Vale entertained the rest of the morning. A local deli delivered sandwiches for lunch. Everyone reconvened in the dining room despite the tear-stained faces of the Vasquez ladies. When Pennie's iPad notified them of movement in the driveway, James and the bodyguard pulled weapons and checked out the unexpected car through the dining room window.

"It's Vic," the bodyguard said with surprise.

"Uncle Vic?" Francelia asked as she jumped up to see for herself.

Pennie peered out to the middle-aged man striding towards the front door. A dark sedan idled in the driveway.

Daniela rushed to open the front door where the president hugged her vice president. They hadn't seen each other since the lockdown. "Vic, why are you here?"

"I've been trying to catch up with you since you left the country!"

The bodyguard had his own question. "Where's your security? You shouldn't be here alone."

Victor Cano gave the bodyguard a curious stare. "Some things need to be handled alone. I didn't want any witnesses today." He peeked into the dining room, "Oh, good. Francelia is here also."

His demeanor didn't sit right with anyone in the room, so when Vic reached into his coat pocket, James tackled him. Before Vic could finish retrieving the unknown item, he was facedown, wearing handcuffs.

"What's the meaning of this?!" he shouted.

Without answering, James searched his pockets to find what the man was reaching for… Only to find a small digital camera. He kept searching to see if Vic had any weapons.

"Seriously? You Americans are so aggressive! Unhand me!"

Daniela interrupted, "We're all on edge, Vic. What are you doing here? Who's in the car with you?"

The bodyguard wasted no time drawing his own gun and heading to the car. It didn't look like the smartest way to approach potential danger, but who was Pennie to judge. She took it upon herself to move Karolina and Francelia behind her and back into a corner to minimize their exposure to any threats.

When the bodyguard came back into the house, he brought a scraggly man with him. They appeared friendly. So much so, the bodyguard put his gun away. The man looked around the room without saying a word. Pennie hoped someone would make introductions—this situation made her wildly uncomfortable.

Then Francelia shoved Pennie out of the way to get to the man.

"Padre!"

Daniela said nothing. Tears streamed down her face. She eased towards her husband.

"*Mi amor,*" he whispered as he enfolded his wife and daughter in his arms. It had been a decade since Carlos had seen his family, but the time lost melted into nothing as they embraced.

Reluctantly, James removed the handcuffs from Vic and allowed everyone to have a reunion ten years in the making. Francelia got the Father's Day she needed, and things might fall into place for the family.

EPILOGUE

The Vasquez family went through many adjustments after that happy reunion. Daniela stepped down as president, allowing Victor Cano to step into the position. The United States offered emergency visas for them. They relocated to New Orleans so Francelia could start school at Tulane. Karolina managed to stay in contact with JJ and Nick, and she explained their brush with terrorism. The brothers graciously agreed to help Francelia acclimate to college life.

Karolina and Pennie spent a few days in New Orleans as well to ensure the Vasquez family settled in nicely. It made for a wonderful respite from the prior few weeks of chaos. Within the next couple of weeks, Karolina would be moving back into her apartment and getting ready for her senior year at the University of Memphis.

Overall, Pennie was ready for her own next chapter to begin. As satisfying as she felt offering a safe haven for Francelia, the experience left her mentally exhausted. She immediately returned to her Krav Maga classes and ran with Peach to work out the pent-up energy from her time in lockdown. Despite the routine, she still suffered from some gloominess she couldn't explain.

When her nieces came back over for a weekend, Pennie's soul was refreshed. Children did that to her. She snapped out of the funk she was in and looked forward to the future again. She trusted that God had a plan for her life. For a husband and children... For blessings upon blessings.

It was time. She felt it in her bones. Pennie was ready to take a hold of the next installment of her life instead of allowing life to have a chokehold on her...

AFTERWORD

Upon completing this book, I had a change of heart about the Pennie Nichols Mystery Series. Originally, this series was intended to have eight installments. As it turns out, Pennie has more to tell. I've added at least one more book as of now, and I'm excited to see how her character will develop.

When this series is wrapped up, I have to determine where to focus next... Another series or some standalone novels? Since everything I do is by the seat of my pants, I suppose we'll find out together in the near future.

ABOUT THE AUTHOR

Deborah Marcum

Photo by Pietra Gois

Residing in the suburbs of Memphis, Tennessee, Deborah is a proud graduate of the University of Memphis. She has enjoyed hosting exchange students, serving at her church, and traveling. She also has a passion for animals and met her husband while working at a veterinary clinic.

BOOKS BY THIS AUTHOR

A Pennie Saved

Book one of the Pennie Nichols Mystery Series... where it all begins.

A Pennie For Your Thoughts

Book two of the Pennie Nichols Mystery Series... stumbling across a dead body in the animal shelter left her frozen in fear, but only for moment. Pennie must find the killer before she becomes the next victim.

Cost A Pretty Pennie

Book three of the Pennie Nichols Mystery Series... Teamed up with Chip for another undercover assignment, Pennie frantically searches for a missing girl on the east coast without regard for her own personal safety

Lucky Pennie

Book four of the Pennie Nichols Mystery Series... Despite the distractions by her new career and her new love interest, Pennie refused to allow underhanded scheming take place that aimed to fix the results of a major golf competition.

Worth Every Pennie

Book five of the Pennie Nichols Mystery Series... With time on her hands, Pennie found a cold case file to research. A case that started in her very own neighborhood after a woman went missing in a storm fifteen years earlier.

Rabbit's Foot Lucky

This standalone book features Pennie's neighbor Kennedy... With the help of a studly fireman, Kennedy shielded an orphaned girl from unknown threats while performing her own investigation. She quickly found herself knee deep in a blackmail scheme involving powerful politicians. As everyone close to the child turned up dead, Kennedy feared she was in for the fight of her life. It would take a network of new friends and allies, and maybe a little luck, to unravel the mystery and make it out alive.

STAY TUNED FOR BOOK 7 IN THE PENNIE NICHOLS MYSTERY SERIES

Made in the USA
Columbia, SC
20 January 2025